Where
Thunder
Sleeps

Where Thunder Sleeps

A Novel

David Cope

SUNSTONE
PRESS

SANTA FE

Sunstone books may be purchased for educational, business, or sales promotional use.
For information please write: Special Markets Department, Sunstone Press,
P.O. Box 2321, Santa Fe, New Mexico 87504-2321.
Cover image › David Cope
Book and cover design › Vicki Ahl
Body typeface › ITC Benguiat Std
Printed on acid-free paper
∞
eBook 978-1-61139-373-6

Library of Congress Cataloging-in-Publication Data
Cope, David, 1941-
    Where thunder sleeps : a novel / by David Cope.
        pages cm
    ISBN 978-1-63293-058-3 (softcover : alk. paper)
    I. Title.
    PS3603.O42828W54 2015
    813'.6--dc23
                                2015006207

WWW.SUNSTONEPRESS.COM
SUNSTONE PRESS / POST OFFICE BOX 2321 / SANTA FE, NM 87504-2321 /USA
(505) 988-4418 / ORDERS ONLY (800) 243-5644 / FAX (505) 988-1025

Acknowledgments

My sincere thanks go to my wife Mary Jane, without whose encouragement and patience this book could never have been completed, Keith Muscutt, whose expertise in writing has helped me immensely, Larry Prescott, whose editing is always spot on, Jerome Stanley, Anatole Leikin, and Ron Garst whose comments and suggestions helped immensely, and to the many others whose advice on this manuscript was extraordinarily helpful. I'd also like to thank all the authors whose books helped me find my way in unknown territory. Any mistakes of omission or commission in this book are entirely mine.

1

I was born in 1977 in Brooklyn, New York. I don't remember much about that day, even though it was likely the most important one of my life. And my parents' lives, given that I apparently slid into reality not fifteen minutes after my mother went into labor—or so she claimed—my father acting as a surrogate midwife by cutting the cord and then tying it.

Some of this background may explain my neuroses, one of which is a desperate fear of spiders. Though to hear my mother tell it, that fear only appeared when I saw my first real one, a daddy-longlegs, so gentle and docile it ran from me rather than I it.

Another neurosis, at least my mother called it that, was my penchant for reading books and thereafter spouting quotes or strange facts from them as the situation warranted.

Like telling her that most household dust consists of human skin cells, and that the average human will shed forty pounds of such dust in a lifetime. That Jack London once said that he would rather turn to ash than dust when he died. Most of the time I had no real idea what these facts and quotes meant, except that knowing them made me feel smart. And occasionally my mother would agree with me.

My father, my birth father that is, told me a story that took place when I was about ten years old. Many years ago now. We were a lower middle-class family and he a plumber by trade, but he seemed very wise to me. So I listened carefully to the few words he chose to impart.

The story went like this. A married woman told her husband about a month before Christmas that she'd had a dream the previous night of receiving a beautiful pearl necklace. Her husband, with great confidence, told her that she would know what that dream meant if she'd wait a month or so.

About a week before Christmas, she told him that she'd once again dreamt of the necklace and asked what it meant. He told her that she would know what it meant if she'd only wait a week or so.

On Christmas Eve, she told him yet again about the dream she'd had about the pearl necklace and he told her she'd know what it meant if she'd wait until the next morning.

Of course, on Christmas morning this woman couldn't wait to open her one present from her husband, a wrapped box about the size she knew would fit a pearl necklace. When she opened the wrapping and the box, however, she found not a necklace, but a book whose title was, *The Meaning of Dreams.*

At age ten, unfortunately, I didn't actually understand what my father meant by telling me this story. However, when he died some nine years later from a long bout with cancer, my mother married a rich man, actually many times over rich, and we moved to a home overlooking the Atlantic Ocean from Long Island. His home. Interestingly, this new husband *did* give my mother a pearl necklace and many other fancy things.

I then went from attending a junior college in Brooklyn to New Haven, Connecticut and Yale, and then eventually on to Boston and Harvard for my graduate degrees. For I, too, was rich. At least in the sense that my stepfather gave me whatever I wanted. After all, he loved my mother, and she me, and he wanted to impress her and me as much as possible.

By the time I was twenty-five, though, both my stepfather and my mother had died in a tragic car accident, and their will granted me a portion of the fortune. It was a large enough sum so that for two years I couldn't get enough of it. The most expensive cars, the most beautiful women, the most wonderful wardrobes one can imagine.

Nothing but the best.

The first year, though, proved that I couldn't live the rest of my life that way. The cars weren't *really* mine, they were my bank's. The women didn't *really* love me, they loved my inherited money. The clothes I wore weren't *really* mine, they were uniforms of my supposed financial status. And it was in realizing these things that I finally understood what my birth father's story had meant. What you get is not always what you think you want.

Regardless, however, I then set off to see and experience the world. My second year with unlimited funds. And I made it through Europe, Asia, Africa, a part of South America, and eventually returned to my home country, America.

At that point, however, I had to settle down and live within the guidelines my mother and stepfather's trust fund had established for me. Monthly allotments of relatively modest amounts for the rest of my life. I reined in my ambitions and took off in an old Plymouth to see the parts of America I'd never seen before.

Thus I found myself in Holbrook, Arizona one late summer's day staying in a motel whose name escapes me even though I am now sitting in one of its drab rooms staring out the window at the large cumulus clouds gathering in the western skies getting darker and more threatening by the minute.

I had driven to Holbrook in my 1975 Plymouth from Albuquerque, New Mexico, where I'd spent the previous night. The hotel in Albuquerque had a layout of brochures of various places to visit in the area, and one of these brochures was incredibly beautiful. With pictures of the Petrified Forest National Park, Utah's Canyonlands National Park, Grand Canyon National Park, and Monument Valley. I figured these and other places would keep me busy for a few days, and introduce me to the wonders of the great southwest.

The room in Holbrook they'd given me was typical middle-class Americana, on-the-road neutral in every way.

Above the bed hung a painting of a western canyon of no particular denomination, as if its competition, the real thing, wasn't enough. We needed to be reminded of our whereabouts.

The bedspread was fractured with several hundred versions of one of the famous mittens of Monument Valley.

The outside wall of my room was a floor to ceiling window divided at the halfway point by a large sliding-glass door. Outside, since the motel lay on the edge of town, was a great desert with no particularly notable views except extreme distance with low hills on the horizon.

The rest of the place contained a television that had a 'do not use' sign on it, a nondescript carpet, a bathroom, and a stand next to the bed with a lamp and a telephone. Not exactly home, though at least somewhere to hang my hat. What did I expect for thirty dollars a night?

I was feeling a bit morose at the moment, since I'd recently broken off a relationship with a woman I'd known briefly back on Long Island. Or, rather, she'd broken off with me having discovered that while I was known as one of the richest men around, my foundation and trust fund made my wealth untouchable, at least by her.

It seemed to me that I couldn't really trust anyone. Money and pearly necklaces were, apparently, the prices necessary to have a worthy relationship with a member of the opposite gender.

So I watched the clouds ponder whether or not they were going to pummel Holbrook with rain or pass it by. The man at the front desk had told me they'd been threatening for many days in the past month, though not a drop of water had touched the ground that he could remember. Just a bunch of huffing and puffing, signifying nothing.

Maybe I was about to bring him and Holbrook some good luck, though, for as I watched, spits of rain splattered my room window like giant bugs racing for cover on an automobile windshield.

And, just as it had begun, the rain tapered and the storm wandered away, apparently more interested in somewhere else to end the drought that plagued Holbrook and surrounding areas most of the year.

All this excitement made me hungry, so I headed out to find a restaurant of interest.

As I walked past the front desk, I mentioned to the man there, the one who'd checked me in, that the ancient town of Calma in the Atacama Desert in Chile had never had rain. Never. Not one drop.

He nodded, smiled, and swung his hand around in a half circle as if telling me that Holbrook was second on the list of the driest places on earth. And I left him there to ponder his choice of locations to live.

In all my travels, here and abroad, I've always tried to find the strangest foods and places to eat those foods. The more mom and pop a place looked, the better. I wanted a taste of the local cuisine. And, the fact that I didn't allow myself to carry any manner of credit cards and liked to keep my cash in a strong box in a little vault in my locked-up Plymouth's floor, meant I didn't carry enough money in my wallet to pay for anything lavish. A simple, local bistro would do fine.

I found such a place about three blocks from my hotel room. This one was perfect. Constructed out of splintering aged wood, it announced its name with a sign placed in its lone window.

The Diner.

That was it. No frills.

The only name I could imagine any less revealing would have been called *Food*. But *The Diner* would have to do for now.

As I entered the place, the smell from the kitchen caught my nose by surprise. A mix of various spices including chili peppers, and the dull scent of something roasted being the most prominent.

The place was dark, though I could see four tables each seating two, and six booths, each seating four positioned next to the walls in a semicircle around the tables.

To my right was the kitchen, currently being tended by a woman cook who I could see beyond the single large opening which, apparently, served as a temporary home to the waitress who would then serve the costumers. This cook, wearing a waitress-type gown, labored heavily, and I supposed then that for tonight at least she would most likely assume both roles.

There was only one other person in the place, and he sat directly across from me wearing a fedora dipped down to cover his forehead, and overalls, the kind that farmers and, I suppose, ranchers tend to wear.

As I watched him, he dipped a tablespoon into a bowl of green soup with an untouched, so far as I could see, full glass of what looked like water to his right.

So delicate were his movements, that it appeared that each of his slow dips into the green liquid were precisely the same. He'd dip, bring the spoon to his lips, sip silently, and then repeat this process, again and again. After a minute of watching him, I noticed that he gave the spoon a quick lick with his tongue after sipping each time, enjoying every last bit of whatever was in the bowl.

He didn't appear to notice me or anything else for that matter. He could have, for example, looked out the lone window in the room above him, a horizontal oval of a thing set deep into the wall with no view I could see. The glass of this window was opaque from dirt or grit or steam, I couldn't tell which. And in the deep recess of the window sat a tiny sailboat of the kind one often finds in stores along a seacoast somewhere, certainly not here. It looked as delicate as the man's motions as he ate his soup, or whatever it was he was eating.

I must have become mesmerized by the view, for I suddenly felt a tug on the sleeve of my shirt and turned to find the waitress-cook looking at me and asking me something in a language I'd never heard before. I must have looked confused to her then, for she quickly changed to English and asked me did I want to sit down. And where. I told her I did, and right here next to the door would do fine. And so that's where I sat. And that's where she left me, holding the menu she'd handed me before she'd left to return to the kitchen to do whatever she'd been doing back there before.

I glanced over my possible choices for the night's meal, and didn't recognize a single dish listed. Obviously in a language I didn't recognize. The prices were low and that pleased me, though eating broiled rattlesnake did not.

I looked back at the waitress-cook and noticed now that her skin was dark brown, and her hair was that wonderful jet black of natives and Mexicans. Except the menu was not in Spanish. I could have read that.

So I glanced across the room toward the man still working on his bowl of green soup. His skin was dark as well, but every other feature told me he was Anglo, especially the white beard he sported that I'd missed earlier because of his balletic eating habits. Yet he'd ordered without trouble apparently.

Taking another look at the menu, I noticed that the words were written in strange ways. Some apparent English syllables were set apart with single quotes and many vowels had accents above them. The first item on the menu, for example, was azee' hókániltsoh. And the rest were equally impossible to read.

I looked at the waitress-cook, and when she happened to glance toward me I motioned her to come help.

She smiled, wiped her hands on a towel at the side of the opening put there for such things I guess, and came through the door to stand by my table.

And she continued to smile at me.

I asked her if she spoke English.

To my amazement, and continued confusion, she said, "no." Plain and simple. She did not speak English, even though she did. At least a few words of it. I suppose that these would be the words I'd have chosen to learn were I to speak whatever language she and the menu spoke.

Apparently I had three choices. Seek help from the man sitting across the room from me, point at a couple of items and hope for the best, or thank her and leave to look for someplace else to eat. I decided to try them in order.

First, I cleared my throat loudly, hoping to get the man's attention, didn't get it, so I asked him if he would mind helping me. The waitress-cook looked in that direction to see what the man would do, and he continued to do nothing except continue spooning pea soup or whatever it was into his mouth with smooth precision. I waited the requisite amount of time for him to reconsider and gave up.

Time for a second shot at it—point and hope for the best. At this juncture, I was willing to take a chance. After all, who knew what great culinary feast might be waiting for me in those wondrous wafts of aromas my nose had received when I'd entered this place? *The Diner*, if memory served.

So I did. I turned the menu in such a way that both the waitress and I could see it clearly, and pointed to the first item. She smiled at my success in fixing the situation, and penciled my choice down in the notebook she carried to register orders properly.

I then pointed at the second item on the menu and watched her eyes. She blinked, and then shook her head slowly back and forth. Not a good idea apparently.

And thus we spent the next few minutes working our way down both sides of the menu until I, or rather she, had accumulated enough food for me to eat. At times, as we did it, she stifled a laugh. I'd join in, and we played a rather ridiculous game of hide and seek.

When she finished writing everything down in her notebook, she left me to wonder what to expect.

While waiting, I could play a game with myself trying to guess what I'd ordered. Giving odds on whether it would be jackrabbit stew or lizard steaks. I didn't. For my mind kept wandering, as did my eyes, toward the enigmatic man sitting across the room from me who had either purposely avoided responding to my query for help, was deaf, or himself unable to speak English.

He'd finished his soup, taken a drink of water from the glass to the side of his bowl, and now put his elbows on the table and sat staring into the empty dish in front of him. So intently, that I thought he might be attempting to read the tiny morsels he'd not been able to take from the bowl as one might to read tealeaves in a cup. For his fortune.

And he sat like that until my food came. Not moving so far as I could see. As if everything that mattered lay in the bottom of the bowl into which he looked.

The first item on the table turned out to be a beautiful artichoke. While not native to Brooklyn, I'd eaten them before, and understood the mechanics of doing so. The waitress-cook placed an empty bowl not unlike the one the other patron was staring into next to that artichoke into which I could put the leaves after I'd scooped off the meat from their bottoms with my teeth.

Next to that came what looked like mayonnaise for dipping the leaves. At least I thought it was mayonnaise. It was white.

The remainder of the meal was unintelligible. Nothing at all that I recognized by shape, form, smell, or manner of preparation. I was completely at a loss.

There were knives and forks. Those I recognized, and several napkins that looked useful.

And there was a plate of what appeared to be Nan, the East Indian bread cooked in a Tandoori oven. Nothing else reminded me of East Indian food, so I tucked my expectations away in my mind so I wouldn't be disappointed, and began with the artichoke.

2

When I was twelve, my birth father occasionally took me to a particular amusement park on Coney Island south of Brooklyn. These were exciting times for me since they were my first occasions to see, hear, and experience the world at large. People from different countries, speaking languages I'd never heard, and all with the same wide eyes as I had.

One of the acts I saw there included a man who could do amazing things. Not just amazing in terms of twelve-year-old boys, but to people of all ages. This magician, who had the words 'prestidigitation,' 'legerdemain,' and 'conjurer' inscribed on the wall behind him, hocked his wares out front of a small building, where the real thing apparently took place inside for only a dime admission. And the first time I saw him do his thing, I was hooked.

While he looked at no one except me, he rolled his sleeves up his arms, showed us the fronts and backs of his empty hands, fisted his left one, smiled, and gently tugged a beautiful red satin scarf from inside that fist with his right. That, alone, would have been incredible enough. But he smiled once again, showed us the large scarf, pushed it gently back into his fisted left hand, said some magic words over it, sprinkled some magic dust thereupon, and once again showed the front and backs of his now empty hands.

First not there. Then there. And then not there.

Magic.

He went on to show us more tricks and then invited all to join him for the disappearing woman act inside. Some went, others kept walking.

My father looked down at me, smiled, and asked me if I wanted to see a woman disappear. I shook my head back and forth, wondering as I did how the world could continue with all these women disappearing, and he took me to the next person hocking their wares.

While we walked, I realized something important about myself. Apparently my brain had switched on at the appearance of the red scarf. For from that point forward, I hadn't really seen the other tricks and had stopped caring about the disappearing women. I wanted to know how the scarf had appeared and then disappeared. After all, the magician certainly knew how it had. How had he done it otherwise? And, from the word 'magician' he used to describe himself, he certainly didn't expect us to believe that the scarf *really* had appeared and disappeared in some rational way.

It was a trick. But how a trick? How did it work?

I needed to know these things. Desperately so, I thought.

That night, with my stomach stuffed with cotton candy and red ropes from the amusement park, and aching from them, I lay in bed trying to figure out how he'd done such a beautiful thing.

What were the possibilities?

And so I spent much of that night and part of the next before I figured it out.

With my reverse engineering in mind, the next time my father took me to Coney Island I sought out the magician's lair and waited patently for him to appear once again to present his magical talents. When he did, he surprised me by demonstrating a completely separate range of tricks, sans the red satin scarf.

Had he figured out that I'd discovered his secret?

No, that wasn't possible. I was one of many thousands of visitors that ranged through the amusement parks at Coney Island.

I waited for him while he and many others entered the building to see the woman disappear and until it came time for him to resume his sales pitch to other unsuspecting and naïve victims.

When he did, though, he ran through the same litany of tricks he had earlier that day.

This time, however, when he left to enter his arena of deception, I grabbed his coattail and asked him where he kept his magic rubber thumb. And that stopped him short.

He looked down at me, winked, and asked me what rubber thumb I was talking about. I told him about the hollow rubber one in which he kept the red satin scarf.

He asked who'd told me about that rubber thumb. Only magicians knew about it.

I told him I'd figured it out on my own.

Perplexed, he stared at me to see if I'd lied to him.

Apparently satisfied I hadn't, he patted me on the head, smiled winningly as he had a habit of doing, and then reached out to shake my hand.

And then he surprised me. As much as I'd been surprised to that point in my life. He welcomed me into the profession of magic. Into the wondrous world of now you see it, now you don't.

Then, before I could thank him in some way, he returned into his disappearing woman arena and no doubt wowed several dozens more of the thousands of others he'd entertained over his lifetime.

When I found my father again and we returned home that late afternoon, I knew my life with magic wasn't over.

Back in Holbrook, I mulled these thoughts over in my mind as I finished my artichoke. And leaned back and reviewed the remaining dinner in front of me. Three different dishes of food and a beverage, none of which looked vaguely familiar, and all of which smelled both good and evil.

And beneath that sweet and sour odor was the ever-present waiting teardrops from freshly cut onions and hot chili peppers.

As I prepared myself for the dangerous possibilities, a woman walked through the same door that had brought me into *The Diner*. A blonde woman, no less, with the white skin of someone even more out of place in this town and this restaurant than I. Maybe in her early forties, she was moderately attractive and had that way about her that some women do of complete confidence.

She stopped when the door closed behind her and turned toward the waitress-cook and got her attention by clearing her throat.

Once she had that attention, she spun off a series of unintelligible words at which point the waitress-cook nodded her head and smiled.

The blonde woman turned and looked at the man sitting opposite me still staring into his empty bowl of green soup, and nodded her head as if she recognized him.

She then turned toward me.

Without a second's delay, she asked if I would like to know what I was about to eat.

In English.

I must have smiled then, for without hesitation she took a couple of steps to my booth and sat down opposite me. She pointed to each dish in turn, explaining that the bread-like pancakes were in fact waffles without the grids on their sides, without sugar, and without syrup. Called fry-bread. Made from corn. She thought I'd find this interesting and useful for soaking up the various sauces from the other dishes.

Then she looked more closely at a bowl full of fried somethings, sniffed them twice, and told me they were a kind of chicken-fried chicken without the chicken. The chicken had been replaced with armadillo. In other words, boneless breasts of this mammal covered in a kind of cornmeal and roasted in an oven for a couple of hours.

From there, she explained that my drink was concocted mostly of water squeezed from what white people called beaver-tail cactus because of its flatness and shape, with the added flavor of squeezed tarantula. She'd said 'white people' as if I was one and she was not, which I found surprising.

The next dish, which to me looked and smelled like lamb, was muskrat parts baked in corn. Probably leftovers from the fry-bread. I was surprised. Muskrats, as I remembered them, were semiaquatic. Not much water around here I'd been told. Maybe she'd had them flown in from Louisiana.

And, if that weren't enough, she explained there was nothing exotic about the peaches and ice cream, the taste of which was enhanced by wild honey.

The ice cream, she confessed, was made from spider eggs, the species of which she didn't know.

Great. Tarantula and its eggs? The hated spider, bane of my existence.

I told her then that honey is the only natural food made without destroying any species of life.

She nodded and then added that honey is the only food that doesn't spoil.

We were both of one mind, apparently. Honey was by far the best food on planet earth.

She ended by telling me that I had fine taste in food combinations, and she envied the meal I was about to enjoy.

I asked her how she'd gained her culinary knowledge. She explained that she owned and managed *The Diner*, had invented many of the dishes on the menu, and that she would have been happy to have waited on me had she not been called away by a slight emergency of someone having collided with her car in another part of town.

I told her I was sorry, but she explained that it was a non-starter in that no damage had been done to either car.

Then she told me to eat. She wanted to wait and watch, she said, because she wanted to vicariously experience the taste of each dish as it took its time developing in my mouth. And, of course, to find out what I thought of the food.

And so she did.

Each dish was different. Wildly strange, though more than interesting. And I rewarded her interest by nodding my approval.

And meant it.

Somehow, and without any particular spice that I could recognize, the food was delicious. Cooked with obvious pride and care. And I told her that.

She thanked me, stood, and turned toward the kitchen. Before she got there, though, she turned again, and walked over to greet the man who was still staring into his empty bowl of pea soup, or empty of some other strange green concoction.

Once by his side and with her back to me, she again spoke in that strange language I'd heard earlier. When she finished, and though I could no longer see him, I heard the man speak back to her in something like the same language.

She nodded and let him be.

Once she'd disappeared into the kitchen, she really disappeared. For, unlike the waitress-cook who I could still see through the glass-less window, she turned the other direction and out of sight.

I looked back at the man in the booth across from me, and he'd returned to staring into his empty bowl. A strange ritual, though apparently only strange to me, as the others took it for what it was. Not a deviation from his normal behavior as I'd suspected it might be.

As I finished my food, I realized that I'd met two people and seen one other in the diner and had not one name, nor had they mine. Why this struck me as odd, being in the town of Holbrook, Arizona, for the first time in my life, I didn't know, but it did. This was probably the reason for my wanting to eat in out-of-the-way places. The sense that I needn't know people's names or them mine. That I was in a special spot, not simply another version of a restaurant that existed in several thousand other places.

As I finished my meal, the man sitting in the booth opposite mine rose slowly and deliberately, turned, and without saying anything to anyone strode out of *The Diner* and the door closed behind him. He walked like someone trying to swim in a sea of marbles, each movement a combination of small jerks. Painful to watch, but apparently it worked for him.

While he'd taken his time, the act so surprised me after watching him sit in one place for so long and moving so little, that I wondered if I'd imagined him. But no. As I looked at his table, the empty bowl and the now half-glass of water were still there.

After sitting for a time letting the food find its rightful place inside me, I asked for my bill. Of course, since the only person who would have heard me was the waitress-cook, I didn't actually ask for it by saying anything, only watched her until she looked up, and then raised my right hand and rubbed my forefinger and thumb together in a kind of universal sign for folding money.

And, of course, she had no idea what I was signaling. So, she smiled beatifically, turned her head, and rifled off a sentence that once again baffled me. Sounding, even after I'd now heard several examples, even more strange and confusing.

If that were possible.

As I half expected, the blonde woman soon appeared at the door to the kitchen, walked over to my table and, though she certainly already knew the answer to my question, asked me what I thought of the food.

Without hesitation, I told her it was incredible and I envied her skills as well as that of her helper in the kitchen.

She was pleased and asked me if there was anything else I wanted.

I told her nothing else, and asked for the bill.

At first, she looked confused by my words. This, in turn, confused me. After all, eating food in someone else's restaurant meant compensating for it. She must have known that. Though she apparently didn't.

Then, she surprised me again. She asked what I thought the meal was worth. Not sure I'd heard her right, I told her that it was worth 'every penny.'

She smiled then, and asked me how much money I had. That being a stranger question than the previous one, I told her that I had a twenty on me, and could get more if that were not enough.

She screwed up her face for a few seconds, and then told me that my twenty was much too much, and would I think her asking for five dollars be an inconvenience.

I told her it wouldn't, that I thought her food and good company was worth far more than that.

She smiled again, something I was not only getting use to, but enjoying more each time I experienced it.

And she repeated that five dollars would be plenty and I gave her the twenty-dollar bill.

She took it, and, for a second I thought she'd changed her mind. That since I was willing to pay more, why not?

No sooner had she left my table than she returned with one five-dollar bill and a ten in change. I let her place it in my open palm and then took the five and put it on the table as a tip. Ten dollars for that meal was still a grand deal as far as I was concerned.

That was when I got my first scolding. She waved her right forefinger back and forth in front of me, and continued doing that until I picked up the errant five and put it back in my pocket to find the ten I'd placed there before.

It was then that I realized she reminded me of my aunt, my birth father's sister. A kind woman, who had scolded me in the same manner. And many times, I might add.

Then my hostess invited me back for dinner the next night. Coyly. As if for a date.

While not prepared for such a thing, it was a quite pleasant consideration. On the flip side, though, I worried about my eventual reaction to what I'd eaten that night. Maybe I'd liked the food, but my body, after a careful sampling, might not like it as much as it roamed through my digestive tract.

Watching me wrestle with a yes or no answer, she told me that more people are killed each year by being struck by flying champagne corks than by spider bites. Was she planning on serving me spider soup on top of the ice cream? Spider soufflé? Spider bisque?

Not wanting to be upped, I told her that yes, people on balance were more afraid of spiders than death. And I further nodded in the affirmative as she smiled. I'd found a comrade in meaningless facts.

When I finally rose from the seat in my booth and walked outside, it was very dark. The stars above had sprinkled themselves out in familiar ways with the Milky Way creating a path toward the south where I could see Scorpio, appropriate for this desert country, seeking its way west. The clouds had dispersed completely. No relief this night.

I walked slowly to let the food settle. It was clear to me that I'd found another very strange place in my journeys, one made stranger by the feeling that rather than foreign, it was welcoming, as if I belonged here somehow.

And I liked that feeling.

As I continued my short walk back to my motel, I watched my step and was glad of it. For I'd just missed putting my left ankle in harm's way. A scorpion, possibly the famous bark scorpion I'd read about and knew was very dangerous, had its tail with stinger cocked and ready for action. Its pincers were raised and open. Nocturnal, the damn things covered the desert here I'd been told, and the smaller they were the more poisonous. This one was quite small. Either a baby, or a killer on the loose. I pulled my foot away and almost fell on my face.

Then I remembered that if you put a drop of liquor on a scorpion, it will instantly go mad and sting itself to death. Another one of those incidental and useless facts that, I suppose, was useful if I had any liquor on me at the time. Which I didn't.

"Welcome to Arizona," I said aloud for the scorpion to hear. Then I found my way to my room without further incident.

3

My mother was an Irish Catholic and brought me up in that religion. My father had no religion whatsoever, though I always assumed he was a protestant given his family background in England. They never fought about it, he never attended Mass with my mother and me, and the conversations we had over dinner and other meals never touched on the subject. Maybe the two of them discussed it after I was asleep at night. Whatever they did, they kept it secret from me. For all I knew, my father had followed my mother's tact of patience, letting her argue herself into confusion and then agreeing with her.

I remained with the church until I was fifteen years old, which is saying something given the occasional knuckle pounding with rulers the nuns gave me in grade school, and the various punishments dealt out for being tardy or pulling a fast one on someone in high school.

But last until then I did, at least until a priest giving a homily told a story one day that set me off. The story was actually simple enough. Two old men were close friends and both loved the game of baseball. They agreed that whichever one of them died first would figure out a way to communicate with the still living one about whether heaven had baseball. Then one of them died. The other one, believing in God and that his friend was in heaven, waited patiently for the message to come. And come it did. One day his friend's voice appeared in his mind saying,

'I have good news and bad news. Which do you want first?' The still living man recognized the voice of his friend and told him, 'the good news.' So the friend in heaven told him that indeed he'd found baseball there. So the still-alive friend asked, 'then what could the bad news possibly be?' And the dead man said that the living man was scheduled to pitch that coming Friday.

Everyone in the church laughed at this, even me. However, as I did, I couldn't figure out what this story could possibly have to do with religion. Apparently, once finished telling the joke, the priest had the same problem, so he rambled on about various aspects of what he'd told us and ended with something along the lines that indeed the story proved there was a God. After all, if there was a heaven there had to be a God to have created it. A dog chasing its tail. It shouldn't have bothered me that much, but somehow it did. The camel's back broke.

The minute my mother and I left church that day, I began arguing with her.

How could she take this idiocy?

She proclaimed that it was a story meant to liven us up for more serious matters.

I, of course, argued that it had not been published in the joke section of the church bulletin where it belonged, but in one of the more important parts of one of the priest's obligations, his opportunity to explain the readings presented earlier in Mass. This was, I said, a lie among truths.

I felt so proud of using her own logic against her at that moment that I felt suddenly grown up, able to think for myself.

Were I to have left well enough alone, I might have escaped the hell that was to follow, except I couldn't restrain myself. I added to my argument a reverse of her advice to me, that maybe it was indeed a truth among lies.

And that did it.

She lit into me like an army of my teaching nuns had in grade school. Her patience had run out. Maybe this is what had happened to my father at one time, and that's the way their arrangement worked out, but I hadn't known this side of her. Not in seventeen years of being her son.

And as we walked home, every stored up bit of anger in her worked its way to sunshine and I heard things about myself, God, her, the devil, and I can't remember what else. And none of it, not one shred of it, pleasant. In the least.

When we arrived home, she'd released most if not all her pent up venom and left me sitting on the porch in the swing they'd put there for me to swing in when I was younger. Whereupon I decided I was no longer a Catholic.

Enough was enough.

I wasn't sure what I was, though it certainly wasn't a Catholic. Since I knew so little about other religions, I couldn't claim them either.

I knew about atheism, but that to me was as ridiculous as believing in God. Who knew enough about such things to either know whether God existed or not. At least Catholics called it a belief, not the 'I know there is no God' declaration by atheists.

And agnostics, those people who said they didn't know. Could be. Maybe not. Wishy-washy as far as I was concerned.

So I decided then and there to become a member of the Procrastinationism religion. I would put off thinking about it until someone or something came along and gave me an answer I could understand.

In the meantime, I'd not give it another thought.

Not long after that, I went to junior college and, though I knew my mother wanted to talk about this problem, it never came up. Possibly because we both knew it might erupt again and neither of us wanted that. She, of course, knew I no longer attended Mass, Communion, Confession, or any of the other accouterments of Catholicism. I worried about her and what she might think of me, though it never came up again. Even when I stood before her that final time not long before she died. For that I was sorry. Fifteen years of attending Mass together, and then not, and not having spoken of it again seemed childish. Except there it was.

I chalked it up my new religion: Procrastinationism.

My father became ill with lung cancer when I was nineteen. I was attending said junior college in Brooklyn at the time and living at home. Somehow his condition had remained hidden until, when diagnosed, it had reached stage IV, long past any reasonable chance to save his life.

At first, though the news was dour, our family suppressed our tears and things remained fairly normal. Then within that first month following diagnosis, he began having severe coughing fits and spitting up blood. Clearly, as much as my mother and father wanted to keep things quiet, even from us, life had to change. And radically so.

The first thing to go was his job. Whatever arrangements he'd made with his company were none of my business, so I had no idea how my mother and I would get along without the breadwinner of the family. But tending to a dying man came first, and I took leave from my studies and stayed home to attend to business there.

My mother, who'd always been a strong woman, lost it then. She couldn't bear to see my father in his day-by-day worsening condition. So it fell to me to give him his medications, sit by his bedside, and slowly watch him waste away.

Life poses many challenges, but watching your father die before your eyes must be among the worst.

Each day brought changes. Not surprising since the doctor had given him only three months or less to live.

Seeing him change from a strong and vibrant man to an emaciated ghost of a human in such a short time was terrifying.

Initially we spoke of the Mets, the Jets, the Nets, the Yankees, and the Giants, though neither of us were sports fans. We joked about the movies we'd seen, the memories of my youth, the time I'd broken my arm while attempting to climb the drain spout on the side of our house. And we reminisced about the old days when we'd go to the carnival on Coney Island and watch the magic shows. Great memories for both of us. Our times together weren't many, though when they occurred they'd been rich, and for me at least, profound.

Unfortunately, as the drugs became more potent and the end neared, he went from coherent and occasionally happy, to disillusioned and discouraged, and then to fatalistic, completely incoherent, and beyond morose.

I'm told there are stages to this process that everyone goes through. I'm sure there are and that he made his way through each. None of this information, of course, made anything easier.

It was hell for him.

And it was hell for me. A different hell, but hell just the same.

My mother grew more distant as time passed. For her, somehow, my father turned into something she'd never married. Like milk gone bad, she couldn't tolerate his dying like this.

When he slept, I read.

When we spoke, he did most of the talking. Or mumbling.

Our conversations, no matter how they started, ended with philosophy. Since my father had never been religious, he wasn't going that direction even as he died. So we spoke not of the earth's religions or great philosophers, but of our own beliefs, however uninformed they might be.

I remember one such occasion when he described an axiom of the theater. Where actors walk out of a scene and ruin it because they aren't really going anywhere except offstage. Directors, he told me, at least the good ones, made their actors understand that when you leave one place, you're always going into another, and that audiences could tell from the way you walked and the look on your face whether you were going to another place or simply offstage.

This notion made quite an impression on me. His implication being that he wasn't really dying, only transitioning from one room to another. His metaphor worked. Like him, I guess, I became convinced that no matter how painful it might be for him, he would make it somewhere else and was actually looking forward to it.

I suppose at that point, he kind of ascended in my mind. Where once he'd been my father, he now became my guru. A messenger of life. Even though he was dying.

We even talked of where I'd been before I was born. I'd studied Hinduism in school and was aware of reincarnation and karma. This was less certain and more like relinquishing oneself to the inevitable. Not looking forward to being a cat, a rock, or a planet, or whatever in the next life, I didn't buy it.

Of course, by the time we'd graduated to these discussions he was pretty well out of it and, I suppose, I'd joined him. At least part way.

We couldn't afford either a month-long hospital stay or a live-in nurse, so it was up to me to give him his medications. Some by mouth and some intravenously. The latter being where I nearly lost it and joined my mother. But I was determined that my father not die alone, even though he insisted that we continue to live our lives normally whether we wanted to or not. So I stuck with it and learned the art of needles and veins.

As the days proceeded onward toward the inevitable, I grew tired, anxious, and most of all fearful of how I'd take it when it happened.

I supposed then that there were stages for the bereaved that each of us goes through as well as for the victim, though I didn't know these either. I just suffered along with him, though not nearly as much physically.

Near the end, it took forever.

His arms were now sticks. How thick and muscular they'd been when I was a child. He'd seemed invincible then. No way could he die. And here was that very man, wasting away in front of me.

He remained in a coma for the last few days, and the only thing that kept him alive was the food and liquid impressed into his arm. And, who knows, maybe my hopes that somehow he wouldn't die as I sat there next to him.

And then, he passed. No fanfare. No announcements. I could tell without feeling his pulse. Or lack of it.

The air in the room remained the same.

The light from the lone window looked the same.

Of course, as I knew I would, I changed. For something was missing from my life and forever would be. Until I myself took this route.

I remember sitting there staring at him. So calm and peaceful. Imagining him somewhere else. In another place. Another room.

And I cried. I wasn't sure why, exactly, but I did. For him? For me? For my mother, who'd not seen him for days at that point? It was a long and good cry. Until I ran out of tears.

And the room had still not changed when I finished. As if the universe considered it another day in an infinite number of days. And that this was happening in so many places with so many different people, that two more or less didn't really make much difference.

When I called out from his room to my mother, she didn't want to come in. She told me she didn't want to see death. As if it were a thing in itself. As if my father's body had been replaced by something called 'death' and in seeing it she'd have to admit to herself that she too was going to die.

And then I knew that while I'd been intensely angry with her for leaving him alone in his time of need, she'd suffered far more than he or I. She'd been alone. And now she knew that seeing him would remind her of that.

Of course, I didn't really imagine that she'd thought these things through as I had, only that that's what she really felt. Below all the façades she'd manufactured to separate herself from life for the few months she'd had to.

She did look in the open door for an instant. And then I let her head rest on my shoulder in the living room. Away from him, she acted as if he was still alive and somehow ashamed of her for fearing his presence.

Of course it was I who had to attend to the ensuing details. Arrange for the police to investigate as they do all deaths. Arrange for the coroner to take his body away to have it cremated. Arrange for the medications still remaining to be confiscated, so that my mother and I wouldn't take them. Arrange for a time when our neighbors could stop by to give their condolences.

Truth be known, however, I delighted in these activities, since they took my mind away from what I was really feeling and place them on something menial though necessary.

The night of his death, after everyone had left except my mother, and knowing that the days ahead would be spent arranging his funeral, I sat and thought long and hard about myself and what this meant for me.

I felt guilty, of course, thinking of myself at a time when I should be thinking of others. Except I didn't give a damn. It was a turning point in my life, and I knew it.

What would I do now that he was gone? Had I attended school only because he'd wanted me to? Had he even wanted me to go to school?

I didn't really know these things. He'd never told me in so many words. I'd simply toddled off as so many others my age did. Maybe to get away from home.

Where the hell was I going in life? Incredibly, I realized then that I was also dying in a way. At least part of me was. I had no idea what I wanted to do with my future. No direction. I'd wandered along knowing that somehow things would be taken care of by my father. And now I had no father. His heart no longer beat with mine. I was alone. With an aging mother who had no idea how to move through life without a husband to show her the way.

That really scared me. Was I to become her virtual husband? No way.

And so I whiled away that entire night thinking these thoughts and others. Mostly about me.

It was frightening to realize that those things that most people think about long before I had, had never occurred to me.

As expected, my mother took herself into a kind of walking coma. She cleaned the house and fixed meals for three as if nothing had happened. A temporary insanity. Some part of her knew he was gone. The part that kept her from calling him to dinner or to get ready for work. The part that would admit the truth didn't exist for her yet.

I let her be. Why not? The realization would come soon enough. It had to. Didn't it?

In the ensuing days, I searched the Internet for websites that would educate me on what my father might have wanted by way of a funeral. I had no idea what lay in store for me.

I gathered that a Catholic funeral wouldn't do. He'd had plenty of opportunity to attend Mass with my mother and me over the years and had never indicated the slightest desire to join us. Just said goodbye, and then kept doing whatever he'd been doing at the time.

My computer search proved quite enlightening. Aside from the usual Christian, Jewish, Hindu, Islam, Buddhist, Baha'i, Quaker, and Sikh customs, I found ethnic traditions from around the world. From Africa, the Native Americas, China, Mongolia, Samoan, to Japan, Hmong, Greek, and so on. None of these, unfortunately, fit my father's proclivities.

In desperation, I sought out alternative customs including Scientology, Wiccan, Asatrú, and Atheist. Embarrassed that of all of these assembled I knew so few. Even the ones I'd heard of I knew little. I finally settled on Humanistic, believing if nothing else, that my father was certainly that.

I read everything I could find on Humanist funeral services, and discovered they actually had a certain basic organization. For example, they begin with an introduction stating the name of the deceased, followed by a reading that contains the nature of death, the names of the family of the deceased both dead and alive, various musical selections, some kind of appropriate reading of poetry or philosophy or fiction, personal remarks from members of the immediate family or close friends, and a recessional of some sort.

Vague, but a recipe I could use as a template.

However, would my father have approved?

He didn't dislike religions. Just never showed a preference or discussed God or gods that I could remember. Maybe he was an agnostic. Didn't have a clue and refused to believe in anything he couldn't fully understand. Did agnostics have funerals?

Back to the Internet. As confused as me. So Humanist it was.

My mother helped not at all. If fact she begged me not to have a funeral. So I changed it to a memorial service. She told me she wouldn't come. So I decided to hold it in the house. Where could she hide?

Finally, so exasperated with her I couldn't stand it anymore, I gently sat her down and told her that I didn't want to attend either. No one did. But for his memory we had to do it. That it would take most likely less than ten minutes. And, before she had an opportunity to say no, I told her that she had to do it or risk never seeing me again for the rest of her life.

That did it. She looked down at the floor, shook her head woefully back and forth, tucked in her chin, and then nodded.

With that as a token gesture, I asked her if we could do it the next day.

The sooner the better, she told me.

And that was it.

I gathered the neighbors together, such as there were neighbors who knew him, and parceled out the duties, the primary one of which was to read the poetry or philosophy or fiction that would be the meat of the short celebration of my father's life.

The one neighbor I knew well, a man nearly my father's age and possessing the baritone voice of God himself, actually volunteered to do the reading I'd dreaded having to do myself. I almost kissed him. All that remained was to find the verse. He had no ideas. Neither did I.

Back to the Internet.

I'd just sung the Brahms' *Requiem* with the junior college choir—in the tenor section, not the solo—and loved the part 'Death where is thy sting.' But I also knew that it came from Corinthians in the New Testament and immediately gave it up for its religious reference.

The part I wanted read,

Behold, I show you a mystery;
We shall not all sleep, but we shall all be changed,
In a moment, in the twinkling of an eye, at the last trump:
for the trumpet shall sound,
and the dead shall be raised incorruptible,
and we shall be changed.
For this corruptible must put on incorruption,
and this mortal must put on immortality.
So when this corruptible shall have put on incorruption,
and this mortal shall have put on immortality,
then shall be brought to pass the saying that is written,
Death is swallowed up in victory.
O death, where is thy sting?
O grave, where is thy victory?
The sting of death is sin;
and the strength of sin is the law.

It fit him perfectly. Then there was William Blake whose works I loved, and I chose this passage,

O life of this our spring!
why fades the lotus of the water,
Why fade these children of the spring,
born but to smile and fall?
Ah! Thel is like a wat'ry bow,
and like a parting cloud;
Like a reflection in a glass;
like shadows in the water;
Like dreams of infants,
like a smile upon an infant's face;
Like the dove's voice;
like transient day;
like music in the air.
Ah! gentle may I lay me down,
and gentle rest my head,
And gentle sleep the sleep of death,
and gentle hear the voice
Of him that walketh in the garden
in the evening time.

I tried to show my mother, but she would have none of it. And so I gave up on her and spent that night preparing food and drinks myself.

And at ten the next morning, dressed to their nines for the occasion, all those invited appeared and sat where they could.

I said a few words welcoming and thanking all who had attended, we played music from someone's iPad, and then my friendly neighbor began reading from Blake in that mellifluous voice he had.

And that's when it happened.

My mother let out a wail, some loud sobs, and cried for several minutes as everyone in the room stared at her.

It was a momentous occasion for me.

She'd not once looked saddened by his death until that moment. Now the damn had broken and the demon loosed.

Even when she'd stop, she'd wait a couple of seconds, and then start over again.

When anyone tried to console her, they looked at me, and I shook my head. This was my mother's time. In her own way she'd loved him to the very end. And now she had to pay for his loneliness of her, with her own of him. Not a bad thing. A good thing.

Eventually, maybe twenty minutes worth, she more or less gave it up out of sheer exhaustion. And she sat there with her head bowed, afraid no doubt to look up and see everyone staring at her.

And my neighbor friend, bless his heart, continued to read from the Blake poem I'd picked out for this occasion.

By the time we'd covered all the bases, my mother had carefully tucked her emotions back into their proper places, wiped her eyes carefully so as not to mess up her mascara, and stood with the rest of the group and received each and every one of their condolences with a gracious smile and nod of her head in thanks.

After that, we had what little food and drink I'd been able to make available, and everyone left. Except, of course, for me and my mother.

"Well," she said to me. "That went quite well, don't you think?"

I had no response to that. She'd obviously ignored the memory of her reaction during the service. So much so, I guessed, that it would never see the light of day again. For her, none of her display of love and affection for my father and sorrow over his loss had occurred. She'd withstood the entire service, if that's what it could be called, and was very proud of herself.

As the rest of that day wore on and we both spent our time word-lessly cleaning the house of the crumbs and other bits of mess that had been made here and there, she began whistling. I had no idea what. Or why. Just whistling.

I'd never seen her so happy. So without care. It was as if nothing had happened. Not my father's death or the quasi-funeral that morning. Maybe she'd become single again in her mind, and I didn't matter any longer. Just a houseboy helping with the tasks.

I had no idea.

And this went on for about a week. I had nowhere to go, nor did she.

We played gin rummy, watched an old black-and-white film on one of the pay-per-view channels on television, ate in silence, and time morphed as it always does, irrevocably onward.

Then, without warning, everything came to an abrupt halt. She'd gotten bored or something, and returned in full force as my mother. And I had no idea which her I preferred. The somehow guiltless tenderer of chores and pretense, or the all-business mother who'd suddenly realized she'd not been doing her job.

She even went into his bedroom and cleaned it as if nothing un-toward had ever happened there. She did, though, avoid the urn that contained my father's ashes now sitting on the mantle of our fireplace. Other than that, no more mention was made of him, his job, his place in our lives, or what we were to make of ourselves now that he'd left us to our own wits.

4

After a fitful night with little sleep, I got out of bed, washed, dressed, and visited the motel's continental breakfast. What a letdown. Plain yogurt, sweet rolls that reeked of sugar and preservatives, and coffee that tasted like liquid refried beans. Not a pleasant experience. Maybe I'd been spoiled by my previous night's dinner into expecting things exotic rather than ordinary.

While eating, though, I decided to stay a few more days in Holbrook. So, after what barely passed for food and drink, I raided my strong box in the Plymouth, and paid up front for three more nights.

And, when I'd finished my morning ablutions, I found myself once again driving Interstate 40, this time headed east toward the Petrified Forest National Park maybe fifteen miles distant.

The sky was clear, the temperature already quite warm, and, without an air-conditioning available other than the warm wind, I shoved my left elbow out my door window, let the oncoming air ride through my hair, and enjoyed the morning.

So lost was I in the midst of my travels, I'd forgotten what day of the week it was. A Tuesday maybe. At least a weekday, I guessed.

As I drove, I noticed the other traffic. Almost entirely semi-trailer trucks going both east and west. The summer visitors from the east had gone home and put their unhappy children back in school, leaving the highways and byways to the truckers. America's veins dealing its well-stocked red blood cells to the towns and cities that huddled like bees around hives along the rarely clotted Interstates.

When I arrived at the gate for the slightly more than mile-high forest, I paid my admission—actually I paid for a ten-day pass since I suspected I would otherwise need many far more expensive individual passes were I not to have done so—and parked in the area reserved for such not far from the entrance.

Though I'd seen pictures of this area, none had prepared me for the contrasts between earth and sky. Unlike the desert around Holbrook, here there were mountains of a sort, or at least hills with rough peaks on top. And what hills these were. Most of their sides were slate gray to white, bleached no doubt by the sea that had at one time covered the area. And along the shanks of these gray and white hills were strata of different shades of white that represented, no doubt, long standing shores of that ancient sea that had slowly evaporated to the sky leaving behind the salts of its waters.

What struck me most strongly, however, were the summits of these hills that, like islands in that ancient sea, were rusty in color giving me the impression of the famed Nipples of Venus truffles I'd once eaten with great abandonment in my travels.

Among the relics left behind by the shallow sea that had once filled the area between the islands, were fossilized tree trunks, some many feet in diameter. While called 'trunks,' they're no longer parts of trees at all now, but minerals having slowly replaced the original bodies of those trees. Amazingly, these rocks looked exactly like the real thing, at least from afar.

I wandered my morning away looking at these ancient remnants, at the meager vegetation no doubt due to the heavy salt in the sedimentary remains of the lakebed, and at the badlands that surrounded much of the area.

Speckled here and there were petroglyphs from various natives that had occupied the area some thousands of years earlier, dug out from the rock and lasting due to the impossibly low rainfall in the region. A drought in this part of Arizona meant no rain at all, with the average most likely between one and two inches a year.

I saw a coyote, with its pointed ears and ribs showing a lean summer. And it saw me. I'd heard that natives called them 'tricksters' because they disobeyed rules with their cunning. Usually for good in the end, as a kind of hero God, they were nonetheless full of mischief. This one looked starved and thirsty and heading my way. I couldn't remember whether they were dangerous or not, though this one looked harmless enough. And alone as far as I could see.

Not wanting to feel stalked, I whistled and raised and waved my arms as if beckoning him forth. He stared at me for a second, stuck his tail between his legs, and loped off in the opposite direction.

I could have stared at the riot of colors, the abnormalities of the moonscape-looking land, and the detritus of the surrounding messages left by ancient tribes for the rest of the day, so wild and uncommon their vagaries. For some reason, though, I had an itch to travel. And, by then, to eat my lunch lest I forget. So I rejoined my Plymouth and headed for the nearest diner I could find. And I found it in a tiny berg named Chambers.

This diner was housed in a motel and apparently, aside from a lonely gas station, represented the entirety of the town.

According to the sign upon entering Chambers, it had zero population, though it had its own zip code and off and on ramps from the Interstate in both directions.

There was also a strange sign stating the illegality of hunting camels in the state of Arizona. The irony of creating and posting such a law where no camels existed was not lost on me. Who knew, though, maybe they once had.

Most interesting to me, however, was that Chambers stood at a sort of half crossroads, an L-shaped connection with Highway 191 going north and onto the Navajo Indian Nation where I hoped to get a view of Canyon de Chelly, a National Monument I'd heard many interesting things about.

My lunch consisted of an overdone cheeseburger, a million grease-covered French Fries, and a glass of Coca-Cola. Oh, and lest I forget, a very large bottle of ketchup to cover any and all tastes that this food might otherwise send my way.

The meal caused my bowels to send me a signal to poop, and should I forget to mention it, I found the passage of said poop a reminder of my previous night's dinner with its hot chili peppers. This secondary reaction to that wonderful meal was indeed unexpected. But, given the nature of my lunch, welcome nonetheless.

I contemplated a dessert, but gave it up after a look at the menu. Instead I bought a Hershey's at the front desk that reminded me of a little known fact that chocolate averaged eight insect legs per bar. And more worrisome, that we consume roughly eight spiders while we sleep at night over the course of our lifetimes. Where I got these bits of minutiae I couldn't remember. They both cheered and disgusted me as I left this ridiculous version of *The Diner*.

As I walked back to my car, I looked across the desert and saw a prairie dog mound with several of the little beasts standing and staring in my direction. They'd stopped their munching on various grasses they'd collected from the area, but likely not warned the others, at this time of day most likely already underground to avoid the heat.

The mound they'd built looked more inviting than my motel did. Well ventilated, with plenty of ways to get in and out, and neatly kept. And it was several prairie-dog stories high. I'd read somewhere that they channeled rain down into their own little water table to save it for dry days, which here probably meant most of the year.

And I got back in my Plymouth and moved on.

As I drove through the mostly flat landscape, I saw two lonely clouds in the distance rise up into huge popcorn-shaped white monsters, with the bottoms dark and as flat as a straight line on graph paper. And, for some reason that I'm sure Freud would have had a field day with, I thought of my mother. She'd been the perfect foil for my father. He would get some sort of wild fanciful idea in his head that she and I both knew wasn't going to work and, instead of arguing with him, she'd let him argue with himself, sometimes for hours on end. Then, when he'd finished, he'd always ask her what she thought. She'd tell him that she agreed with him, a line that never ceased to amaze me, especially since it worked. My father would then have to revisit what he'd said for fear that he didn't really know what she—or he—meant, and then eventually agree with her. That it was all nonsense.

Just as my father with his story about dreams of pearl necklaces who'd taught me a wise lesson, my mother once told me something that had stayed with me as well. Hers, though, was a simple one-liner. Not told as an interesting story. She said, and quite out of the blue, that a lie can and often does appear within bunches of truths. That hidden there, it could easily be taken as a member of those things around it, and pass for one of them as well.

For some reason, probably because her telling me this came seemingly from nowhere, it took hold of me in a striking way. Mainly, I think, because she'd heard it from me originally.

And since that time, having her verify my own logic, I always took each element of an argument on its own merits, waiting for the lie that often hid itself behind truth. While my discoveries of such lies in stories often made me lose the thread of what they really meant, they also indicated that I'd found flaws where none otherwise existed. And I learned that science and religion, two strange bedfellows, were most guilty of committing those hidden lies.

By the time I'd reminded myself of these memories, I found myself in the town of Chinle, Arizona, a small village on the Navajo Indian Nation about two miles east of Highway 191 on Indian Route 7, and about half a mile west of the Canyon de Chelly National Monument Visitor Center.

As I passed the Farmer's Insurance building and the Holiday Inn, I stopped for gas at an independent station nearby. I filled my Plymouth's tank with regular—since I was convinced the higher-priced versions were identical to it—and watched the clouds I'd seen earlier nearly cover the sky and the sun with darkness. Apparently Chinle had a better position or altitude for rainfall than did Holbrook.

Almost immediately, my prediction proved true, and I sat in my car underneath the cover for the gas pumps and watched first hail and then rain pound the desert around me.

The sounds on both the metal above and the cement below were so loud I had to close my window to hear myself think.

And the lightning and thunder came nearly simultaneously. No slouch this, the sudden storm continued for at least fifteen minutes with water rushing down the street after filling the culverts, and I thought for a minute it would raise my Plymouth up off the ground and carry it and me along with it.

It didn't.

And, like the near storm I'd experienced the night before, this one stopped as abruptly as it had started and the sun reappeared.

Within minutes most of the water had been swallowed by the thirsty land and, aside from the increased humidity and the fast retreating clouds, I could hardly believe there'd been a storm at all.

I paid for the gas and again retreated to the safety of my Plymouth. As I sat there considering my options, I realized the truth in my mother's and my own statements so long ago. That even in this land, where the truths were that life was mostly born of heat and lack of water, I'd experienced a lie of sorts. The most strikingly strange storm I'd ever witnessed. Delivering to the earth huge doses of ice and water. And did I really want to go into Canyon de Chelly with the chance of facing a similar lie in terms of a flood as I walked on the sands below high cliffs in the wake of the creek, stream, or river that had carved that very canyon? And the answer I gave myself was a definite 'no.'

I had seen a couple of photos of Canyon de Chelly—pronounced de shay—in the motel in Holbrook, and they were impressive. Thousand foot patina-striped walls at the bottom of which lay a winding canyon amid large cliff dwellings and a sandy wandering stream at the bottom.

Indeed, this was a place to see.

But not for me.

Not today.

Not with the recent memory of such a billowing giant in the vicinity.

And so I made my way back to Highway 191. And, since it was only a little past two-thirty in the afternoon, I turned north instead of south. Not sure what had possessed me, I continued deeper into Navajo country, toward what I saw by the signs along the road was a town called Many Farms.

The country around me had progressed or digressed from a chaparral kind of terrain to mostly sage and bunch grass. Flat with small hills in the distance. No clouds, which apparently had flown south for the upcoming winter season.

And, once again, I thought of my mother.

A gentle woman given to bouts of asthma now and again. She neither smoked nor drank and gave the impression of infinite patience, as she'd often shown with respect to my father who was pretty much the opposite.

She was also, I suppose, quite attractive to the opposite gender, causing my father an occasional fit of jealousy that my mother put to rest with her usual grace.

How the two of them had met, fallen in love, married, and then had an only son, was beyond me save for the adage that opposites attract. Not that they fought a lot, they didn't, but mostly because my mother wouldn't let it happen. Her winning strategy for all potential arguments being, again, intense patience.

My arrival at Many Farms lacked any fanfare whatsoever. To my left were a convenience store, two gas stations, and mostly farm implement businesses. To my right was a turnout for Many Farms Lake. There may have been more to it than that, but before I could actually take stock of the town, I'd passed it northward and had to make a U-turn back toward the Interstate.

There was one thing of which I was sure. The Navajo Nation must have the lowest population per square foot outside of Montana and Alaska in the U.S. I'd passed two cars I could remember, and had only seen one person, the man who'd taken my money at the gas station in Chinle. And he'd been a gringo, no less.

As I drove back to Holbrook, I felt strangely detached. Not lonely exactly. Some sort of separation between me and the land through which I now drove. It was as if I was floating within a dream of some kind, in which my body was someplace else.

Last night I'd tasted and felt a deep sense of connection with the people I'd met and the food I'd eaten, and now the precise opposite. And I decided then and there to again visit *The Diner* where I'd seen the man staring into his empty bowl of pea soup, the apparently native young waitress-cook, and the blonde manager of a restaurant in the town of Holbrook, in the vast emptiness just beyond the Navajo world.

What was I missing?

5

After my father died, life with mother provided me no end of confusions. I thought I knew a bit about magic and its misdirections. What I'd learned, however, was nothing compared to what she gave me. And it came naturally to her. So naturally in fact that when I pointed out the process she'd used to her, she denied it, claimed she'd not done anything on purpose, or ignored me entirely. It was tough sledding. At least until I saw Chloe for the first time.

I'd met Chloe in high school briefly, though she'd hung around with a group that didn't much interest me. In fact, no group interested me. In the least. I was a loner. And so she went her way, and me mine.

Then I saw her in a coffee shop one day, maybe two months after my father died, and I barely recognized her. Dressed to the nines in a professional women's suit and looking ready to tackle the vaunted Wall Street tycoons.

I re-introduced myself to her and she smiled and invited me to sit down. I did. And we talked like we'd known one another our entire lives. Though it was definitely not love at first sight, it was damn close.

And we began seeing each other. All, of course, to my mother's great concern. Who was this slut I was seeing? What would come of me if I continued seeing someone with no future? And on, and on.

Interestingly, my mother at this time had begun dressing herself

more formally. Using makeup. Altering her hairstyle in ways more allur-
ing. At least as I thought she thought of it.

This concerned me no end. I'd read Oedipus, after all, and knew
the potential problems these actions brought to mind. At least my mind.

Chloe, however, was a real looker. At least this newer version of
her. But why was I comparing the two of them?

And my mother knew how to dress provocatively. Not by showing
anything, you understand, by obviously *not* showing anything, an art
I quickly learned had been lost through the generations. At forty-five,
my mother was still in her prime and quite attractive with full war paint
applied. Though I wanted nothing of it, I still had to admit it was so.

To counter her attempts, I stayed away from home far longer than I
needed to, took up smoking briefly, and wandered around Coney Island
again to remind myself of the days with my father there. And, of course,
I often took Chloe along with me.

Of course I was mistaken about my mother's intentions, for the
time I spent away from her she spent wooing suitors. Especially wealthy
ones. After all, in her mind at least, we were slowly going broke. We were
about to lose the house. And with it our ability to cope in the modern
world. Like eat and drink and poop in other than public restaurants and
restrooms. In short, we were close to walking the streets. I, of course,
kept interviewing for jobs. Unsuccessfully.

In spite of all the tension, mother and son, mother and Chloe,
mother and money, me and money, me and Chloe, and so on, we made
an interesting trio. Made even more interesting since I'd not introduced
Chloe to mother. No reason to bring the red-hot branding iron directly
in contact with the fuse of dynamite. After all, I had no idea my mother
was sleeping around, fishing for a replacement for my father.

So I was incredibly surprised when one night readying myself for
a night out with my beautiful Chloe, a well-dressed and rather pompous
man showed up at our door and introduced himself as the richest man
in Brooklyn. Well, he didn't say that exactly, though he just as well could
have. Clearly, he dressed in style and had the swagger. That kind of 'I
have it, you don't' look of a man who could buy your loyalty in a minute,
and turn around and sell your ass in a second.

My mother, claiming that he'd come early and apologizing for her
son's presence and how awkward this made things and how sorry she

was that we'd met in this unusual way, had planned it perfectly. She'd obviously told the man of me, and rigged it so I'd have to save my questions until later, after I'd met him.

We sat in the living room that would soon be someone else's living room if we didn't get some money fast, and discussed the price of things and the usual state of politics.

It was riotous fun, and over none too quickly.

I excused myself with a smile and apology, and headed out to see my fast-becoming fiancée. With a guilty conscience about ever imagining my mother as considering a potential incest complication in our lives.

As I walked to meet Chloe that night, I tried thinking of this man as my new father. But it wouldn't do. He was pompous. Smug. Arrogant. Fastidious. And so on. It wouldn't work.

Of course, he was also rich. Probably owned half of Brooklyn. And what did I really care anyway? *I* wasn't marrying him. He wasn't *really* my father.

Try as I might, however, I couldn't stop thinking of what my father would think of him. My father. The most unpretentious man I'd ever met. Full of earthy qualities to be admired by anyone and everyone I knew. A man among men. And all that. And the more I thought of these things, no matter the money, the angrier I became.

Chloe quietly cut through the bullshit and made me understand that the choice was not mine. My mother would make hers, and who knew whether hers was only a date or the real thing? Of course, the real thing was money, not love. Of that I was sure.

Nonetheless, this episode remained with me for days. Especially when I finally got a job as a low-paid staffer of a stock investor delivering packages across town on a bicycle yet. At fifteen an hour. With overtime and pedaling at night, we kept our house and ate regularly. Though the latter was unnecessary with mother having her dinners paid for, and I spending more and more time with Chloe's parents who loved meeting their daughter's beau.

And things progressed on both fronts. Mother with her billionaire as I eventually found out, and me with my high-level Wall Street ladder climber and her parents. Of course, my low-class job as delivery boy for the giants of industry seemed oxymoronic amidst those climes, but what the hell.

My mother then made a big night out of nothing, I thought. My first dinner with her and her boyfriend. At his house, yet.

And it *was* a big deal. His house, that is. Three story mansion out on Long Island facing north and within a mile of the shoreline. Took us an hour to get there in his limousine. Maybe he was a trillionaire rather than a billionaire. But who's counting? A million here, a million there.

We had aperitifs in his library with caviar on the side. Looked like a pound of it. And his books, many of them first editions, covered wall to ceiling with a twelve-foot high roof and two ladders to wheel around for getting out-of-reach ones. And organized according to the Dewey Decimal System. He told us that he even had a librarian on site twenty-four hours a day to fetch books for him. Maybe a zillionaire?

I'd brought Chloe along, and she gaped right along with me. Especially when we entered the dining room with a table that would fit a football team and their wives or girlfriends. Or whatever. I don't remember the number of courses we had. Seven at least. Beginning with true *hors d'oeuvres*. Bruschetta, two small half-buns covered with garlic, olive oil, tomato slices, basil, beans, and I don't know what else. Apparently the caviar hadn't counted. The *consommé* was a bouillon of various vegetables in a cup. The third course—I could at that point still count them—was poached salmon with mousseline sauce and cucumbers. And that followed in turn by a large filet mignon, lamb in mint sauce with creamed carrots, a Romaine punch, roast squab and cress, cold asparagus vinaigrette, *foie gras*, all ending with a Waldorf Pudding of apples, walnuts, and raisins with a hint of nutmeg. I had no idea what most of these things were, so our host graciously announced each of them in turn before we devoured them.

Conversation was polite and mostly begun by my mother. She spoke of our host's great accomplishments which were, as I remember them and in order of importance, inheriting his fortune from his parents, building an advertising agency that apparently had been the first to require their clients to offer the same number of buns as their associated hamburger and hotdog packages had, and investing wisely over the years, building upon his inheritance many times over. Impressive credentials for a handsomely dressed idiot who probably hadn't yet learned to tie his own shoes.

I said nothing. Chloe said nothing. Our host introduced the courses of the meal. Mother did all the talking. Looking and sounding like the man's wife already.

And our host loved it. All of it. My stepfather to be? The replacement for my father?

No way.

So I told this to Chloe as we left the place, quietly walking behind the host and my mother on the way to the limo. She smiled and whispered that the man was rich. No more bicycling. No more cheese sandwiches. No more groveling. Live with it.

I could see her point.

Then she put the capper on it.

Not your decision anyway.

And, of course, she was right. My mother could make up her own mind. I wasn't a kid anymore. I didn't have to live with the man. And so, as I watched her kiss him gently on the lips and then let him help her gently into the car, I realized this might be better than having a *real* new father, someone who might actually compete with my real father.

I had it made in the shade.

Or so I thought.

Six months to the day after my father died, my mother and her rich benefactor were married. Of course, I attended. Alone. Chloe had decided my obsession with my new stepfather exemplified my anal nature and decided to find someone else to agree with her. Ours had been an interesting relationship at the beginning. Of two parts lust and one part argument. I regretted losing her, though not so much as to want her back.

The morning of the ceremony, my mother's betrothed sat me down to have a heart to heart talk. This amazed me, for as I watched him sit across from me, a heart was the last thing I thought he could buy. He certainly hadn't shown much of one himself to present.

He told me that he wished to be a real father, not a token one. That I was free to live with them for as long as I wanted and no matter what I decided, I would wont not. Nothing in that I could possibly argue with. So I didn't. I thanked him instead.

He further told me that he'd never met anyone like my mother, and that he planned to make her the happiest woman in the world. I doubted that, but that he was going to try made me happy as well.

He asked me what I planned to do with my life. And, of course, there he had me. I'd never given it much thought. I'd always let things happen to me rather than make them happen. I didn't actually tell him that, I let him figure it out for himself based on what I'd said.

He advised me, in ever so non-insistent terms, that I should attend a college of worth. Say, for example, Harvard or Yale, and major in something of worth, say business or economics, as if making money was the only reason to continue living. This made a certain amount of sense coming from him, though I didn't buy a shred of it. Money is great. I knew that. He knew that. Except you can't buy everything, I thought. Though I didn't tell him that since this was, after all, his wedding day.

I did tell him I'd give everything he'd said the deepest consideration I could and would let him know as soon as I figured it out for myself. He apparently understood, or at least that's what he told me, and we concluded the step-father-to-be advice to me at the precise time he was called to join the procession.

I'd opted out of being best man, train holder, or usher for the event in hopes I might get away early and drink for the rest of the day at a local bar. So I sat on the sidelines as the ceremony took place.

And it was a grand performance. Catholic in every way. I still didn't know if my new stepfather was Catholic, except he knew the drill and the priest gave him communion, so he must have been. Either that or he was a damn good actor willing to risk eternal damnation for his performance.

While my mother and I had only a few friends, the moneyman had hundreds. The place that seated nearly a thousand was full. It was a big deal. Full costumes, parades down the center aisle of the church, and all attending dressed appropriately. Unfortunately, like my father, I was now a non-denomination Humanist not feeling at the moment very humanistic.

I didn't really understand what was bothering me. The man was rich beyond avarice. My mother was happy. My real father was dead. And, as I saw it, I shouldn't give a damn one way or the other.

Was I sad or mad I'd lost Chloe? Or that my mother wanted this idiot instead of my father back? Or that I had no life to speak of?

Each of these was good enough of an excuse to feel miserable as I watched the ceremony. Taken together, they were overkill.

I shouldn't have felt bad, I should've felt absolutely terrible. Even though I didn't give a rat's ass about who my mother screwed, in marriage or not, it was too soon for her to forget my real father. Or maybe I was just telling myself that. Maybe I wanted her to miss my father for the rest of her life. No other man was good enough to replace him.

Time to see a shrink. And I could afford one now. So I did. And I chose one that cost almost five hundred bucks an hour. Why not? Wasn't my money. And my stepfather wanted the best for me. Nothing less would do.

Of course, as I often discovered in life, competency and cost are inversely proportional. And this guy proved his worth from minute one on. As in, I did the talking and he tried his best to stay awake.

No suggestions. No comments. Just more of the same.

'And why do you think that?' he'd say.

And on, and on.

'Why did you break up with what's her name?'

'Chloe?'

'Yeah.'

'I didn't. She broke up with me. She'd had enough of my complaining about everything. Especially my mother's new husband.'

'Why do you suppose that is?'

'Because the guy's a stupid son of a bitch.'

'Hmm.'

He said that a lot. As if he was actually thinking, not merely counting the hours to make more money.

Two sessions and I'd had it with the schmuck.

And with psychiatry in general. Even the drugs weren't that good.

So, as that summer wore on, I decided to return to school. Not the junior college I'd previously attended and graduated from, mind you, but a *real* university as my stepfather insisted I call it.

Hello, Yale. Hello, New Haven. Hello nothing except more of the same.

Bored teachers lecturing to bored students who wanted nothing more than to party and screw. Not me among them, of course, but that was the gist of it.

So I endured the two requisite years to graduate in the middle of my class. Absolutely nothing to distinguish me from my classmates, literally none of whom I knew. In fact, were twenty-five years from then a reunion held, I'd not recognize a one of them.

I majored in something called Modern Age because it was the only major that had no focus whatsoever. Right up there with Management. Classes in everything possible, guaranteeing that whatever your interest was, you could find it somewhere in the available courses. All of these, of course, at beginning level, and thus I graduated knowing a little about everything. Better as far as I was concerned than knowing a lot about only one thing and, therefore, nothing about anything else.

And, so engaged was I with the college experience, I got into Harvard for my graduate degree, a masters in Communications.

As vague as Modern Age? Yes.

Of course, I was smart enough to know that with my grades and background I'd not gotten into Yale or Harvard without my stepfather's help. He, of course, had paved and paid my way. And for that, I suppose, I was grateful.

At the same time, he never showed his face to me during those years. Nor allowed my mother to either. They took off for parts unknown with nary a word about their destinations. Vacationed their asses off. This was fine with me, given I had the house and servants to myself whenever I wanted. And a library to die for.

The few women I wined and dined were full of class and far beyond my level of experience. They spoke with strange accents, alluded directly and indirectly to their status in life and how important they were, and gave me the willies. Believe me, there are levels to which men will not go to sleep with a woman. I've had first-hand experience. Lots of it.

During my three years getting my master's degree, I thought over the nagging question of what the hell was I going to do with my life?

Did I have a goal? Could I remain this way forever? Simply forget about doing anything except lazy my way toward infinity?

When I asked myself these questions seriously, I kept coming up with nothing. Absolutely nothing.

And on graduation day, sitting with the rest of the graduates waiting to be handed their diplomas, looking over the crowd that included my mother and stepfather, I had no more idea what the hell was going on than I'd had when I'd been ten.

No drive. No ambition. No intent other than waiting for something to happen that would tell me what to do.

And then it occurred to me. Simple. So simple I'd spent all this time overlooking the obvious.

Nothing.

I'd majored in it, specialized in it, loved it, was good at it, practiced it daily, preached it to myself and others, and generally considered myself the world's authority at doing it.

Nothing.

Of course, I couldn't tell anyone that. After all, nobody does nothing for a living. Even the very rich claim alternates to that way of life. So my problem wasn't about what to do with my life, only to give doing nothing a respectable name.

Adventurer. That was it. Meant nothing as far as I was concerned. Like traveler with more pizazz. Adventurer.

And so, when I met with my mother and stepfather in the crowd and they asked me the inevitable question, I told them that. I would be an adventurer. Travel the world in search of adventure. Like so many of the greats before me. Sir Edmund Hilary, Thor Heyerdahl, John Goddard, Jason Lewis, and the list went on and on.

Of course, I had no idea what I was talking about. None of those men and their accomplishments meant much of anything to me. I was only interested in avoiding conflict. And, from the looks on their faces, I had.

My mother looked absolutely proud.

My stepfather looked confused at first, and then proud as he saw my mother's reaction. After all, the one thing I could say about the man was that he loved my mother, and anything that made her proud made him proud.

And so I became an adventurer, *nee* a 'do nothing.' And proud of it as well.

Life was good.

6

I thought these thoughts until I arrived back at the motel I temporarily called home, the one in Holbrook, Arizona. And it was there, like a rattlesnake following a mouse, that the storm that had bullied me and my Plymouth in Chinle already once that day had found me again.

The sky had that nearly black incendiary look that precedes real violence from the heavens. Maybe the gods had seen fit to punish me for fighting with my mother since she'd been on my mind. Whatever the case, I parked my car, locked it securely, and rushed into the motel lobby just as the hail arrived.

The manager smiled at me as I passed him heading directly for my room. This I had to see out the broad window there facing south.

So, as I opened my room door, I could see that the hail had already stopped, no rain had followed, and the sun had already begun peeking around a leftover cloud.

Once again the storm had been hijacked someplace else at the last minute, and whatever bits and pieces of moisture had fallen here were already evaporating to make more clouds to rain down on another part of the desert.

No longer dispassionate about my day, I immediately decided to change clothes and visit *The Diner* again. It had been a long time since my covered-in-ketchup hamburger and fries lunch, and my mouth was watering for exotic foods with an under layer of chili peppers.

So I raided my suitcase on the luggage rack near the door, took a shower, climbed into my new gear and headed out the door for another culinary surprise.

The earth around me had already swallowed what little water it had received, and the sky had returned to its usual taciturn self. The teasing clouds had disappeared into the distant mountains, and I could feel what little cooling the ice and water had provided vanishing as well.

Another hour at least before sunset, and the town of Holbrook had one final crack at heating up its citizens.

When I arrived at *The Diner*, the large window still displayed its sign and below it 'Open.'

As was the case the previous night, the street in front held no cars and no pedestrians walked the streets nearby. As if the little restaurant was plagued with some kind of strange disease that kept people away. Not me. I strode confidently up the two steps to the door, opened it, and without any hesitation, stepped inside.

It was as if I'd never left. There before me were the empty tables and booths in the cool darkness with a lone man sitting under a small oval set-back window delicately dipping a tablespoon into a bowl full of green pea-soup liquid, raising the spoon to his lips gently, sipping the spoon dry delicately, and then repeating the motions over and over again. To my right was the large opening beyond which the same young woman with jet-black hair was cooking something. And to my left was the place where I had sat the previous night, looking the same as it had except for a menu already placed in front of where I'd sat, as if someone expected me. Of course, I didn't believe that to be true. Someone else must have sat there during the day and left it there. Or maybe I had left it the night before.

The girl in the kitchen looked up, saw me, smiled, and with a free hand gave me a little wave with her fingers.

I returned the gesture without any hesitation, and being a creature of habit walked to my vinyl seat, sat down, and picked up the menu. Of course, why I did the latter was beyond me, I couldn't read a word of it. Yet it was the thing to do, so I did it.

As far as I could tell, none of the words on the menu had changed places or been replaced by new entries. Maybe it was the exact same menu I'd used previously, I couldn't tell. And I still had no more idea what these words meant except, of course, for azee' hókániltsoh, which I presumed meant artichoke in what I now guessed was the Navajo language. How the other dishes I'd had on the menu were connected to one another I had no idea.

Not wanting to press the issue, I placed the now closed menu back on the table in front of me, looked around for help, found none except for the waitress-cook in the kitchen who was too busy to tend to me at the moment, and found myself once again staring at the man sitting across the room from me. He, in turn, paid me no mind whatsoever, just dutifully fed himself like clockwork from, I now noticed, the quite deep bowl in front of him.

He hadn't changed the least bit since I'd last seen him. His fedora tipped over his forehead, his farmer uniform with its blue suspenders hefted over his broad shoulders, and his eyes and apparently thoughts intently focused on his meal.

His white beard hadn't changed either, still so white that it looked almost blue in the darkness, somehow lit from within like a buried automobile headlight might through sand. Whatever made me think that, made me shake my head back and forth. Not known for creating word images, I thought it strange to say the least.

I hadn't heard her come in, but when I looked up the blond woman who'd saved me from embarrassment the previous night was looking down at me with a notebook and pencil at the ready. A grin playing across her lips. And she asked me what I had in mind to eat.

Not having a clue, I suggested that whatever I'd eaten the previous night would be fine. I'd liked it very much then, and I would surely like it at least as much now.

This, however, did not sit well with her, because before I'd gotten the words out of my mouth, she was already shaking her head indicating no. She then told me that repeating meals was not a good idea. I would expect the same wonderful surprises and only be disappointed. A surprise, she told me, was only a surprise if you didn't know what was coming.

And with that she asked my permission to let her fix me a different meal and did I trust her enough to do that. Not having any other idea how to proceed except by pointing my fingers at things on the menu about which I knew next to nothing, I granted her request.

When she'd written her choices down on her pad, I added that did she know that cockroaches were known to live at least nine days after their heads had been cut off. In other words, before they starved to death. And then I quickly decided I shouldn't have asked her that.

She smiled again, this time broadly, and headed back to the kitchen, nodded to the waitress-cook, said nothing to her, and disappeared. I found this particularly strange.

Had they worked out something in advance of my arriving?

How could that be, for how could they know I'd be here tonight and not trying out some other maybe more popular place in town for dinner?

Or had they worked out a plan for feeding Anglos in here? After all, I couldn't be the first to find the menu indecipherable. They must have a planned menu going for the first few days until such customers got the hang of things and could order for themselves.

None of this, of course, really mattered. If this meal were as good as the last one I'd had here, it would have been well worth it.

So I sat back and waited.

And, of course, my eyes drifted to the only other thing besides the waitress-cook in the kitchen that moved. The man sitting across from me. And the strange oval window under which he sat. The one with the sailboat in it, and the opaque glass through which I could see nothing. At least nothing that made any sense.

He was definitely a white man. Nothing about him looked Indian, though truth be known I'd not yet seen an Indian since I'd been in this part of the world. Except maybe the waitress-cook.

His skin was definitely white, though deeply tanned. His eyes, or rather eye since I could see only one of them, now stared directly at the business at hand. Crinkled with age lines, as was his face, at least the part of his face I could see above his beard. The amount of hair I could see below his hat in back was streaked with gray, though light brown not black, giving me one more indication that his ancestry was European and not local. The delicate motions were the most persuasive in giving him away. The precision in which he ate suggested upper-class nobility rather than a result of a stark living made from the local dry desert landscape.

He again gave no indication that he knew of my presence or that I was looking at him. So engrossed in his simple act of eating soup that I believe nothing could have persuaded him to even glance my way. Were I have suddenly jumped to my feet and yelled something strange, what would he have done?

But I didn't do it. He was quite a sight already. Nothing like I'd ever seen before in my life.

It was then that the blond woman, definitely not native, arrived with her hands and arms covered with plates of steaming food, quite different than that she'd served me the previous night.

No artichoke of bowl filled with mayonnaise. No nothing that I recognized.

She smiled as she set the dishes in front of me, leaving the glass of something I didn't recognize for last. I pointed at it and looked at her, and she reminded me that it might taste better if I were surprised. I nodded, though I wanted to remind her that this had not been the case the previous evening when she'd identified the various dishes for me.

I began with a large bowl of green liquid that, not surprisingly, looked exactly like that which the man seated across from me was now finishing. And, whatever I expected, I quickly found substantially different. Rather than some kind of soup, this was a thick mud requiring a strong set of digits to bring to my mouth. Once there, though, I ate a full spoonful. And, whatever had once reminded me of liquefied peas disappeared completely. This was a mix of flavors, none of which I could immediately identify. Bunch grass, pinion, and cactus being the only greens I'd seen since entering Arizona from New Mexico. Maybe this was these, squashed together to form a thick green cold broth.

Pungent was my first thought, then hot, as a tear formed in my left eye. And after that, sweet, sour, and brutal in that order.

Not that it wasn't interesting. It was. Only that it was unforgiving. No prisoners.

So I puckered up and swallowed.

Maybe I shouldn't have, for it then made it's way south with a distinct trail following it down. And then a definite, rock solid 'thump' in my stomach.

Good God, I thought, how could I eat the full bowl. My entire body lit up like a Christmas tree. And with only one tablespoon of the stuff.

I closed my eyes for a few seconds, and when I opened them the blond manager, or owner, or whatever, was seated across from me.

Watching. She had a slightly wicked look on her face, or was I imagining it? And she asked me what I thought. And I would have answered her could I have opened my mouth at the moment. But I couldn't. Not a chance. While I tried to talk, I thought once again of the man seated across the room from me. He'd eaten a full bowl of this volcanic greenery both nights I'd been here.

How was that possible?

And showing no outward signs of having any reaction whatsoever except possibly genuine pleasure.

When I regained my voice, I looked at her and asked her what was in that green slop I'd just eaten. Though I didn't use that precise language.

She replied that she'd discovered it herself one day when she'd forgotten to clean out the remnants of goat's milk from a pan she'd left in the sun. A few days later it had magically morphed into an algae of some sort. Given her curiosity, she'd eaten some of it and found its taste somewhat curious. And the actual algae was not only non-toxic, but delightfully awakening. Like a cup of coffee providing a dose of caffeine. So, she'd taken to using many pans and goat's milk to create lots of the stuff, and thus her new dish had been created.

And, so far, she added, no one she knew had died. Good to hear.

And some, she then added, had become habituated to it. Like, for example, the man sitting across from me this very moment, who had, apparently, at least as far as she could recollect, had had a bowl of it a day for at least the past five years.

All this was far too much information for me to swallow at once. Instead, I pointed at the remainder of the food and asked, maybe demanded might be the better word, of what it consisted.

Again, though, she told me I had to try each dish first. Then she would tell me.

And with that, she stood up and returned to the kitchen to once again disappear while the waitress-cook continued to make concoctions. For whom, I had no idea. Maybe *The Diner* had ghosts who filled the place I couldn't see, and were now busy gulping down these mysteries with gusto.

I glanced over at the only other patron I could see in the place and watched as he glided the tablespoon from bowl to his mouth without the slightest sign that he was eating wild algae of little or no known ancestry. Up and in, down and scoop, over and over and over again.

So I looked back at my own set of plates and bowls. One looked like baked wood, another similar to the number two excretions of a human child, and yet another like a bowl full of fried cockroaches. I knew my imagination was getting the best of me. But I didn't much care. After my first taste of algae stew, I wasn't sure I'd been right in returning to this place. Maybe I could feign that I was a moth, many species of which I'd once read didn't have mouths at all. They live off the food they consumed as young caterpillars.

However, I stayed the course and forked a black turd into my mouth. And, to my delight, it tasted wonderful. Not at all like a turd, not that I had that much experience with such things. More like a strange version of a sausage made from a mixture of parts of various animals. The spices were reasonable and quieted the growing sense that the algae had reversed direction and was heading upward rather than further down.

Another dish looked like dead beetles. At this, I blanched. I remembered that a quarter of the world's population was beetles, and no doubt someone had to eat them. Why me?

And so it went, as I sampled everything in front of me with increasing interest. Before long I was dipping each in a batter of algae and finding the taste even of that growing on me. Of course, my imagination still wondered if I might find myself the next morning singing 'it isn't easy being green.'

The beverage of the evening was the biggest shock of all. An apparent mix of lemons, limes, grapefruit, peaches, grapes, and something I couldn't quite identify. But it went down easy and accompanied the food in a complementary way. Once again, the manager had fooled me. This was delightful and surprising.

And, of course, that's when she appeared again to join me in my booth, asking what I thought of what I'd eaten.

I had to say that it had been memorable. Clearly a new experience.

And she smiled, that beatific smile she had when she knew she'd won a minor victory in life.

Then, of course, I made the mistake of asking her what, in fact, I'd eaten. Having fulfilled my side of the bargain she had to come through with hers. So, in rapid succession, and before I had a chance to react, she told me that I'd eaten a bowl full of fried cockroaches—no surprise there—a bowl of jackrabbit testicles, a snake of some kind that she thought was probably a type of garter her cook had found in the garden, and baked wood bark from a nearby cottonwood tree. After she saw the look on my face, she added that my guess on the contents of my drink was mostly correct and that the added unknown ingredient was honey gathered from a local wasp nest.

After a moment of silence and I'd taken all this in, I asked her how it was possible for wasps to make honey. She told me that the *polistine* wasps did, and that they're plentiful in temperate regions and easy to collect by leaving paper out for them to build their nests. It seemed, at least according to her, that these wasps produce some of the world's finest honey.

I was, of course speechless at her wide vocabulary of foods and knowledge of the types of plants and animals in this region of the desert. Of course, all this was postulated on my current state of disarray as the fried cockroaches argued their way into my lower intestines and battled the green algae there.

When she rose, I pulled out the ten left over from the previous night and handed it to her.

She, of course, stuck it in her pocket and returned a five to me. I was in no mood to argue over this idiotic amount of money and headed for the door and my way back to my room as quickly as I could make it.

After I left, and as I walked along in the darkness, I heard a nightingale singing in the distance. I recognized the repeated figure followed by one of a few different hiccup sounds.

Comforting.

A way to remind myself that the world was all right. That danger doesn't necessarily lurk around every corner. Or that darkness benefits the victim as much as the stalker. Same disadvantage. Something like that.

I felt at peace with myself and my place in the universe. For no reason I could think of, except maybe the dinner I'd just eaten.

As I approached my room, I began to believe that my sudden urge to evacuate all that I'd eaten was more from the contents I'd learned of than from the actual food itself.

And I was right.

When I crawled into bed with the curtains on my floor to ceiling window opened fully so I could see the night sky in all its glory, I felt relaxed and ashamed of myself.

Had I become a bigot in my own way? Not willing to take chances anymore?

And, when I did, finding myself on the verge of exhaustion from the experience?

7

One day while in my new home—the castle—for the holidays, my stepfather took me aside and told me some things about himself. He asked that I remember these if ever I should find a use for them. All true, he claimed.

He began innocently enough with him living at home, the very one in which he now lived but at that time with his parents. His father, a successful banker and innovator in the world of business and finance, was the patriarch of the family and ruled with a stern hand. But, he claimed, not so heavy that it didn't include leniency for minor offenses. Thus, and for example, he never included physical violence, not even spankings. At the same time, he was not shy of handing out plenty of hard labor. Thus, though rich, my stepfather had plenty of opportunity to feel punished, and possibly severely so. Even though, he said, his father had loved him. Of that he was certain.

His mother, on the other hand, was a tyrant. Whenever his father was away, which was often, she wouldn't shy away from beating the hell out of him. She was, he claimed, a 'witch.' Like one of the three Macbeth faced in Shakespeare's play, only not just to stir the brew and chant evil incantations for the spirits or the devil to do their bidding, but more fiendish things.

His father had died from cancer, much as my own had, for which

I gained a certain amount of familiarity with his plight. And when this happened, his mother had fully released her wrath on the world around her. She drank hard and heavy, she swore like an infantryman, and she brutalized every one she could possibly brutalize. Her son especially so. For it was he, she was convinced, that prevented her from catching a new husband and to live a happier life.

He warned me then, that she would be visiting us for the holidays and that I should keep as far away from her as possible. I'd either lose it and murder her—for which he'd be eternally grateful but which would not turn out so good for me—or take a beating the likes of which I'd never received before.

He had me so believing his description, that when this 'witch' finally arrived with ten tons of baggage as if she were going to move in rather than visit, I hid away in my room waiting for the walls to tremble and the floors to shake. I was twenty-one by this time, and his little lecture had had that much effect on me.

When called to dinner, I more or less snuck in and took my seat, fearful of looking up at this sinister shrew for fear my eyes might become locked on her Medusa face and I'd live forever thereafter as a body in stone.

Except she addressed me right off.

"And you must be the son," she said. And her voice matched one of the three witches that I imagined Shakespeare had in mind.

So I looked up. Now or never.

And she was a witch. In every detail. Tall. Skinny. Ugly as sin. Scraggly hair. No makeup. Thin, wiry, downturned lips. Eyes that bore holes through me. Dressed entirely in black. It looked like she practiced her part when not busy pulling the claws off kittens.

"Yes," I said. Meekly, I thought.

"And what do you do?"

"School," I replied.

"So?"

"So? So what?"

"What are you studying?"

"Communications," I said.

She looked astonished. Her eyelids, which certainly had a life of their own, vee'd into her forehead.

"What did you say?" she said.

"Communications," I repeated.

"What in God's name is Communications?"

I wasn't quite sure what to say at that point. I could try saying the word 'nothing' or 'adventurer,' though I didn't suppose that would do anything except anger her more.

So I said once again, "Communications."

I think she may have made a sound, though if it meant anything I didn't understand.

"It's an important major," my stepfather tried to bail me out. "You know, mother, one of those majors where you study many things rather than one so you'll be good at everything when you graduate."

"Poof," she said, with that hissing sound she had. "Sounds like he'll know next to nothing about everything to me."

"No," I said without thinking. *"Absolutely* nothing. And about everything."

And the table went dead silent at that point.

If that were possible.

Thank God she decided to ignore my outburst.

"And what do you plan to do with this degree in knowing absolutely nothing about nothing?"

"Nothing," I said.

My mother, for one of the first times I'd seen in my life, actually smiled. And for that, I felt greatly relieved.

"So, if I've got this right, you're going to school with the intention of learning nothing. That so?"

"Exactly," I said. By now I'd gotten into the rhythm of it. She was all bark and no bite. I could take her in a second. Might be a bitch with glares, but she was a wimp down deep.

Then she did something completely unexpected. She stood, pushed her chair back with one of her legs, slammed her napkin down on her plate, turned, and, without a word, stalked out of the room.

She was amazing, I now realized. Not only a witch. The *perfect* witch. One so practiced at it, she set the traps wherever she went. And pulled them shut at exactly the right times.

I had no idea how to respond. Nor did her son. Nor did my mother. Nor did the two waiters standing helplessly aside.

And that was that. We sat for a time. For no reason I could think of. Nobody spoke a word.

Finally, I said, "Well that wasn't so bad. In fact, I thought it went rather well."

Her son, my stepfather, and my mother looked at me as if I'd just landed in an alien spaceship.

"I'm hungry," I said, and looked at the waiters. Having no idea who was in charge at that moment, they both turned and headed for the kitchen.

"Better lock your bedroom door," my stepfather said. "Just to be safe."

And he didn't smile as he said it.

My mother kept on staring into the far distance. She'd not only met her match, she'd been a water boy for the lowest minor league team and watched Joe DiMaggio step to the plate and send one over the right-field fence.

And we ate in silence.

When we'd finished dinner and a liqueur served, my stepfather offered me a cigar.

"I wished I'd done that just once," he said. "Just once. My boy, you're a genius."

I had no idea how to respond to that.

But I gave it a try.

"Are you an only son?" I asked.

"Yes."

"You should have had some brothers. And maybe a sister. Maybe eleven in all. A football team. You might have had a chance. I may have gotten away with it tonight, but only because she means nothing to me."

"She means nothing to me, as well," he said. "But I'm her son, and that means something to the world."

I watched him as he sipped his liqueur while attempting not to toss his cookies.

"Is she going to expect you to come up and comfort her, or convince her to return to the table?" I asked him.

"No. Not ever. My father wouldn't allow that."

"So she's done this before?"

"Plenty of times."

I found myself having new respect for this stepfather of mine. I wondered if I could have survived under the same roof with the shrew.

"I'm sure she has off days," my mother, in a different mode than I'd ever seen her before, said.

"This *is* one of her good days," my stepfather responded.

For the rest of her visit, my step-grandmother never looked at or spoke to me. I was not there as far as she was concerned.

This, of course, made me incredibly happy. Somehow, having lived with my mother no matter her minor league status, my psyche had practiced the art of dealing with witches, and this skill I didn't know I had had helped me through a difficult period.

And when she left two days after our encounter, she remained aloof, never glancing my way.

Was she afraid of me? Of my wicked wit? Of my biting tongue? Of my wry humor? Or simply sick of me already? Of my nothingness?

As her chauffeur drove her away in a cloud of exhaust, I realized that her visit had actually cemented a small though important bond between myself and my new stepfather. This was a good thing. We had a common event that we could remember. A memory that we shared.

My stepfather was as chained to the earth as we all were. Maybe more so in some ways. And for that, I could feel a sense of kinship. If not the real thing, something at least as substantial.

One day many months after this incident, while on vacation, my stepfather decided to drive from Carmel south to Los Angeles taking Highway 1. I couldn't blame him, for that route along the Big Sur held some of the most incredible scenery I'd ever seen in my life. I'd only been there once with Chloe on one of our jaunts to get to know one another better, but it had been the highlight of our brief yet tumultuous relationship.

The route begins with the southern portion of Carmel Highlands, the place where castles reign and where the old man should have lived rather than on Long Island. The road then travels along high cliffs to Cambria south of Hearst's famous castle. Along the way, visitors are treated to thousand foot precipices, waterfalls some falling directly into the Pacific, views of the ocean's turquoise waters, and extraordinary natural bridges. And more. Much more.

Somewhere along in there—it's hard to tell from the police report exactly where—they met someone traveling north at a high rate of speed. As it crossed the median line into their lane of traffic, my stepfather tried to avoid the vehicle by veering off the highway without guardrails and found himself and my mother in midair falling ever downward into the vast Pacific below.

I was in New Haven when I got word and felt immediately shell shocked.

My mother couldn't die. How was that possible?

I could imagine her wasting away in an old-age home, but not like this. Not when her mind was still active and she could misdirect accidents like this. Magically sidestep them. Place the car somehow back on the road around the next turn. Except she hadn't done that.

And I immediately grabbed my computer and looked up how long it would take for a free falling body like a car to fall one thousand feet. Eight seconds the web told me. Eight full seconds of knowing you were going to die. Watching the water come head on. At two hundred and fifty-six miles an hour. Or so the same site predicted.

The cops recovered the car and bodies and asked if I wished to come and identify them. I told them no. To have them shipped back to Long Island where I would handle the funeral. And from that conversation I learned that I was not the executor of the estate. That my step-grandmother was. Jesus. What a thing. Not that she could change anything in the will, if I cared, but that she could make a mess if she wanted. And, of that I was sure she would. Making messes was her profession in life. As assuredly as doing nothing was mine.

I couldn't sleep that night. All I could think of were those eight seconds. What went though my mother's mind during that ride off the cliff? I'd been told that because of their speed, they'd catapulted far enough out to avoid any landfall along the way.

Weightlessness for eight seconds.

Did her life pass before her eyes? Did she think of me? Of my real father? Or was it too quick for any of that? Did husband and wife say anything to one another? I love you dear? Something like that? And what was it like when they hit water?

Immediate death, or something more like my father went through, but a million times faster? First here, and then gone.

Then, of course, I realized I was alone. With my mother gone, my family was gone. Every one of them. Not that it really made much difference. Since my father had died, things had not been the same. My mother was her own man, as it were. As was I.

I tried to remember the cliffs along where they must have died from memories of my one-time visit there. Scary enough when you're driving safely and with no one coming directly at you. When they'd met their fate, they'd had that split second decision. Divert and risk going over the edge, or chance surviving a head-on collision? Or was there no opportunity to think at all? Just react. Instinctively.

Every time I fell asleep, I found myself in that car, riding the air, falling, ever falling into the deep blue sea, and waiting for the inevitable. No sense in worrying if I'd survive or not. I wouldn't want to survive. Not from that height. I'd want to die as quickly as possible.

And time, of course, would go slowly. Or I guessed it would. Move like a clock ticking in a sea of molasses. Every second extended to make me feel the full effect of knowing I was going to die and, most importantly, how I was going to die. Of course, we all knew the first part of that already, just not the exact second. Or minute, hour, day, month, and so on.

And I'd wake up sweating and breathing hard and scared out of my skin. I'd get up, pace for a while, drink some coffee to avoid dreaming that dream, and hope I'd somehow never sleep again.

My father had died slowly. Had the time to follow the steps of death to their irrevocable end. My mother not so. Had she had premonitions before it happened? And what did she feel when she first saw that car aiming head on at them? Was she frightened? Or was she resigned to her fate?

None of these thoughts had occurred to me when my father died. Maybe because it took so long and we'd had so much time to work out the details in our minds. To put things to rest in ways they cannot be put when someone drives off a thousand foot cliff and dies in eight seconds. Or so you hope.

Try as I might, I couldn't find the energy to feel the same about my stepfather. He wasn't an evil man. I didn't hate him. I didn't have any real association with him at all. Could that have been different? Had my stepfather been too much a rival for me to find it in myself to understand he was a man caught in the stream of life like everyone else? No better, no worse. And certainly as fragile as the accident had proven.

Except no matter how hard I tried, I couldn't place myself in his head.

What had he gone through during those final seconds? Had he thought of my mother? Did he really love her? Or did he think of his billions of dollars? And how he'd miss them?

Had someone been able to provide me with this scenario several weeks before it happened, there's no way I could have foreseen what a mess it would make me.

Maybe it was the way they died. Or where they died. So far away. Or that I hadn't been much of a son to either of them.

Adventurer? Hell I wasn't even very good at doing nothing. I was shitty at that as well.

And so I waited for their bodies to return from California by airplane. The executer of the will made that happen, bless her damned heart.

I waited in the big house on Long Island. In the empty rooms where I'd never hear their footsteps again. Maybe that was it. Maybe when my father died I knew my mother's would still be around. Now, there would be no footsteps of anyone I knew around.

I was truly alone. For the first time in my life.

I'd been alone before, sure, and even hoped at those times I could even be more alone. Though now that I was more alone, I was terrified.

Their bodies arrived in long casket-like boxes and were taken to the mortuary for whatever mortuaries did to them. My step-grandmother would take care of all that.

But I wanted the opportunity to say goodbye on my own. And so I had it. All of maybe a minute's worth. I was granite by that time. I couldn't feel anything, even for myself.

Whatever the universe had in store for me, as always, would be what it had in store for me.

No choice. So I returned to the big empty house and waited. For what, I wasn't sure. For who, I wasn't sure. I wasn't sure of anything. Except, I suppose, I was damned sure I didn't want to face *the witch*.

The bitch. The shrew. The harpy, old biddy, nag, backbiter, fishwife, harridan, muckraker, ogress, and whatever other synonym fit. And lots of them did.

My step-grandmother. Ever again. Ever, ever again. And so on.

Of course, I did have to face her. At least one more time. And she'd smile when she looked at me and order me out of her son's life. Forever. I was a good-for-nothing slob and should be on my way.

Of course, the first part of that was a compliment.

Unfortunately, the second part meant that for the first time in my life I had nowhere to go, and no one to go there with. And, maybe important as well, no money to live on.

Crap.

8

The old battle-ax took care of the funeral arrangements. That was fine with me. Though my mother had died as well, it was her son, his car, and him driving. Besides, I'd taken that burden on with my father, and one funeral was more than enough for me.

I should have expected a surprise and a surprise is what I got when one of my stepfather's servants handed me the funeral day's schedule. A service in the cathedral, then a memorial service in the house, followed by a long procession of cars to the burial site. And then another short service run by the priest before the bodies were lowered into the ground.

My stepfather was apparently Catholic, as I'd suspected. I didn't care about that much. I'd been one at one time too, and I supposed still was. I'd not been to Mass in a long time, but I hadn't been excommunicated. Had I? About that I didn't really care either.

As I scanned down the list of events and who was doing what and searched for my name, I found it. In a place where it shouldn't be. Where it couldn't be. No way.

My step-grandmother had patiently waited to get her revenge. For there on the docket of the memorial service, in the place where the eulogy for the couple was to take place, was my name. Spelled correctly and listed as the lone presenter. Beside that was the scheduled amount of time she'd allotted me. Twenty minutes.

Twenty minutes of comments about a man I barely knew and a mother who'd damn near driven me nuts while alive.

The hellion had bided her time, waiting for the precise moment to stick in the pin. She was getting even for that night at the dinner table.

How could I get out of this? Feign sickness? Simply leave like she did at the meal when we first met? Shoot myself? Shoot her? What the hell was I going to do? None of my options, of course, actually included giving the eulogy. That was unthinkable. I had nothing to say. Absolutely nothing.

Two days until the fateful hour. The memorial service invitations had already gone out. People, none of whom I knew except her, were expecting great things from me. Or some drivel that would put them to sleep. Maybe a reading of an epic poem about death by Homer? A chapter of a novel by Hemingway or Steinbeck? Something that would relate to the deaths of her son and my mother?

The bitch had done it all right. I'd already suffered more than she had in a couple of minutes after seeing my name. And I knew then that we had entered into a private war. That somehow, in delivering my eulogy, I had to get even. I was not going to go easy on her. It may have to be subtle, but the knife would be sharp and deadly. The last act of a man already being driven mad by a witch. Maybe something from Hamlet?

And so, for two days, I no longer suffered the imagined deaths of my mother and stepfather in that car falling a thousand feet into the Pacific, but planning my revenge on the wicked witch of the east. Making every moment count. Ensuring that when the knife slipped into her, it would be the end of our brutal war.

Little did I know that she'd already guessed that, and had thought of a perfect retaliation.

Knowing that someone else would be reading a list of accomplishments of my stepfather and my mother planned so that I couldn't plant my own versions in my eulogy, my speech had to command some other view of their lives and untimely deaths. Something soaring. Something with grandiose views of the universal meaning of life and death, of love, of generosity, of the far reaches of heaven and all its glories. Something beautiful in words, poetic in rhyme and verse, and containing such hidden sophistry that no one could see the bunk beneath the frosting.

Then it struck me. A simple solution. This would not be a eulogy about the dead couple at all. It would be a revelation, however indirect, about *her*. The witch. Something that everyone in the place would know to whom I'd directed it, though having no direct proof of it. I'd have to hide it in such a way as to protect myself, returning the pain she'd dished out tenfold on her.

So I searched for famous eulogies on the Internet, looking especially for irony. And the very first one was perfect. I shall not reveal here the source, though those familiar with the greatness of the man who first delivered it will recognize the beauty of his words here and there. I did not, of course, copy it word for word, but took the material as a model from which I made my own version.

As the hour approached, I saw hide nor hair of the shrew. She'd somehow made herself invisible. At least to me. Well and good. I might have wilted under her hateful gaze. Shied away from my determined goal. Instead, I actually looked forward to my reading. And of watching her face as she realized to whom I actually spoke that afternoon. And that everyone else in the room knew it as well.

When the fateful time arrived and the crowd stilled as I made my way to the lectern she'd borrowed for the occasion, I dramatically unfolded the pages I'd typed, and began to read.

This afternoon, we gather in the quiet of this wonderful house to pay our last tribute to this man and woman who have played such important roles in all our lives. Now, as the curtain of life has closed on their time with us, they are committed back into the eternity from which they came.

(pause, clearing of throat)

These children of God—innocent and unoffending—were the victims of a most vicious and criminal act made by some uncaring and mindless individual. And yet they died nobly.

(pause, clearing of throat)

And so, this afternoon they have something to say to each

one of us in their death. Something to say to those of us who still live. Those of us who remain safe behind the walls of their castles and their fortunes.

(long pause, clearing of throat, and glancing at the witch)

And if we could hear their voices now in this very room, they would tell us of the blatant hypocrisy they'd faced during their lives and survived it. Of the stale bread and hatred they suffered from those whose very position in their lives should have provided the opposite.

(glance at the witch)

And so, my friends, they did not die in vain. God has a way of wringing out good from evil. Unmerited suffering is redemptive. Their spilled blood tell us many things, not the least of which is that those who've sinned so mortally should be forgiven, no matter that they sit in this very room and haughtily believe they have done nothing wrong.

(long pause, clearing of throat, and glance at the witch)

And so I stand here this afternoon in front of all assembled, and say that no matter the darkness of this hour, we must not despair. We must not become bitter or violent.

(glance at the witch)

No. We must not lose faith. We must continue to believe that the most misguided among our brethren can learn to respect the dignity and worth of all.

(pause)

Including her own son.

And with that, the witch, as my mother had at my father's service, suddenly wailed, sobbed, and cried in the most obvious ways imaginable. As if she knew I'd made the eulogy about her.

Most everyone watched in shock as she continued her spectacle. As if she'd known in advance what I would say and had rehearsed this episode for just this moment.

I waited and watched as well. An actress at her peak. A perfect performance.

And it lasted about as long as my mother's had. Maybe my mother had told her about that. Given the witch the nod.

When she finished, punctuating her ending with a deep shuddering deep breath, I realized that I'd not finished, though my allotted time had transpired long ago. That everyone had turned to me to make things well again. To complete this eulogy with the same panache with which I'd begun.

So I did.

Death comes to every individual. There is an amazing democracy about death. It is not an aristocracy for some of the people, but a democracy for all people. Kings die and beggars die; rich women die,

(pause)

and poor men die. Old people and young people die. Death comes to the innocent and to the guilty. Death is the irreducible common denominator of all.

Death is not a period that ends the great sentence of life, but a comma that punctuates it to more lofty significance. Death is not a blind alley that leads the human race into a state of nothingness, but an open door that leads into life eternal.

(pause)

And so today, you do not walk alone. You gave this world wonderful children.

(glance at the witch)

With meaningful lives.

(pause)

Good night sweet prince and princess. Flights of angels sing thee to thy rest. Death, where is thy sting? Death, be not proud.

(I tried not to wince at this motley collection of quotes)

To die, to sleep no more. And, by asleep to say we end the heartache and the thousand natural shocks that flesh is heir to. Tis a consummation devoutly to be wished.

These final words from Hamlet said, I stopped and stared into the audience.

And the witch was gone.

She'd somehow sneaked her way from the crowd and had no doubt gained their sympathy in the process.

No one said a word. No applause, not that I expected any. Especially given the performance by the witch that had far exceeded my own.

So, I gathered my pages, turned, and walked from the false stage and out the front door.

And into the waiting arms of the witch.

She had the bulging eyes and the hair of the devil itself. She shook from head to toe. With not a single sign left of her crying fit. She was, most definitely, mad as a bloody hatter.

I had no idea what to do.

But she did.

She gritted her teeth, stared me down, and said, simply, "Come to the reading of the will."

And with that, she swung around and walked away from me toward the back of the house. If I hadn't known better, she almost walked on the air itself, her feet never touching the ground.

At that moment, I knew I'd been converted somehow. Into what I wasn't sure, but there *was* a devil. I'd seen it. Something so incredibly without feeling for anything except itself that nothing else existed. Except, maybe, just maybe, other devils.

Like me for instance.

When I returned to my room, lying on the bed was an invitation to the reading of the will. And at the top of the single sheet, proudly stated for all to see, was the witch's name followed by the words 'executer of the estate.'

Interesting. Could executers receive an inheritance? They were supposed to be above that. Weren't they? Completely without prejudice. I could hardly imagine that my father-law felt that way about his mother. Then again, maybe that's exactly the reason he made her the executer. She wasn't getting any of his money.

Then again, she probably got her money from her husband or her father, and didn't need any more. Knowing her, though, whoever *was* getting the man's dough was most likely going to spend the rest of their lives fighting off her contestations for the legality of the document.

Didn't bother me either way. I couldn't imagine that someone who I'd known so briefly would bequeath me a fortune. Or part of a fortune. No matter that he apparently loved my mother and considered me his only son. Though I was not even that.

So I attended.

Sat in the back of the room where several other wannabes waited for their names to be called. For their lives to be changed by the almighty buck. I was a nobody. Interested in nothing. True, I would've liked to have had some funds to deal with the witch. And to keep a roof over my head and a meal a day to keep on living. While I did nothing.

But the will itself was short and sweet. The witch never looked at me. She simply sat at the provided desk, pulled the will from a sealed envelope, smoothed it out carefully, and read the two sentences steadily as if the force of law stood behind those words. And, I suppose it did, not knowing much about those kinds of things.

The first sentence named a foundation to which my father-in-law and my mother had willed more than a billion and a half dollars. This foundation sought to eliminate Alzheimer's disease forever.

The second sentence, to my amazement and gratitude, willed a smaller amount to me for two years to spend freely, the remainder of which would serve as a trust from which I could only have a certain amount each month for my continued survival. The will was specific. A few millions of dollars for me to spend, and after two years the amount I hadn't spent became a sort of pension based on the interest the trust drew. Just the same, I figured I was set for life.

And my desire not to shout for joy amidst the gloom of the room almost got the better of me. But I resisted and remained in my seat. Ashamed that I'd thought of celebrating given my lifetime goal of doing nothing. Of course, this bequeathal would make that possible.

The witch stared at me, as did all the others in the room. And not with kind eyes, I assure you. There were, apparently, more witches in the world than I suspected.

With that accomplished, and no other business to be conducted, I got up and resolutely left the room. As did most of the others who'd attended.

It was quite a sight. Though somehow I knew it wasn't really over.

So I took the bull by the horns. I hired an accountant to protect my money for the two years of freedom I had to spend as much as I wanted, and then I had him protect the trust fund that allowed me an allowance to live on from then on for the rest of my life. Small in terms of money, though not so small when considered in relation to ordinary mortals.

And then I set off to see and experience the world.

And for whatever reason, she contested nothing. In fact, I didn't hear from her again for some time.

9

When the reflection of the sun lit my face and woke me, I looked at the clock and found I'd slept most of twelve hours.

From what? Sightseeing and dinner at *The Diner*? A little rich kid playing the martyr because he'd lost his parents and couldn't find anything to do with his time except travel and see the sights?

Not wanting to think of such things, I dressed and headed for the front desk and eventually the blandest meal of the day. Without ketchup no less. And when I got there, the person at the counter had become someone else. An Indian I guessed from his darker skin and long straight black hair. Before I had a chance to greet him, he did so to me, wishing me the best of mornings and wasn't it just a very fine day.

I smiled, nodded, and waved all at once and headed for my morning coffee. All the while wondering why in hell American Indians were called redskins. Nowhere except in films—where they painted white actors red—had I seen anyone with red skin. Except, of course, for the aforementioned white people with sunburns.

Man, was I in a foul mood. Too much sleep is worse than too little, I decided, as I collected my cup, coffee, a little cream, and some kind of pastry so filled with preservatives and food coloring that I was sure it posed more of a threat to my health and well being than anything I'd eaten at *The Diner*.

And I ate by my lonesome, as usual, in a corner. Watching parents watch their kids destroy their breakfasts.

I then remembered a line from Kurt Vonnegut's *Breakfast of Champions* that went something like, 'As children we learned that in 1492 people landed in North America to live full and creative lives when, in fact, people had already been doing that here for thousands of years. That year, 1492, was simply the year we began robbing, cheating, and killing them.' Not the way the history books I'd read as a child had it, but very likely the way it had been.

As I made my way back to my room, the Indian manning the front desk, bored no doubt by the weekend job he'd taken, asked me what I had in mind for the day. I told him I had no idea. Just sightseeing, aware that I was confirming what I'd feared earlier on.

He asked me if I'd been to see the crystal forest. That stopped me in my tracks. Crystal forest? I couldn't imagine such a thing, and told him so.

Less than a half-hour by car from this very spot, he told me, and listed the wonders of the Petrified Forest. I hated to stop him in progress, but did so anyway such was my mood. Been there, done that, I said.

He lowered his head and looked at the counter in front of him as if silently begging my forgiveness.

Suddenly feeling guilty, a thing that Catholics, even ex-Catholics, do very well having practiced for a lifetime and becoming world champions at accomplishing, I told him that I'd not spent a lot of time there. Maybe I hadn't seen it. And would he tell me more.

That brightened his spirit, and he asked me what I had seen so as to not repeat his previous mistake.

I told him I'd parked my car at the entrance, gone inside the park maybe a quarter mile or so, touched a few cylindrical rocks that looked like tree trunks, and left it at that. He smiled, as if he'd realized he hadn't been a fool after all. That I hadn't seen the crystal forest.

He then told me about a wondrous place on the far south side of the 'rocks-that-pretended-to-be-trees' as he called them, in which I would find a special sight that few took time to discover. That I would never be sorry to have taken my time to do so. He made it sound spectacular, without using any adjectives or adverbs at all.

I thanked him for his referral, returned to my room, and decided to spend the day in front of my air-conditioner watching football games on television. It was Saturday, after all, and given the summer was almost over, the channels would be filled with preseason activities. Who would most likely do what and to whom, interviews with important personnel of important teams, and the like.

Unfortunately, my room's television still had a sign on it telling me it was broken. I considered calling the gentleman at the front desk to get it repaired, but decided not to. I liked football games for the most part, but the talkathons preceding and following them bored me to tears.

So I looked outside at the beautiful blue sky, the distant hills to the south, and the occasional pinion pine scrub that dotted the plains in between.

And, heat or no heat, boredom or no boredom, driving around made sitting in my room seem like the difference between eating month old breakfast rolls and eating filet mignon.

So Crystal Forest it was. After all, I had a week's pass for federal parks and monuments, no reason not to use it.

I drove twenty minutes east and then, after showing my pass to the guard at the station, turned south and headed for what the man at the front desk in the motel had told me was a spot worth seeing. Who knew, it might change my life.

When I arrived at the signed area, however, I couldn't tell the difference between it and the Petrified Forest I'd seen before. Maybe the trees lying on their sides looked more like trees. Or maybe the chunks of them were longer and wider, though certainly not enough for me to tell they were in any other way special. So I'd decided as I parked, that I was going to get myself out of this funk and, if I had to, make these ancient rocks interesting if it killed me.

So I got out of my Plymouth, carefully locked it and its contents against invasion by who or whatever, and took off down the trail where possibly more interesting things awaited me.

I took my time walking to smell the sagebrush around me, sending out its camphor odors after yesterday's rain. As I did, I saw a red-tailed hawk floating on a sudden bank of air above me. Graceful and elegant, it was slowly taking measure of the earth beneath it, looking no doubt for rabbits or other rodents to eat.

I wondered then why I hadn't driven on to California. Why here? Why Holbrook? Why anything?

The hawk had it right. Let the air take you where it needed to go rather than having to make that decision yourself.

Every so often as I strolled along, I came upon a sign telling me interesting facts about the logs of apparent wood that lay around me. They were apparently actual crystal for the most part. Quartz to be exact, riddled with iron oxide or rust to give them the right colors. A cubic foot weighed close to two hundred pounds, and the crystal part, the quartz, was so hard that it would take a diamond-tipped saw to cut it. Which, by the way, was illegal to do those same signs said. These and other facts, while fascinating, did little to change my mind that this was any place special.

Finally, at the signed half-mile point and where the trail U-turned back toward my car, I sat down on one of the larger logs and gave my life some thought.

Here I was, alone, in my mid-thirties, rich though having little control over it, and spending my life traveling around the world.

Was this what I *really* wanted?

Or was I wasting time?

Or at best, filling up my in-basket so that when it got jammed with memories, write the great American novel, or at least something someone someplace might find interesting.

Hell, I thought, even I would find that interesting. My life was one long boring journey to nowhere. And, while anyone with any sense would envy me, I was basically unhappy. Not so unhappy as to break my tradition of doing nothing, but unhappy enough to feel unhappy.

That's when the fickle weather made its return. I hadn't seen it coming. From where I sat, the sky was as clear as clear could be.

Behind me, though, I heard the unmistakable rumble of thunder roiling in the not so distant sky, providing a sign that those caught out in the open might face some rough going.

And, before I could even turn my head, I heard the thump of something hitting nearby and the immediate deafening roar of another something gone terribly wrong in my simple world.

Looking back toward the east now, I could see that a monstrous storm was closing in rapidly on my spot, the dark beneath the clouds looking as sinister as any weather I'd ever seen. And not that far away stood the smoking remnants of a pinion tree which for some odd reason had taken the brunt of the electric shock from the angry gods.

Being clearly half a mile or so from my car, I had no idea what to do. In a minute to two, the sky was going to part and loose upon me rocks of ice that could easily knock me unconscious and pummel my body with such forces as to make me at least wish I was dead if not being so.

I'd worn a sleeveless shirt against the heat of the day, no hat since I thought my mop of hair would protect me from the sun, and Bermuda shorts. Only my hiking boots fit the oncoming storm. Though well worn, they were perfect for walking in mud. That was it. And aside from a single small green plant next to a local member of the Crystal Forest, I had nowhere to hide.

And there I was, standing to face the wrath with precious little between me and my maker.

Was God mad at me? For missing all those Sunday Masses?

Was that what this was about?

That couldn't be. The priests spoke about a loving God, not a retaliatory one.

Were some other gods mad at me for not seeking their counsel since I'd quit the Catholic Church?

Or were there no gods after all? This being a simple accident of nature. And I not so important in the scheme of things. Thus, it wasn't an accident at all. Simply a matter of being in the wrong place at the right time.

And then the first drop of rain hit me on my left arm. Not hail. Rain.

A stroke of good luck? I doubted it, for the drop had been so large and hit me so hard that it mattered little. I curled down on the ground making myself as small a target as possible. Waiting for the onslaught of marble-like raindrops to hit me.

And they did.

I held my hands over my head and gave those drops only my back and the bottom of my shoes as targets. They didn't mind. What had seemed like a simple and uneventful adventure had become the nightmare of nightmares.

The wind kicked up frightening gusts, and my back felt like a pirate being struck continuously by a cat-o-nine-tails.

Hurt like hell. Luckily the pain was everywhere. No place was any less painful than any other. And, as I thought whoever was in charge would be kind enough to spare me the full onslaught, it got worse.

I opened an eye between my bicep and forearm and saw that I couldn't see anything except bouncing water drops covered with dust.

The lightning and thunder continued unabated, one atop another, and the pain grew worse. Maybe the storm would kill me. It surely appeared as if it could. I knew there were forty-five miles of nerves in the skin of every human being, and all forty-five miles of mine were screaming at me at the moment.

Without thinking, I rolled over onto my back with my knees up against my stomach, my elbows touching those knees, and my head pinched between my arms to take it on my front side. I had no idea if this would be any better than my previous position, but at least my back would get a break from the torrent of rain pounding down on me.

And then it stopped. As I'd seen it do previously. No sign of slowing down. No diminuendo of sound and flashing lights. Here one second, and gone the next.

I waited anyway, crouched in a fetal position on my back waiting for whatever had caused it to return to finish me off.

It didn't happen.

The passing storm had done its job and was off to somewhere else to provide its dramatic wonders.

And I lay there like that for several minutes, taking stock of what had just transpired. My kidneys, liver, intestines, private parts, arms, legs, head, and so on. Attempting to find permanent or life-threatening injuries, but finding none except a continuous pain all over. Of course, I really had no idea what crises my body really faced. Wasn't a doctor. Clearly I could still think straight, and that would have to be good enough for now.

When I finally relaxed and let my body stretch out, I found that, aside from dark blue bruises here and there, I'd survived the ordeal fairly well. I had no idea what my back might look like, though it still felt no worse than my front.

I stopped stretching and then fully relaxed, this time with a sense of having gained an experience. Something that might last me a while.

As I looked up, I considered what the young man in the motel might have expected I'd encounter out here. Certainly not the slightly more real looking petrified trees.

Had he somehow conjured the storm? To give me that little extra punch to make my trip more interesting?

Or something more sinister? None of that made any sense, but why not think it, along with my thoughts of various gods with demonic plans of their own to stoke my growing paranoia.

And then I turned my head to the side and found a bystander nearby, one I'd not seen there before. It looked like a tiny version of a yellow striped blue and gray dinosaur. With a flicking tongue, bright five-toed claws, and red dots along his sides. His eyes looked bored, half sleepy, and he ranged from roughly four to five inches in length. Then I revised my first statement. While I hadn't seen one outside of books, I recognized it as a Collared Lizard, whipping his tail back and forth across the sand on which he stood staring at me. Directly in my eyes.

I stared back at him. Or her. Maybe only they knew their gender. I certainly couldn't tell.

He looked none the worse for wear, blinking occasionally, waiting for one or the other of us to make the first move.

So I did. I smiled at him. Or her.

And without warning, he-she flashed away from me at a speed I couldn't estimate. And was gone before I could blink again.

I sat up slowly, feeling the muscles in my back argue with my every move. As my skin stretched, I discovered my wounds were a bit more severe than I'd originally thought. I hurt everywhere. Nothing a few aspirin wouldn't cure, but nonetheless not slight.

Interestingly, my clothes were already as dry as the desert around me. Bruises not withstanding, one could imagine the storm had never occurred.

The clouds in the sky had nearly disappeared. What was left, far in the distance. Late August or early September was apparently the month for such monsoon behavior. Hit and run meteorological violence.

I stood and waited for my body to signal it had suffered enough pain. That my imagination had produced most of the drama. I'd been rained on. Simple as that. The sudden fury and the magic of the storm's disappearance had triggered expectations that had not been realized.

And I slowly found my way back to my Plymouth, climbed into the front seat, discovered from my watch that it was already far past lunch time, and made my way back toward the northern entrance of the Park as if nothing at all had happened.

And, maybe it hadn't.

10

I visited Europe after my first year of aberrant behavior spending my newfound money on wine, women, and automobiles. I'd never been there before, but had read and heard all the good things about it that world travelers tell.

With England as first stop, I spent several weeks seeing the well known and some lesser-known locales. London, of course, was the hub of my activities. I did absolutely nothing at all in places like Shakespeare's Globe Theatre, Covent Garden, the British Museum, Westminster Abbey, the Tower of London, the National Gallery, and a day trip to see the rocks at Stonehenge.

I didn't photograph anything. Or take notes. I barely listened to the tour guides. Just soaked it in, breathed deeply, and tired to feel something. Anything.

But I was empty. Without soul. Buildings, rocks, art, memories having neither relevance to me nor ghosts from the past.

It was, in a word, boring. A perfect way to experience nothing at all except age, something that as an American I'd experienced little of before. At least nothing like this. We Americans, after all, replace things on the spot rather than leaving them standing for posterity. Which, given the way most of our architecture looks, might be the wisest approach.

A sign I remembered seeing in Brooklyn once read, 'Serving America for *Four* Years,' as if it were a record of achievement to stay open for that long.

Then came France, of course. Beginning with Paris.

What a place. The Eifel Tower, the Moulin Rouge, Versailles, Arc de Triomphe, the Seine, and Notre Dame.

And women, of course. Beautiful and seductive women who spoke beautiful and seductive French. Everywhere I looked. The Brooklyn me had dreamt of women like this since age five, and here I was.

And nothing. Like they were manikins. As if to make sure the travel brochures were accurate, they'd all come out of their homes on cue to do whatever their scripts told them to do.

Tuesday? Walk the Left Bank. Wednesday, the Louvre. Next up, Barcelona in Spain, where I visited the Montserrat Royal Basilica, La Sagrada Familia, Fundació Joan Miró, and the Museu Picasso. All great places to wile my days away doing absolutely nothing except breathe it all in.

For last, I saved the *Basílica i Temple Expiatori de la Sagrada Família*, the Church of the Holy Family, designed by Antoni Gaudi and still incomplete after over one hundred years since its inception. Nothing about this place proved anything less than spectacular. Bizarre and yet strangely familiar. But photos would have sufficed for all the good it did me.

In Rome, of course, I saw the Coliseum, St. Peter's Cathedral and the Sistine Chapel, paintings and sculptures by Michelangelo and Bernini, and the Pantheon. I stayed on the top floor of a hotel right next to this domed marvel.

And I toured Venice and Florence as well. What a country. And, of course, the Italian women. Va va voom! Voluptuous and inviting.

I even hired a woman guide and took her out to dinner after our tour together. She spoke English well and included, at no extra cost, an extraordinary Italian accent reminiscent of Gina Lollobrigida.

Nothing about her wasn't perfect. Maybe that was the problem. At evening's end we shook hands and that was it.

No more va va voom.

I couldn't miss Austria, of course, with Vienna as my home base. There I saw the Mozarthaus, the Schloss Schönbrunn Gardens, the

KunstHausWien, and the great Klimt Villa. The latter, the house where artist Gustav Klimt spent his final years painting, was spectacular. Truth be known, in photos at least, he resembled me. Or I him. However you want to look at it. Many of his paintings were positioned unframed on pedestals lending a feeling that he still roamed the premises on occasion. Maybe in the darkest nights, wandering the rooms and balconies, pining for his lost loves of which I'd heard there were many. I even saw a print of his famous portrait of Beethoven with the face of his friend Gustav Mahler—one of my favorite composers—positioned there instead.

No go. No matter his historical importance, Klimt's work reminded me more of bedspreads I'd seen than art. A kind of distanced and morose sense of sexual nostalgia.

Then, on to Budapest and a boat trip on the Danube—not so blue by the way—and a visit to the Royal Palace, the Széchenyi Chain Bridge and Baths, and the Parliament.

Nothing much happening there, but old things growing older. As if their continued existence alone made them somehow important.

And on to Berlin and the Brandenburg Gate, Hitler's Bunker, the Holocaust Memorial, and several other smaller museums. I found it difficult to believe that we let that evil little dwarf with *the* mustache kill so many people and almost rule the world.

And then on to Dubrovnik, Athens, Istanbul, the Netherlands, Denmark, Sweden, Finland, Estonia, Portugal, and so on. All wonderful places hanging onto everything they could for fear that if it were lost, they'd be lost as well. And this was certainly true given their economies, poor educations, and generally worthless art, music, and literature. At least according to me.

I took a third of a year doing nothing except visit places and let it all into my addled brain.

Millennia of wars, wins, defeats, and more wars.

Of the excesses of the rich and the misery of the poor. Of mindless drivel often called art, and extraordinary art often called drivel. Of religious conquerors and their victims. Called converts. Of towers and castles erected as monuments to ego as the poor lay dying in the streets. Of disease and petulance beyond belief.

And all of it saved for us to marvel over. A wonder in itself.

I ended my trip in Cologne, Germany, sitting on the edge of the Rheine looking up at the city's Dom. It's major Cathedral. Blackened by acid rain, standing over five hundred feet tall, begun in 1248 and not opened until 1880, with its Gothic architecture and construction of huge stones without mortar.

And watching the lights on the restaurant boats heading down-river, wondering what the hell I was doing here when I could go two blocks down the street and treat myself to a Whopper at MacDonald's. Or was it a Big Mac at Burger King? Could never remember.

From Mecca to the Wailing Wall, and many points between, I then got a taste, a negligible one mind you though one nonetheless, of the various religions that have played a central, if not *the* central role in the lives of the major populations of the world. From Orthodox Jews and their more moderate youth in Israel, to the hatred the Shiites hold for the Sunni and vice versa in the world of Islam. By the time my month was up, I was more confused than when I arrived. But more knowledge-able, for what *that* was worth.

In Jerusalem, being an ex-Catholic as I considered myself, I took the *Via Dolorosa*, The Way of Suffering, also known as the Stations of the Cross. These representations of the places of the main events during the torture, sentencing, carrying of the cross, crucifixion, death, and burial of Jesus would have to move me.

Believing it, however, did not make it so.

Thus, empty as a can of drunk beer, I pinned my hopes such as they were on my continued travels.

My trip to India helped somewhat. Hinduism, it seems, is a more personal belief system and, while there are several sects and versions of beliefs, I found no wars in the making. Except with the more Islamic Pakistan to the west.

I visited the Taj Mahal, the Ganges River, the Red Fort, the India Gate, the Qutab Minar, the Jama Masjid, and Humayun's Tomb.

More poor than I could count.

Though priceless vistas of the Himalayas.

I also took a separate trip to the Punjabi city of Amritsar to see the Golden Temple, the great Sikh shrine surrounded by water. It was here, I was told, that at night, with the gold dome lit up and reflected in those waters, I could not avoid being enraptured. But this so-called 'Holy Pool of Nectar' was no such thing. Placid, dirty, and lifeless, yes. Spiritual and inspiring, no. Even though many locals bowed in deep reverence to the mammoth building, it remained nothing but that to me.

Old. So what?

In China, I missed the Great Wall, but visited the Forbidden City, Tiananmen Square, and the Temple of Heaven.

I stayed in Hong Kong for a week, taking the tram to Victoria Peak, a boat to Lamma Island, a tour of the International Finance Center and the HSBC Building, and generally made a nuisance of myself by riding the subways and watching the people there trying not to watch me.

My visit to Japan included a walk up Mount Fuji. Not to the top, mind you, though certainly high enough for me. Big volcano.

Next up, the Tokyo Imperial Palace, the Tokyo Tower, and wandering the streets of the city with twenty-four hours of an incredibly hyperactive lifestyle. I avoided Hiroshima and Nagasaki and any other memories of the horrors of WWII. I'm not now sure why. Maybe they weren't attractions to me.

When I concluded these tours, the worlds of the middle and far easts were as confused as those of the west. Only different. More intense. And deadly. Even more linked to the past than Europe in some ways. And less respectful of human life. A downer, though still meaning nothing much to me.

So I traveled the length and breadth of Africa, the so-called cradle of life. Where it supposedly all began.

From Egypt to South Africa. From Morocco to Kenya. From the dunes of the Sahara to the rainforests of Rwanda.

I sailed the great Nile and the less great Sombani.

And everywhere I went, the people were incredible. As different from me as they were from one another, though I'm sure there would be those who'd disagree with me.

In Egypt, I visited the famed Sphinx, the colossal temple on the way to the Valley of King Chefren, the body of a lion with a human head more than two hundred feet long and fifty high. As big as a six-story apartment building. I discovered there that what I'd thought was female was actually male.

King Chefren. Of course. What was I thinking?

I followed that by visiting the Pyramids of Giza, near Cairo, the ones built around 2650 BC from two and a half million blocks of limestone.

From there I took the Wonders of the Nile trip that revealed the relics from one of the world's most ancient civilizations, The Valley of the Kings, with its monumental statues, and the magnificent Kom Ombo Temple north of Aswan on the east bank. It boggled my continuingly clogged brain.

For me, though, the most intense site was Luxor, the ancient city of Thebes. Standing among the huge columns in the Precinct of Amun Re in Karnak. It brought me the closest to feeling awe I'd ever been. Each of these megalithic seventy-ton pillars held dozens of large engraved cuneiform scripts over four-millennia old. Va va voom, indeed.

Next was the Djmaa el Fna in Morocco, the world's most exciting town square. There, in the heart of Marrakech, I saw snake charmers, henna-painters, storytellers, date-sellers and orange juice vendors selling their wares. At night, tribal drummers, dancers, and mobile restaurateurs sold their grilled meats, breads, and salads as the smoke rose above their stalls into the wee hours. I relished my meals there, though I still felt something was missing.

Exotic yes, enlightening no. And I even walked on the Sahara dunes there as well.

I toured with Berbers from Zagoura and camped in Tazzarine, where runners from all over the world complete the weeklong *Marathon des Sables* each spring.

And I visited the Draa Valley between the Atlas Mountains, where kasbahs made of red earth rise into the sky.

In Kenya, I watched the rhinos at the Solio Reserve in the area between Mount Kenya and the rolling peaks of the Aberdare Mountains, where large numbers of them run free.

And in Rwanda I had a close encounter with a mountain gorilla in the Rwandan rainforest who reminded me of the witch back on Long Island.

And then on to Mount Kilimanjaro in Tanzania. Africa's highest peak at nearly twenty thousand feet. I could see why they called it the 'island in the sky,' its dormant volcano having ripped off its lid thousands of years in the past. I actually took a shot at climbing it, rising through lush rainforests through alpine meadows, and finally across a barren lunar landscape to reach a twin summit, often above the clouds. I never made it to the top.

Who cared?

From there, I caught sight of the great migration in Tanzania, a year-around continuous march of more than a million wildebeests and several hundred thousand zebras making their annual migrations, the animals moving from the Ngorongoro Reserve in January, up through the Serengeti around June, and arriving at Kenya's Masai Mara around September. And then, of course, all the way back again.

Victoria Falls—also called *Mosi-oa-Tunya*, or the 'Cloud That Thunders'—in both Zambia and Zimbabwe, is the world's most majestic water spectacles I was told. Over four hundred feet high, they were once recorded flowing at nearly forty thousand cubic feet per second, doubling that of Niagara's highest level. I got sick there, tossing my cookies over and into the waters below me above the falls. So make that forty thousand and *one* cubic feet per second.

After that, I visited the Bazaruto Archipelago in Mozambique by air, taking the ten-minute helicopter ride out to the Azura Retreat on Benguerra Island.

I followed this with a visit to Nyika Plateau National Park, Malawi's largest, giving me more than a sense of the wonders of southeast Africa, the most unusual place I'd ever seen. A plateau cut by numerous rivers by way of waterfalls off the eastern edge of the mountains.

I could easily sit and watch the antelope and zebra attempt to escape from the leopards. In fact, I got lost there by wandering into heavy bush and losing north on my internal compass. Frightening for a time, until I caught up with some locals who kindly guided me back to my host group.

In Malawi, I visited Mount Mulanje, the highest mountain in central Africa. I saw monkeys, hares, voles, and a huge crop of butterflies. Lake Malawi, one of the largest lakes in the world—called the 'Lake of Stars' by Dr. Livingstone, I presume, who trekked there in the nineteenth century—supposedly containing more tropical fish than any lake in the world. How anyone knew this was beyond me, though I didn't really care either way.

My brief stop in Namibia included the Spitzkoppe, various granite peaks in the Namib Desert with the highest rising over six thousand feet. Its name was in German of all things and meant 'pointed dome,' probably referencing the Matterhorn. Its resemblance, however, was lost on me.

And the Sossusvlei Dunes, which developed over millions of years, and resulted from the Orange River flowing north and then returning again with help from the surf. I never figured out how that worked exactly, but what the hell. Makes for a fun story.

I climbed the dunes for incredible views of the Deadvlei, a ghostly expanse of dried white clay punctuated by skeletons of ancient camelthorn trees.

And I didn't miss the famed Fish River Canyon, fifteen hundred feet deep in spots, and more than two hundred miles long. Its rift is second only to the Grand Canyon in size, and during the dry season is characterized by beautiful turquoise pools. Avoiding another lost episode by remaining in the large Humvee that the local government had somehow procured from the U.S. army, I also tried to swim there. Shouldn't have. Like taking a dip in a dirty hot tub. Not my cup of tea.

In Zambia, I caught the Lower Zambezi River, with canoers chasing hippos, as elephants and other animals drank from the river.

And the Nyiragongo Volcano in the Eastern Congo was not to be missed. Nearly two miles wide and containing a lava lake, this volcano is one of Africa's most active. Its last eruption in 2002 displaced nearly half a million people. All this history I noted, never having appeared in the textbooks I'd been forced to study in Catholic school in my youth. A shame.

In Botswana, I saw the Makgadikgadi Pans, dried-up salt flats in the Kalahari Desert, a forbidding landscape formed by a huge lake that dried up millennia ago.

And I watched the Baines Baobabs sitting close to the entrance of Botswana's Nxai Pan National Park, the fruit there apparently tasting like sherbet.

I tried it. And it did.

During all these tours in Africa I encountered many wonderful and different peoples and cultures. A big place. Mysterious and full of sights, sounds, smells, tastes, and touches that few other places I'd visited had. And still my wants, whatever they were, had not been fulfilled.

I finished my trip with a visit to Table Mountain, South Africa, that makes Cape Town, one of the world's best beach cities, also one of the world's most photogenic as well. I took a cable car ride to the top of the mesa, and saw the great views, fantastic sunrises, and sunsets.

Finally, I walked the streets of Johannesburg wondering if apartheid had really bitten the dust. As much as Mandela had worked to achieve that goal, it still, apparently, had some ways to go.

All this, and nothing. I wasn't bored, exactly.

But not fulfilled either. Maybe I was not supposed to be. Maybe I was learning something.

Who knew?

My final overseas trip took me to the Western coast of South America. On the drainage opposite that of the Amazon.

I began by landing in Lima, Peru, and then slowly working my way down the Pacific coast toward the tip of Chile, that long slim country that has long been a friend of the U.S.

While in Peru, I flew from Lima, a European-like city of Spanish descent, to Cuzco, an Inca City of natives from the area. This took me from sea level to well over ten thousand feet. Into the high Andes south of the equator.

Wandering around the city on my own, I met a beautiful young woman of mixed races—or so she told me—who gave me a royal tour of the place, from the Temple of the Sun to the Catholic Churches of Spain reminding me of the schooling of my youth. These churches were often built atop the ruins of more ancient native cities. Damn shame.

Regardless of my immediate attraction to my guide, I found her drifting away from me, no doubt due to my distant mind viewing everything in third person.

From there I visited the famed Machu Picchu ruins of like altitude, taking the standard tourist route by train along the Urubamba River, a tributary of the Amazon, and then a bus up the switchbacks to the extraordinary ruins themselves. I'd seen many photos of the area, though none prepared me for what I saw there. A large city literally growing out of the mountain. Roughly five hundred years old, it's only been during the last century that it's seen the light of day, Hiram Bingham and his crew from Yale of all places excavating the ruins from the jungles that had surrounded them and then temporarily claimed them as their own.

From there, I rented a car and took it south to Lake Titicaca, the highest freshwater lake in the world at well over ten thousand feet. Half in Peru and half in Bolivia, my destination was the Bolivian side near which stood the ruins of the great Gate of Tiahuanacu. This monument, a large single-rock arch, boasted an engraved calendar that suggested the year of construction was significantly shorter than the length of our current year based on predictions of the previous speeds of earth's rotation. All meaning that it could be as old as twenty-six thousand years.

While there, I saw a white man with a dark black beard accompanied by a beautiful Indian woman who was, surprisingly, carrying what looked like a modern Western medical bag. If memory served, the insignia it had was called a *caduceus*, a pair of wings atop a pole around which two snakes wound their way upward. I remembered it being Greek in origin and carried by Mercury, the messenger of the gods. Why these things struck me odd at that moment, I didn't know, but they did. Unfortunately, before I could speak to them, they'd passed me by, moving on toward the great ruins now behind me.

From there I drove south to *Salar de Uyuni*, the great four thousand square mile dry lake and salt bed in southwest Bolivia, the largest in the world and most likely the highest. Twelve thousand feet above the near sea-level Atacama Desert to the west, I'd found it on the Internet easily enough, with its blank white eye easily visible even when looking at the entire continent at once.

I remember standing and staring out across the geometric salt patterns and seeing nothing except a flat white horizon in the distance. If this didn't generate something in me, nothing would.

It didn't. Even when I stayed at a spectacular hotel near its shore. Nothing. But it didn't phase me, for I'd felt this way for so long it came naturally.

Was I really trying to change something that came without trying? Why?

The next day I came down from the heights into the driest desert in the world, the Atacama, with no known rainfall ever having been recorded there.

Nothing growing. No life except an occasional seagull from the nearby Pacific. I'd been told by an attendant at a gas station in the mountains that he'd heard that some kinds of poisonous scorpions survived here though he'd never seen one.

Neither did I. Occasionally I did see a large pictograph of some kind that had been placed there long ago, but other than those and an occasional passing car, more nothing.

Maybe I should move here, I thought. Chile's a friendly country, and the nothingness and I would get along famously.

I took a side trip north to see the Nazca Lines. These giant patterns and pictures of animals etched into the otherwise white desert could only be fully seen from the sky. The riddle of why any culture would create such things in that manner was curious. And they weren't quickly drawn either. In fact, most were many hundreds of feet in length or diameter and covered many miles of the desert floor.

I took a flyover in one of the local prop jobs and saw them for myself from above. Fascinating and no joke. I wasn't buying the favored myth that they somehow proved that aliens had once visited earth, however. Not that I thought this was impossible, mind you, just that I couldn't see drawings in the sand as that much of a curiosity for a space-faring race to come take a look.

Finally, I headed south again for Cape Horn, the southernmost headland of the Tierra del Fuego archipelago of southern Chile.

On my way there I stopped at the Torres del Paine National Park where some of the most wonderfully grotesque mountains in the world stand. Spires, iced lakes, glaciers, and geological delights everywhere. The pinnacles are worth seeing in themselves. The weather changed nearly every minute, lending the landscape a living aura.

And that was pretty much it. End of my slide show without the slides.

Note that I didn't accidentally ignore Russia, for in many ways it would have brought its own mysteries more to life for me. But working my way through the Byzantine world of passports and visas was not in the cards. I'd already had enough of that gibberish at home.

I left the islands of the world alone as well, including Australia, New Zeeland, and Antarctica, as well as Greenland, Iceland, and Polynesia. They were either too hot or too cold for me. And maybe too exciting for my tastes.

By the time I headed home to Long Island from Santiago, I'd

realized that of all the things I'd seen, heard, and felt, while extraordinary, none had made me feel the way home did. No old castle in Germany, no pyramid in Egypt, no high altitude ruins in the Andes, the Alps, the Sahara, or the Torres del Paine. I guess I'd had it with people and their leftovers.

That's it. That's all. Nothing.

So I returned to that empty house facing north on Long Island that had been bequeathed to me, and listened to the nothing around me.

No footsteps upstairs. No television sets barking their commercials at me. No nothing. And felt fine about it. Not missing anyone now.

And I thought back to the trips that had taken me around much of the world and felt I'd wasted my time. I'd seen many of the great works of mankind, met many interesting people, but nothing had affected me as much as the magic of the familiar.

And from this, I realized the meaning for me, though I couldn't tell you now what that was exactly.

Because I didn't know.

I did know one thing, however. From now on, I'd visit my homeland. America. See what, if anything, it had to offer. Drive across the country, take my time, meet people, and see the land. Here, at least, the monuments of man were destroyed almost as quickly as they were created.

They meant nothing. And nothing was what I wanted.
Still.

11

On my way out of the park, I spotted the Agate House, a building made entirely of petrified wood and built by natives of the area sometime in the eleventh or twelfth centuries. According to the brochure I'd picked up the day before, the house was held together by mud adobe and rocks gathered from the nearby Rainbow Forest. I had no intention of visiting either of these places given my recent experience with the weather, so I kept driving, eventually making my west again toward Holbrook where, I presumed, a restaurant along the Interstate would give me the respite I needed from my recent encounter with nature's fury.

As I came to the off ramp for Holbrook and the motel I'd pegged for food, I drove into the parking lot, stopped, and looked out the windshield at the restaurant. Nothing extraordinary about it, except its name. *The Diner.*

How could this be? Two restaurants in the same town with the same name? How would they be listed in the phone book? Didn't seem right.

Maybe the one here listed the name of the motel first, as in The Petrified Forest Diner, or something like that.

I didn't really care that much, except for the conflict this could create. What if this place was siphoning off the profits from the other, or vice versa. Taking advantage of the situation.

I got out of my non-air-conditioned car, combed my hair back into place with my fingers, and walked to the entrance, determined to find out the reason for this name duplication.

However, no sooner had I entered the place, than a possibility came to mind. A small chain. That was it. No wonder the place in town that I frequented could continue with so few customers. Same owner. The blond manager. One kept the other going.

Satisfied with my reasoning, I followed a waitress in a far too short skirt to an empty booth, smiled at her, and gazed over my menu with the satisfaction of knowing that at the least I had a good idea of approximately what I was going to get when I ordered. Here were all the American notables. Cheeseburgers, fries, milk shakes, steaks, spaghetti, meatloaf, coffee, and the usual things one found along Interstates from coast to coast. Battered not beaten, I ordered a full plate of blueberry pancakes—breakfast served all day and all night—and a glass of ice tea.

As I waited for my food to arrive, I looked around the dining room and, much to my surprise, was shocked to see that most of the after-noon customers were natives, not tourists. On a Saturday yet. Or was it Sunday? I couldn't remember. And all of them brown skinned, not red. They spoke rapidly to one another in a language I was now beginning to recognize. Not by meaning, by sound. The local Indians being Navajo, I then presumed the language had the same name. It had a nice lilt and ring to it except for the glottal stops that often chopped syllables short and made things difficult to follow. And, I imagined, to swallow. At least for me.

I looked myself over as well as I could under the circumstances, meaning no mirror to see my behind. Dirty, yes, though that was not out of place given the hard working clothes of the others in the room.

Exhausted, smelling of sweat, and still hurting here and there, I didn't feel the need to visit either the john to clean up or a doctor. But the desert had certainly had its way with me, and for that I'd learned my lesson. Stay in the car or face the consequences.

When my breakfast-lunch arrived, I made quick work of it, ordered another ice tea, and glanced out at the weather through the large plate glass window that, in a curved signature way said *The Diner* on it. Beyond it, the afternoon looked sweltering and dry. No clouds to the north at least.

I paid my bill, walked to and got in my Plymouth, and made the short trip back to my motel and my room.

As I sat on my bed there, I reviewed my day so far. A simple return visit to the Petrified Forest National Park had become a signature moment in my life. Nothing had really happened, except a surprise.

Where had I heard that word before?

Last night in *The Diner*, a different diner than where I'd eaten my lunch. And it was already three in the afternoon. Time for a nap?

Before I had a chance to review other options, I was out cold. Sleeping like a baby I presume, though it had been a long time since I was a baby. And besides, I wasn't really there then to know much about how I slept.

And I dreamt. Actually not only a dream, for that would be selling it short. It was an *incredible* dream, the likes of which I'd never encountered previously.

This dream took place somewhere in the Midwest. Not sure why I knew that, but it had the feel of the Midwest about it. Certainly not mountainous or near the seas of either coast, so close enough for me.

Why I was in this Midwestern place was beyond me. As far as I was concerned, the Midwest was someplace you had to travel through to get somewhere else. A necessary evil. My apologies to those who live there, but that's the way it falls.

And in this Midwestern dream, I lived with my family of four, a wife, and a boy and girl. This house had many stories for some reason, maybe five or six in all. And in those stories, many nooks and crannies to hide in. And I apparently spent most of my time trying to find my wife and children.

On the day of this particular dream, my house of five or six stories had begun to melt. Floors that had been flat previously had slumped under the force of gravity. Even the roof was giving way. Somehow, though, I had expected this because I knew that the actual structure of the house, the parts that held it together, were not made of wood or metal, but of rubber. And the rugs, floor tiles, and so on, were aware of this as well, and took the easy way out and melted right along with the rest.

With sudden awareness, I remembered that this was our first day living in the town of my first college teaching job and that I'd forgotten the grand party we'd planned for that very day.

Of course, I'd never considered teaching as a career in my real life, but this was a dream after all. My colleagues and their significant others were to attend this party and we were only minutes away from them arriving. This had come to me in my dream as I watched my family disappear, reappear, and disappear again in the melting rubber floor of what I imagined to be the family room. They were having a ball, laughing as they tried to climb the melting sides of the floor to reach me.

I screamed as the doorbell rang, and woke up, startled by the reality of it. Not reality itself, the dream. For the moment at least, it had replaced my real reality.

And I was shook from the terror of having made such an important date and not lived up to my responsibility of having my family ready to greet our new friends at the door, as any new faculty member would do.

As I looked around my motel room for any signs that might be left over from my dream, I noticed that the afternoon had waned, and the shadows outside my window had lengthened. The sky was clear with no signs of impending fury from the sky. Of course, I couldn't see behind me toward the front of the motel. There could be a hurricane coming from that direction as far as I knew.

I shook my head trying to clear my brain from the remnants of my hallucinatory imaginings, and stood still for a minute to help my blood move more freely.

And, of course, I thought through what I had just experienced. A rubber house—no surprise there—with a family I didn't have, waiting for colleagues from a department I didn't belong to, to attend a party I couldn't possibly host.

And, as usual, I over-analyzed what my brain had concocted.

Did I want to be teaching instead of traveling?

Or did the dream mean that that was impossible now that so many years had passed since I'd gotten my degrees—hence the rubber-framed house?

Had I also missed my opportunity to have a family? Did I want a family? And on, and on.

As I now paced back and forth on the carpet I noticed had had plenty of that kind of treatment in the past, I imagined myself a teacher, standing in front of a group of graduate students telling them of the vicissitudes of the modern age that had been the core of my own studies.

I could literally see them in my mind, staring off into the distance rather than at me or the blackboard behind me wondering if their destiny would be like mine, and being disturbed by that thought.

I'd tell them of the wonders of knowing things. Beginning with Leonardo and Michelangelo and ending with this very day. In the years between, I'd take them through the Reformation, Columbus, Galileo, Newton, Shakespeare, Voltaire, Bach, Mozart, Stravinsky, the American Revolution, Napoleon, the two world wars, Picasso, Pollock, science, computers, space exploration, and on, and on, and on.

All this gave me a strange feeling of excitement. Gone, of course, the minute I'd experienced it.

My alter ego, the one that hated me, took away what it had provided as quickly as it had given it to me.

I didn't relent. What could I say to my imaginary students to, in a sense, wrap up the whole idea of an education in a single notion? A person, maybe? A single name that summed it all up?

A philosopher certainly, but one not sewn into a single model, but able to view the world as a whole from a satellite above. Without emotionally scarring his or her view of things with personal bias.

Who? And this idea of 'who' suddenly captivated me. Who, indeed?

Descartes? Who reviled the notion that any belief with the slightest doubt could be true.

The first philosopher to turn toward science as the true distinction of the human mind.

Yes, I thought. Descartes was the man. The father of modern philosophy. I would make him human to them.

Tell them of his mother's early death.

How he, his brother, and his sister were raised by his grandmother of all people.

And Catholic, no less. Of course, I might skip that part.

That he lived only fifty-four years, though that was pretty good for the sixteenth century.

Of the attacks and perils he faced by attempting to turn the world away from the imaginary, and toward the real that's so natural to us now, to those students in the room I'd faced in my dream.

And I'd have them in the palm of my hands.

This was exciting, I thought, and before I could ridicule my emotional imagination, I hurried on into my next instructional step with my virtual class, something that, interestingly enough, Descartes would himself have found ingenuous of me.

My God, I thought, I've learned something from my schooling. Something important. At least to me. I was on a roll.

So, I imagined telling them about *cogito, ergo sum*, 'I think, therefore I am,' Descartes' famous line that a friend of mine elaborated to *cogito, ergo sum, cogito*, or 'I think, therefore I am, I think.' And my virtual classroom thought it pretty funny as well.

And, of course, I followed that with Descartes' invention of the Cartesian coordinate system, the first method to link Euclidean geometry and algebra. The one with the X,Y perpendicular lines in both positive and negative directions that we all used in high school to graph two independent variables.

Then, one of my imaginary students in my imaginary class asked an imaginary question. Something like, 'Will this be on the test?' And, while I wanted to go ballistic, I hid my imaginary anger and told the student something I'd once heard on a television show. 'You know,' I told him, 'there's a very large electron microscope at Yale University that can actually see things as tiny as an atom. If I were using that electron microscope at this very moment, I wouldn't be able to find my interest in the question you just asked.'

No one in my imaginary class liked my picking on one of their imaginary classmates like that, so one of them said, 'Surely you can't be serious?' And, following the script of a film I'd once seen, I said, 'I am serious, and please don't call me Shirley.'

My imaginary class didn't like that either, so I let them go early.

As I thought these thoughts, I paced myself right into the room's standing-open closet door. Headfirst. And, for a second, nearly lost consciousness. I definitely needed some pills. Not ones that would further my natural tendency to hallucinate, but ones to take care of the pain in my head and the pains of my skin on my back and legs and arms from the morning's blast of moisture from the sky.

So I closed the closet and opened the door to my room, stepped out, and made my way to the front desk to see if they sold aspirin or any other antidote to pain.

Of course, I could have gotten something stronger from a local doctor given my condition, but I didn't want anything messing with my brain at the moment. For, surprisingly, I felt pretty good. My general malaise about life had made a noticeable shift toward the lighter side. No surer about my view of my course in life than before, I'd somehow gained a slight sense of humor.

Maybe.

I'd traveled five continents of the world and found myself in a remote part of Arizona, where the world around me was slightly dangerous, slightly repugnant, slightly inviting, slightly obnoxious, all at the same time.

Nothing much here to speak of except fake wood, unpredictable weather, people of strange and macabre melancholy, food that ranged from exotic to routinely disgusting, and a sense that at anytime at all, everything I thought normal would slowly slide away revealing a completely unpredictable foundation beneath.

And I liked it.

12

I was pacing around the living room in the old dusty house when someone rang the doorbell three times in succession. Insistently.

Already on my feet and headed in that direction anyway, I made the slight detour and answered it.

Looking shocked and raising her eyebrows from her extraordinary blue eyes, the longhaired redhead with freckles that themselves had freckles stared at me. As if I'd risen from the dead.

She wasn't beautiful. Maybe not even pretty. But she had a certain kind of insouciance—a word I'd decided never to use, even in my thoughts, though had now find the perfect occasion—that virtually begged for attention.

She smiled. Another attractive signal that someone was at home inside her head. And she asked if I was owner of the place. Exactly the word she used. 'Place.'

I answered in the affirmative, and as I did she worked her way past me into the living room without invitation.

Insouciance indeed.

She looked over the place, from the high ceiling to the layer of dust that covered everything. Taking everything in as if she were planning to move in right away, but maybe had second thoughts.

After a moment or two of silence, she turned to me with that smile again and introduced herself as Paulette, the best real estate agent the world had ever known, and did I perchance wish to sell this incredible place.

And then, not missing a beat, and before I could even consider a response, she suggested a price I couldn't imagine anyone ever thinking of offering. And told me she was the person who could seal the deal.

I decided to ignore her canned patter and offered her a cup of tea.

Surprisingly, she declined. And she continued to wander around the room, taking stock of its construction and the furnishings in ways that only real estate agents can.

I felt like I'd been caught with my pants down. It hadn't been five minutes since she'd rung the doorbell, and she'd already cased the joint, offered me far more than the place was worth, refused a cup of tea, and was now standing before me, filling out her high-class outfit in ways both appealing and astonishing.

"Paulette," I said, catching her off guard. "Is this your usual approach to potential costumers?"

She ignored me completely, and asked if she could see the upstairs.

I gave up and pointed the way. And up we went. To the bedrooms.

And I showed her the entire place as she took notes on a legal pad in handwriting no doubt stylized so that people like me couldn't read what she'd placed there.

She wanted to see the closets that, by the way, were mostly empty. She wanted to see the kitchen, the study, the dining room, the pantry, the bathrooms, and the attic.

And all of these so quickly, I could barely keep up with her.

I couldn't imagine what she was deriving from these glances, though she'd seen more of the house now than I'd ever known existed. So many rooms. So many places to hide. So many stories I knew nothing about. And a layer of dust over all of it.

When we arrived back at the starting line, I offered her tea once again.

Not interested. She was a cracker. Fast. Sharp. And with more energy expelled in a moment than I spent in a day. There was very little about her not to like, except that. Keeping up with her would be nearly impossible for any man. Certainly impossible for me. And yet here I was, standing near tornado's edge, locked into her amazing grace.

By the time she left, and that as abruptly as she'd originally rang the doorbell, she'd told me about the contract she'd draw up and have for me that evening over dinner, having both asked me out and answered for me in the affirmative. She gave me the place, the time, and the warning of not being late, and left. I figured we'd be married by nine, and that by midnight she'd be pregnant with our first of many children to come.

I closed the door and immediately sat in the nearest chair to review what had just taken place.

A feminine whirlwind had blown through my life like a jet stream leaving me in serious doubt of it ever having happened.

How had she done it? Maybe it had been her motor mouth. Her intensity. It certainly had not been her great beauty, though she did have certain physical conditions.

More likely, though, she'd quickly read me for what I was. A nothing kind of guy shut off from the world, and ready for a good time. And, not surprisingly, she was right. I'd come from a multi-year tour of much of the world, and she'd provided more of a show than all that put together.

I arrived at the swanky restaurant in Oyster Bay at precisely eight that night. Actually, two minutes before that. Paulette had already been seated and looked impatient with me for coming so late to the party.

She'd already ordered a bottle of New England's finest champagne and was sipping it gently and peering at me over the edge of the glass. I smiled, sat, and readied myself for another round of raw energy from the control freak.

It never arrived. She'd somehow become a new person. Slowly and carefully she spoke of her day on the job and then asked about mine. Of course, I had nothing much to say. After all, I had achieved my life's goal. And I told her so.

She smiled at me. Said she'd never met anyone like me before, and did I wish to marry her. Actually I made up that last part.

And so dinner went impossibly slow. She had things to say. I didn't. So I listened to her and politely ate the food that tasted as bland as the lady she'd turned into.

What had happened? Was she a shape shifter? The opposite of a vampire. Lived during the day and hibernated at night?

By the time dinner arrived, I felt I knew pretty much the entirety of her life. Roughly my age, middle class, happy family, not married, still living at home in a middle class neighborhood, well educated, played the piano occasionally without having much talent, and making a fine living, thank you very much, by selling other peoples houses, and had I thought about her offer that afternoon of selling my place.

While all that might have taken a couple of minutes earlier in the day, it had now occupied the entire meal. I felt like I'd wandered into an apology for her earlier visit.

I told her that even though I owned the house, I couldn't sell it for legal reasons. Those being the trust under which I'd inherited it that forbade me to sell it under any circumstances. That the foundation had decided it must remain in the family.

That discouraged her. So much so, in fact, that her smile turned visibly upside down and into one of the toughest frowns I'd ever seen. On anybody. Male or female.

And with that, we left the restaurant, on my tab of course—after all she was middle class and still working for a living—and she went her way, and me mine.

And, for an instant, I figured that would be the last time I'd see her. And it was. Until I returned home that night.

For as I unlocked my front door, a human body jumped me, and, as soon as I could figure out who it was, we proceeded to do *it* on the floor there on the very rug that on that very day I'd met her. For the first time.

While quick and dirty, it had an animal feel to it that nearly altered my permanent state of mind. Everything about it was instinctual. And Stone Age.

We wrestled like insistent bears, incapable of doing anything else.

If she'd brought an army of mafia along, I wouldn't have cared. It was simply her and me. Sweeping the floor of dust with my and then her back and butts. And mindlessly enacting a primeval act of carnal lust I'd never imagined possible. All with our clothes still on. Or most of them.

When we'd finished, she rose from under me by pushing me aside, stood and smoothed out the new wrinkles in her dress, nodded efficiently as if what we'd done had passed some kind of test, and walked out the door without saying a word.

Still on the floor on my back, I looked up in time to see her dress flailing behind her in a sudden gust of wind.

And she disappeared in the night.

Jesus.

I knew her first name only. Paulette.

She'd made the reservation at the restaurant, not me. I could always ask them, but somehow that seemed ridiculous.

And the days passed. All I could think of was this woman who'd entered my life, changed it forever, and then, as quickly, left it for no given reason.

And try as I might, I couldn't get her out of my mind. An enigma. A puzzle I couldn't solve. More than a bit of true magic that I hadn't felt since my childhood experiences on Coney Island.

She had me. And she probably knew it. She'd danced that lure in front of me, caught me, and now was playing me for all it was worth. And all this, if it was true and I was sure it was, made me angry.

And to get even, I wanted to grab her and do it again. And again. And again. This was madness. She must know I didn't know who she was. Couldn't contact her. And yet she was waiting. Until I couldn't take it any longer.

Then one morning the doorbell rang three times in quick succession. My heart immediately raced at an alarming rate. Did I really want to answer it? Was I ready for her? In any way? But I did answer it.

I pulled the door open, and in she came. In so many ways. On top of me without a word and, even with the sun shining through the open door, we did *it* again. This time with our clothes tossed this way and that, and taking more time.

Maybe two minutes.

When we finished, and both breathing as if we'd finished a marathon, she told me she was hungry and was I ready for breakfast yet and could I make her some eggs please and toast with marmalade, orange marmalade, and coffee.

And with that, and no comment about what had occurred, I followed her into the kitchen where I cooked up a meal of burnt everything which she claimed to enjoy.

And then she watched as I cleaned up afterwards.

We spoke in one-word sentences. We didn't look at one another except as a completely naked couple might in a restaurant full of fully clothed people. Though I still had on my socks. Actually only one of them. With no memory of how I'd gotten that way.

After breakfast was out of the way, she asked me if I could break my contract with the foundation and sell the house.

I was completely baffled by her question.

Had our sexual romps been a preview of her commission? It was true, there had not been much love involved. Maybe not much 'like' involved either.

From my point of view, however, my no doubt naïve point of view, things shouldn't be this way. We'd not talked about anything really substantive besides my selling the house since I'd first met her.

I told her that the deal with the house, the trust, and my monthly allowance was set in stone. That I had no intention or way of changing the terms. That I was a man destined to do nothing with my life, and things had worked out perfectly in the current arrangement. At least so far.

From her expression after I'd finished, I couldn't tell whether my speech, the longest she'd allowed me to make during our brief relationship, made her happy or unhappy.

She simply sat there at the table with her lips pursed and her eyes fixated on the stove, most likely thinking about something else entirely.

Quiet.

And that was saying something given it was daytime.

"Paulette," I said, "what's going on?"

She looked at me in a way she'd never done before.

"Nothing," she said. "Nothing at all."

A few days ago, I would have adored that answer coming from a naked redhead sitting in my kitchen on a sunny late spring day with the front door still open and our clothes wildly scattered over the living room floor.

Today, not so much. There was also something ominous in her voice. Something I couldn't quite get a handle on. But there it was.

Eventually, she quietly rose from her chair, walked out of the room and into the next, gathered her clothes, and completely without any shyness whatsoever dressed right there in front of the open door for anyone passing by to see, looked back at me as if for the last time, and left.

I asked myself what had happened? What had I done? Or not done? Was she insane? Was I insane?

I slowly closed the door, dressed myself for the second time that day, and tried my best to think of anything beside Paulette. Of course that wasn't possible. How could I think of Europe at a time like this? Of the beauties of Africa? Or South America? Or of my planned trip across America?

And so, as I was sure she knew I would, I whiled away the next few weeks having cancelled my reservations for my trip, and thinking of nothing but her.

She hadn't meant that much to me. It had happened so quickly, how could she? Though there it was. Everything revolved around her. I knew, in a way, that it always would. I also knew, no matter my protestations, that she was gone. For good. Not a figment of my imagination. A chance meeting with an energy I'd never thought existed. The candle that burned twice as fast, and all that.

I hadn't dreamt her. Nor the experience. And my nothing had nearly disappeared. As tangibly as if my nothing had actually been something.

I wondered if I could ever get it back. I wondered if my trip across America would do it. That somewhere between here and San Francisco I'd forget about her. At least to the extent that my intense will to accomplish nothing in my life would still be possible.

If only partly so. Mostly by rote, then, I proceeded to slowly piece together my long drive across country. To see America. To lose myself as much as possible in the things I wanted to see, the various experiences I wanted to experience, and to regain my sense of not giving a damn about much of anything that had been so rudely stolen from me by someone I really didn't know.

13

The man at the front desk had changed genders in my absence and was now a beautiful, and I mean beautiful, young Navajo woman dressed in a native costume so brightly colored that my eyes nearly watered from the sight of it. All fresh and clean and smiling at me.

I could hardly believe my eyes. Not that I had any carnal thoughts toward her—though truth be told some did cross my mind for a second—but only artistic appreciation. That she could be my daughter were I a Navajo with a Navajo wife and had brought her up to this point in her life.

Around her neck she wore what looked like a pearl necklace. Not possible. Even considering this region had once been at the bottom of a great sea, I doubted anyone could collect one pearl no less a necklace full from around here. But she was busy and ducked down behind the counter before I could ask her what it was. Probably pieces of shells or potsherds collected from nearby ruins.

When she once again emerged, she asked if she could help me and for a second, so shocked by her reappearance, I couldn't remember why I'd come to the desk. Then it came to me, and asked her if she had aspirin or any other over the counter medicine I could purchase for my headache that, not surprisingly, had disappeared by now.

And she handed me a tin of Beyer and told me it was free for occupants of the motel and would I need anything else.

I shook my head, smiled, and, for a second wanted to tell her how great she looked. Common sense got the better of me. Not an appropriate comment, I was sure.

So I made my way back to the solitude of my room. Lonely now, where I'd only been alone before. Missing Paulette? Already missing the beautiful young lady I'd just met? Missing my imaginary class of imaginary students?

When I opened the door to my room it seemed darker. No doubt by the setting sun, though as I looked out the window I noticed that the sky had clouded over during my brief absence.

And as I watched, a lightning bolt shot out of that sky, hit something no more than a few feet from my window whereupon the pane shuddered as the immediate thunder pushed me backward against the wall. Likely more from shock than by anything physical.

Strange as it might be, and as reasoning a man as I thought I was, I sensed that this was the same storm I'd seen that morning. In fact, the same storm I'd seen over the past few days. Following me across the desert, sensing something in me. Maybe the times I needed to be reminded of its being there, otherwise hiding in the mountains when not.

I reminded myself that according to a book I'd read once, lightning struck the earth on average at least eight million times a day. And with very few casualties.

But I stayed where I was, as far from the window and the outside world as I could. Not actually fearful, but leaning toward caution.

The rain never fell, though, as the clouds moved on into the distance, sorry not to have killed me when they'd had their chance.

How, I thought, do people live in this kind of weather? First hot and dry, and then teased to death by threats of downpours, floods, tornadoes, hail, and, for all I knew, snowstorms in late August.

And I reminded myself that on average, one hundred people choked to death on ballpoint pens every year.

This didn't make me feel better, except it gave me a sense of relief that I hadn't yet been one of them.

As the late afternoon sun returned my senses of wellbeing and normalcy, I sat on my bed as I had earlier that afternoon before suddenly dropping off to sleep.

My thoughts of teaching had mostly disappeared, and recollection of my dream had actually now made me less curious. I was a traveling man, out to see the world, to experience as much of it as I could, and doing that at the moment.

Time for dinner. Where? Could I chance another visit to *The Diner*, the one down the street from where I sat? What would *she* be serving this night? Poached rhinoceros? Broiled lizard toenails? Baked coyote?

Or did I want another steak? No doubt covered in ketchup? The same old food that everyone ate for fuel rather than for excitement?

Had anything served in *The Diner* actually harmed me in any way? And what about the man spooning tablespoons of algae into his mouth and licking the bowl clean of it? Would I miss seeing him again? Would I miss him if I never saw him again?

Without any answers to my many questions, I let their sheer number push me out the door of my room.

When I walked outside, the sun had slipped over the horizon so quickly, I hardly realized its disappearance.

Then, however, the real show began. Sunsets in the desert apparently present the best shows on earth. I'd missed seeing one since my arrival.

Like Monet's *Sunset in Venice* without the water and spire, this one exploded with colors, mostly reds, yellows, and oranges, so well blended I couldn't tell where one ended and the other began.

And it endured, gently projecting its soft hues on the hills behind me.

I stood in awe for many minutes watching it finally dim to darkness. Then I turned and walked down the street to stand once again in front of the splintered-wood restaurant of my choice. The one with the window and signs indicating first its simple name, and second the fact that it was still open for business.

As I strode through the door, the dark interior once again struck me as strange. Was the large window displaying the sign boarded up on the inside? Or was it for the manager's office alone?

On the other hand, the dark felt good, cool, and refreshing compared to the air outside.

The room's tables and booths were, with the exception of the lone man sitting in his usual place, empty. And he, using no doubt the very same spoon he used every night, was busy eating his bowl of green soup, treating every spoonful as if it were his first.

He wore his trademark fedora reminding me of a gangster from a 1940s black and white movie. He still wore his farmer's overalls with suspenders and heavy work boots. And he still stared directly into his food as if his future were written there as in a Chinese fortune cookie.

In the kitchen, though, a change had been made. The blond manager now cooked instead of the waitress-cook that had served me that very first night.

She looked up at me, nodded, and indicated by pointing her chin in that direction for me to take my usual seat in my usual booth. And I did, noticing then that no menu had been left out for me. Rather the table was set as if I'd been expected. As if the blond had already determined my various foods for the evening.

I sat down obediently, feeling a sense of both belonging and of being taken for granted, neither particularly satisfying, though neither particularly uncomfortable either.

Of course, my first upward glance was toward the man who sat opposite me. Who was he? What was he? After all, how could anyone eat that bowl full of green slop night after night and still be conscious no less alive?

His eyes never moved from glaring down into the bowl in front of him. Not a single sign that anything interested him except that.

I looked at his hands. They were as calloused and bruised as my back felt. A working man. Fresh wounds as well as ancient ones.

His boots had been scraped and beaten as they would have had he used them for years. Caked with mud and tied with laces that had broken and been tied together again to keep them on his feet.

His clothes also had that look of exhaustion from wear and tear. Worn at the knees and elbows, a rip near one of his suspenders, and ruffled at both the wrists and ankles by the constant ravaging of who knew what.

As I watched him, I felt someone coming near and looked across the table at the blonde woman who had delivered my dinner and, surprisingly, her own. Apparently I was to have company with my meal this evening. I'd somehow passed a special test in her mind.

She smiled gently at me, and began eating something I could only guess as a salad of some sort. And she closed her eyes in apparent nirvana as she savored what she'd prepared.

What the hell, I thought, and grabbed my fork and mirrored her. Good for the gander, good for the goose.

And it was wonderful. No heat or bitterness. Even a kind of sweetness I hadn't expected. The look of brittle leaves, yet so soft they melted in my mouth.

I nodded toward her and smiled my approval.

Then I worried my eyebrows in such a way as to silently ask her its name. She caught my question as easily as if I'd spoken it aloud and told me it was mouse. One mouse for each of us.

I lowered my head a bit to look over the plate. No sign of head or tail, though I somehow got the impression that she'd cooked the entire little beast. Maybe dropped it into boiling water like a lobster and then chopped it to pieces and made it look like a salad. Or crisped it in a fryer. No matter. Nothing about eating mouse made me anything but sick to my stomach.

Of course, as that thought crept into my head, she wagged her right forefinger back and forth at me again, as if she knew what I was thinking. Like my aunt warning me of what I was missing.

So, I bunched my shoulders in response and took another bite. Delicious. How could I argue with that?

She then drank a blood red liquid that looked more like sap from a dying sequoia than any drink I'd seen before. And when she put the glass down, its color had stained her upper lip like lipstick might a paper napkin. And again she smiled.

Damned if I was going to let her get the best of me. So I took my glass and likewise took a hefty drink. And let it help the mouse on down to its new temporary resting place. I had no idea what it tasted like. Never had had the experience previous. But there it was. Something new and unexpected.

She looked at me, smiled that wonderful smile yet once again, and told me it was the blood of a mongrel dog, one that had plagued the neighborhood for weeks and had now been given its due.

This time my stomach lurched without any conscious help. Except, of course, it stayed down since the finger appeared again, and wished my nausea away.

I was a quarter of the way into my meal at this point, no time to stop now. So I watched her pull what looked like a small part from the body of a still mostly intact something and put it to her mouth as I might a chicken or turkey leg. This, certainly, could be no vermin or mongrel or blood. This was something I would recognize and possibly have eaten before.

So I imitated her action, and soon found myself enjoying the wondrous taste of a dead something or other. Something I'd rather *not* know the name of. And I ate the dish without stopping, grinning mightily as I did, as if I'd killed it myself and knew already what it was.

And she told me it was turtle. Something quite rare in these parts. That it had been captured on the shores of the Many Farms Lake up north and brought here especially to be a part of her wonderful and unique cuisine.

And, she added, the bowl from whence I'd eaten my portion was the actual shell of the turtle, as she'd not had a large enough bowl for it otherwise. And indicated that I should feel all the more special because of it.

From then on we ate in silence, me forgetting, or at least trying to forget, the make and model of my food, and she, I imagined, praising herself for creating such a wonderful meal. And it *was* wonderful. And when we'd finished eating I said so to her.

Then I made the mistake of asking her that since we'd eaten together did this represent our first date.

She did not take that kindly for some reason and so I apologized. And, by the way, looked down at her left hand to see if I'd forgotten to check for a ring.

None was there.

Apparently I'd crossed an invisible line or some other barrier I'd not known existed. Of course, truth be known, I was happier this way. She was at least twenty years my senior, and much more like my aunt than someone I wanted to date.

I'd been mistaken on almost all counts. While she liked me, she said, and I should not take it personally, she preferred another gender which I assumed was women to men, and couldn't we enjoy the evening as it was rather than complicate it with suggestions of dates and the like.

I agreed. Not too readily, I hoped. And she took to smiling at me again. All was well.

That's when I asked her about the man sitting across from me, making it clear as I did that my asking had nothing to do with dates thank you very much, but about his strange mannerisms. Like eating the green algae everyday for however long it had been.

She listened to the way I'd put my phrase with patience, since it actually took me a long time to make it, and then told me that she should let him tell me who he was.

I told her that he never looked my way, didn't seem to know I existed, and that he enjoyed what he did so much that I couldn't possibly interrupt him.

This she took in with intense pleasure, as if she'd somehow gone through the same process as I at some time or another herself, and found it consoling I was now going through it as well.

After a time, she then said that if he wished to tell me the things I wanted to know, he would make it clear that he did.

This was a very strange response. Was I to come in here every night for years before the man with the fedora acquiesced to inviting me into his world? Just to ask him a few questions like why he ate the same meal every evening like he did? I was certainly not that interested in his life. I found him curious, that's all. Maybe because he apparently didn't find me curious. Or even interesting.

She looked like she understood how I felt, thanked me for eating at her establishment, stood, worried her eyebrows for a minute, and finally gave it up.

I got the picture. The five dollars for my dinner. So I dug deep in my pocket, found five ones, and gave them to her. And that was that. Dinner for two in *The Diner*. What a treat.

Then I said, quite out of the blue, that a pound of houseflies contains more protein than a pound of beef. And *that* she loved.

And not having a retort, she left me and went back to her office, or wherever it was she went when she disappeared inside the kitchen.

I sat there for a while longer, maybe a quarter of an hour, and then, without once looking over at the man who'd let me know when and if he was interested in fielding some questions from me, I walked to the door and out into the dark night.

Once there, I found to my amazement the very last thing I expected to find. The sky was clouded over and a soft mist had settled over Holbrook, a near rain that felt cool and liberating.

I could feel the desert around me coming alive again. The air smelled of it. The lights of the motel were surrounded by halos. The few streetlights I could see looked like tired beacons in the distance. And the Interstate made a continuous whirring sound as the tires of the few cars and trucks on it made their way across the damp pavement.

It was a delightful moment in time. As if the gods had released their anger over the earth, had taken a well-deserved break from their persistent watch, and were now sleeping peacefully for the first time since I'd arrived here.

And so, with my dinner tucked neatly away in my stomach and my curiosity waning over the man in *The Diner*, I found my way back to the motel, to my room, to my bed, and into a soft place between the covers there.

Not to dream of rubber houses, or nonexistent faculty colleagues, teaching, or much of anything else.

At all.

14

My first overnighter on my way west was Cleveland, Ohio, a long day's journey into night. I'd never been there but had heard a great deal about the city whose river had caught fire, taking three days for the fire department to extinguish. As illogical as it was to imagine water catching fire, this event had been caused by intense pollution in the Cuyahoga River, mostly with combustible chemicals such as refined oil byproducts covering its surface.

Cleveland was also known for its port on Lake Erie, one of the lesser lakes in the great lake's region, that then contained one or more floating islands consisting primarily of phosphorescent algae clumping together with similar pollutants so at night they could easily be seen glowing by aircraft flying overhead.

With these strange images in mind, I found a high-rise hotel near the downtown shore area and immediately looked out the windows of my room in hopes of seeing otherworldly images similar to those I'd imagined. Or maybe some new ones.

Unfortunately, I was disappointed. Apparently, the city's management had since 1969 tended the environs more carefully, and the city looked damned good. Home of the Rock and Roll Hall of Fame, of the Indians, Browns, and the Cavaliers sports' franchises, and of the well-known Cleveland Orchestra.

Beside the downtown area, the rest of the city was, at least in the view of the local newspaper I read, much the same as I'd imagined it. The west side middle-class working white, the east side near downtown as ravaged as Detroit, and the southeast side, the so-called 'heights' area, consisting of the principle upper classes. As typical as any eastern city can get.

When the installed knocker on the door to my room slapped three consecutive times, my first thought was that Paulette had followed me here.

Was that possible? Yes. She was certainly obsessive enough. I hadn't looked in my rearview mirror that often. So I immediately imagined her jumping me as I opened the door, sprawling us out on the floor with that door still ajar, and doing *it* right then and there.

It was, however, someone who'd forgotten his room number and had expected what he thought might be his wife's big smile waiting for him. Instead he got my disappointed grimace.

Disappointed? Just what *was* I expecting to find in Cleveland? I certainly found no Indians, American or otherwise. Nor brown people. Nor cavalier people, though I hadn't searched that hard for them. Not yet anyway.

Hoping to rid myself of memories of Paulette, I ate in a fancy upper class strip club. A waste of time, though the teasingly mostly-naked ladies held a certain fascination for me.

Afterward, I drove the length of the city's lakeside, looking out over the waters hoping to spot one of the floating islands.

No luck.

Before hitting the sack that night, I took a slow three sixty around the hotel to get some fresh air and met three individuals I wouldn't soon forget.

The first, a pimp if there ever was one, tried to sell me a blowjob with one of his harem, a young man of great potential he said. I continued on without saying a word.

The second was a young man, not the one to whom the pimp had referred I assumed, who tried to stick me up with a finger pointing at me from his jacket. The worst imitation of a gun I'd ever seen. I told him 'no thank you,' and left him standing there.

And third, a man with a bottle in a paper bag, as whacked as I'd ever imagined anyone being, who said to me, inexplicably, 'Welcome home, partner.' I hoped he wasn't right.

Once back in my room, I tested the tenth-story windows for strength to ensure I couldn't walk through them in my sleep, closed the drapes to avoid seeing the city sprawl of lights, and tried to sleep.

As tired as I was from driving and seeing the sights, I couldn't get there. No dreams therefore. No more knocks on my door. Paulette or otherwise.

By four in the morning, I gave it up, and drank one of the instant coffees brewed in hot tap water and headed west away from the coming dawn.

While driving from Gary, Indiana, to Evanston, Illinois, is only forty-five miles, it takes nearly two hours to get there. Thus, Chicago, like many Mid-western cities, really had no there, there. Or maybe too many theres. It was difficult to tell.

With the exception of its lakefront position, O'Hare Airport, and the Sears Tower, I never actually knew where I was as I drove by. Of course, the signs along the expressways helped a little, though they often promoted smaller nearby towns and cities more than the singular nature of the city with the broad shoulders.

Thus, with little disagreement from my intuitive side, I plodded onward toward St. Louis and eventually Kansas City, my real destination for day two of my cross-country sojourn.

Along the way I saw the Gateway Arch—the six-hundred and thirty foot tall half parabolic sculpture along the Missouri River, seen several major league baseball stadiums, driven far enough away from Branson, Missouri, to avoid being replicated there, taken a brief ride on a showboat, visited Busch Gardens, discovered that the actual Kansas City is not in Kansas anymore Toto, and gambled briefly in a reservation casino. Not exactly France or Italy, though what the hell. Tomorrow it would all be torn down and replaced by something else anyway. I liked it.

Arriving about dinnertime, I ordered a well-done famed slab of Kansas City beef straight from the local stockyards. When it came, I wondered immediately what the rare would have looked like—the live steer walking by having just been brand-ironed?

I again did a three-sixty around my hotel and met people from the area. Still half expecting Paulette to show, I was disappointed to find a representative of the Seventh-Day Adventists attempting to provide me with peace of mind, another pimp who I tried to hook up with the Seventh-Day Adventist, and a strange little man with a completely bald head skipping a rope near the hotel entrance. I asked him what he was doing and he told me he'd heard from Christ that day that the world was about to end. I asked him how long I had, but unfortunately he'd apparently skipped that part.

I looked up Paulette on the Internet that night. For all such women with that first name living on Long Island and engaged in one form or another in real estate.

No go. Maybe I'd imagined her. Made her up to fill my libido with promise of things to come. No, I wasn't that imaginative. Nor could I have created such an improbable being. The long red hair, the freckles with freckles, the raving blue eyes, and the smile that could put you away for keeps. And well, of course, there was that certain something about being hijacked when you least expected it.

That night I slept like a dog in a high mountain meadow on a warm summer's day. Paulette visited me there briefly but ruined things by morphing into the great witch of Long Island who had fingernails as long as Edward Scissorhands, and a shrill screech resembling the infamous chalk scratching a blackboard. That, not unlike her own.

And I woke in a sweat, remained awake, and once again left town in the dark before anyone except the truck drivers dared face the pavement.

Driving down the eastern side of Kansas, into and through Oklahoma and the panhandle of Texas, and on to Albuquerque, New Mexico, is a trip worth missing. Not even faux hills are legal in most of this area, with the flat land extending as far as the corn can see. Until the southern edges of the Rockies appear to the east of Albuquerque.

The movement of the continental plates had apparently decided to save this western part of the world from complete boredom.

I thought for a moment about going north to visit a college buddy of mine who'd found a teaching job in North Dakota. Or another not college buddy friend of mine now spending his days in a Washington state prison of some kind.

But I didn't turn.

Didn't know them that well.

I stayed in a hotel to the west of downtown near Old Town in Albuquerque, where the plaza still boasts a gazebo where bands and orchestras still perform on certain afternoons. Or so I was told.

So far my trip had not disappointed me. Not much to see. Not much to do. Nothing to keep me from being myself and plodding onward into the far horizon where everyone I met and everything I saw lived up to my hopes.

It and I were both a lot of nothing at all.

I considered taking a side trip to Santa Fe, only an hour north and east from town, where there were more art galleries than any other city in North America except the Big Apple, a nearly outdoor opera house where the best of the best from the Metropolitan sang during the summers, and the American natives sold the real McCoy while sitting outside in the shade.

But I decided against it. The lure of the west beaconed me. The Grand Canyon, Yosemite, the great Pacific, and even Big Sur where my mother and stepfather had driven into oblivion together.

That evening, I wandered along Central Avenue, part of the famed Route 66, where in the 1950s it boasted nearly one hundred motels, many of which were brothels of both good and ill repute.

Things had changed over the years apparently, as I was not propositioned once, and the number of hotels had clearly diminished several-fold over the years. I did, however, find many of New Mexico's less fortunate, the University of New Mexico's main entrance, and more than several Mexican restaurants offering signs of the best Hatch green chili available in America.

Having advantaged myself of the latter, I spent the evening cooling off with water from my room's basin and a cold shower from not having thought of Paulette until I returned from my long walk.

And I further avoided any other reminiscences by looking out my fourth story corner window up toward Sandia Peak and the ranger station at the end of the nearly three-mile long tram there.

Strangely enough, the in-room television included many cable channels one of which was showing *Lonely are the Brave*, a great black and white film from the early sixties with Kirk Douglas, Gena Rowlands,

Walter Matthau, and many early sequences of Albuquerque from the days before it had grown to its current sprawl. And a long manhunt up the south side of Sandia ending at its high ridges. Maybe this was the first sign of things to come, as tomorrow I would head west toward Flagstaff through Indian country.

I couldn't imagine that would disappoint me.

15

I woke the next morning feeling, well, beatific. Maybe the mouse or the dog blood I'd consumed the previous night had had some influence on my natural dopamine output. Or maybe my endorphins. Or maybe seeing green not of the algae kind outside my window made the difference.

While the sky was clear again, the nighttime drizzle had obviously had an effect on the desert. Tiny pricks of grass or some other kind of groundcover had reaffirmed its existence in the garden beyond my plate-glass window. For what had previously been the color of rocks alone, now had the signs of life that made me want to smile. And even the cacti looked radiant. And some flowering plants had taken what little substance the universe had given them, and made the most of it by generating new buds here and there.

Maybe I'd discovered the secret of desert living. A little water goes a long way. Maybe a little of anything goes a long way out here. And maybe it should elsewhere on earth as well. Unlike places that had plenty of everything as well as people taking it for granted.

With these thoughts in mind, I headed once again for the front desk hoping I might see the young Navajo woman there again, looking equally as refreshed as the desert.

But she'd been replaced by a man, a white man this time, and one I'd not seen before. While he looked friendly enough, I realized that I'd seen plenty of white men before, and though I had nothing against white men, I'd much rather look at different types of people occasionally. Particularly ones with fresh expressions and wearing wonderfully colorful dresses. Especially young ladies.

Not wanting to dwell on what some might consider pedophilia, even of a benign sort, I once again made my way to the dining room for another batch of precooked food, no doubt made in kitchens some hundreds if not thousands of miles from where I now sat eating their culinary monstrosities.

Except for me, the dining area was empty. Must be a Monday or Tuesday. Couldn't remember. As I finished my breakfast, I realized I had nothing planned for the day and tried to recollect what other sights I'd seen advertised in the brochures I'd read in my room. Nothing outstanding.

Apparently, within a two-hour drive, the landscape looked pretty much the same.

As I signed for my meal adding the bill to my room tab, I rose and headed back. On the way, I walked past one of those aluminum racks with hundreds of different postcards, most of which were copies of those placed in front. One of them leapt out at me. Not actually out of the rack, but caught my attention. I took it out. What I saw there was truly amazing. An ancient town of some sort desperately hanging to the top of a cliff overlooking a vast canyon below.

I looked at the back of the card. Walpi, it said, on the Hopi Indian Reservation, First Mesa. That was it. So I paid a buck for it at the front desk and returned to my room to see what treasures my brochures held of this place.

When I spread them out on my bed, I found no sign of the word Walpi or Hopi. Strange. I'd left my computer home for this trip, wanting to find my way on my own. However, I'd seen a guest use one near the front entrance of the motel. So I made my way there with postcard in hand and, after waiting patiently for two kids to stop playing a video game so violent I had to look away, I searched the Web for any further information about this Walpi place. And found it. Off the beaten track only an hour and a half or so from where I now sat.

So there it was. My destination for the day. A way to waste time until dinner to see if the stranger who sat across from me in *The Diner* was ready to talk yet. Or at least recognize that I existed.

The directions to Walpi were easy enough. East on Interstate 40 for eight or so miles, then north on 77 to 264, then twenty miles west to First Mesa.

I filled up with gas at the nearest in-town station, and headed out, with the sky clear of clouds in every direction including up.

As I drove, I remembered something about the Hopi. A reservation within a reservation, the outer and larger one belonging to the Navajos. And something about a place called Big Mountain, a legal battle that the Hopi had won granting them property the government thought more rightly belonging to them rather than the Navajos that lived there who then had to move. And something about the Hopi, a Pueblo people meaning they'd crossed the straits separating Alaska from Asia millennia ago where the Navajo were late comers from the same general area, most likely no longer recognizing their relatives from earlier times when they arrived.

Tribes and cultures, I thought, ain't they a wonderful reason to kill one another to make it easy for the white man to come and decimate the both of them. Or was I simplifying things too much?

When I arrived at First Mesa around noon, I found that the post-card had not done the view I saw justice. Not in the least. Walpi was a pueblo located at the end of a thin and high mesa whose multistory buildings joined with the rocks below them so seamlessly that I couldn't tell where one ended and the other began. While not Machu Picchu in Peru, the scale was staggering. A lone one-way washboard dirt road led from the main drag past two intervening villages and ending at Walpi.

As I parked, I looked up and saw something as out of place as a condor in Alaska. A contrail spreading its parallel lines across the sky above and, for a minute or two, actually producing shadows on the cliff walls.

For a second, these actually took the form of a strange creature about ready to step out of hiding and wreck havoc on whoever happened to be in its way. Me, for example.

But it softened and then disappeared, as if it had never been there at all.

When I then wandered around to get a better view of Walpi from a distance, I literally bumped into a man who introduced himself as a tour guide, and who asked me did I want what looked like a one-person special tour to keep him busy for a while. We agreed on a price, and within minutes, without lunch, I was on my way out and up onto the mesa itself.

And this is when my life began to transcend. A view down toward Blue Canyon started it. Not really blue, per se, the rocks in some distant past had folded back onto themselves into impossible shapes. Like someone overlapping frosting onto a cake.

Then I got my first view of Walpi. From a distance. It seemed for a moment like a castle nestled in a billowy cloud in the sky. Separated from the earth, and somehow perfectly placed to counteract gravity.

My guide, apparently unaware of the extraordinary view, moved on without stopping. And the road led us through two villages separating us from our destination, those being Sichomovi and Tewa. And the mesa slowly narrowed towards its end point.

As we walked, he spoke of Kachinas and their importance to the Hopi way of life. Made by men to instruct young women to the Hopi way of becoming adults—an interesting approach to gender differences. Kachinas, or more rightly katsinas, were, he said, constructed of cotton-wood tree roots with each figure a ceremonial god of sorts.

I'm sure I lost track of what he continued saying as we entered Walpi proper, with its small plaza around which the town grouped.

He introduced me to the lower chambers of some of the buildings where the *sipapu*—a chamber to the gods—was located in the floor of the religious kiva.

Interesting words these kachinas, kivas, and sipapu. They meant very little to me, but each time I heard them, I zoned out. And looking out over the other mesas and into the far distance, I realized what an extraordinary place this was. I'd never experienced such a place in all my worldly travels.

Then my guide told me that for the first time in well over a thousand years, Walpi was today no longer permanently peopled with Hopi Indians who only visit their village now on weekends. This, he told me, because water and food are so difficult to bring to the cliff dwellings by hand on a daily basis.

That fact, and the far-away mushrooming clouds to the north, added to a strange sense of fear and *déjà vu* I'd experienced before in my life, though never this strong. It was as if I'd been dropped here from someplace else, softly landing unexpectedly in someone else's body, someone else's mind, someone else's past.

And, as I looked at one window in particular, one on the second floor of an adobe structure, I saw a shadow move across its glass which added, no doubt due to my feeling of displacement, to that fear and *déjà vu*. The shadow disappeared as quickly as it had appeared, but I was certain I'd seen it. Someone there. Then gone. Me? Had I split into two pieces, inseparable though different?

My guide then brought me back to reality, at least my version of reality, by asking me if I had any questions. Since I had no idea what he'd been talking about, I shook my head no and noticed that he, too, had changed. In ways I couldn't delineate or describe, except that he had.

And a stray cloud then shadowed us for a second and then disappeared. Was I imagining all this? It certainly was a place where one could concoct all manner of such wanderings of the mind.

Then my guide smiled, and everything blew away as if it had never been. I was standing in a street in a village high up on a mesa in northeastern Arizona with a guide I'd luckily found who was touring me through the architectural antiquities of his Hopi civilization.

That's it. That's all. Anything else was a flight of fancy. A dream. Some crossed wires in my mind. Signifying nothing.

We walked back to my car without a word.

I'm sure the man must have thought I'd gone silent for some reason he couldn't figure out, that I was probably this way by design, and that he'd find a more loquacious customer around the next corner. For my part in it, all I could do was shake my head to clear the inner clouds now matching those ballooning on the horizon, and say goodbye. When I did, he looked at me straight on and seemed a bit worried. Like maybe I'd had a stroke or something. I hadn't. I knew that. I'd simply wandered into a strange land and had been put out of my regular habits.

My stomach returned me to normal as the tires of my aged Plymouth hit pavement again. It was near three in the afternoon and I had at least another hour and a half before eating. My stomach growled as if unhappy with my reasoning, though it was what it was.

As I drove east, I noticed that the thunderheads now approaching with severe rapidity, were coming directly for me from all directions except east. That I was luckily traveling toward my lone escape route.

Relieved, I pedaled it up a notch and reached seventy, opened my driver's side window, and let the hot wind blow in my face and through my wild uncut hair. And with that, I hoped, my brief experience with strangeness would leave me and return to wherever such experiences go.

In Keems Canyon, I found a gas station food mart combination, more like a Brooklyn convenience store than a restaurant.

I filled the Plymouth with gas, and me with a prepackaged turkey sandwich and two cans of cola, the brand of which I didn't recognize.

Turned out I'd bought gas for both my car and me. And, thanking my open window and the wind roaring through it, I kept racing east being chased by the late summer storms of northeastern Arizona. They had kept up with me all the way so far, and maybe even gained a bit of ground during my hasty retreat for gas and lunch.

I arrived at highway 77 South, stopped, looked in that lonely direction, watched as the lightning danced across the desert floor, and kept going. This road would take me to 191, the route going left up toward Canyon de Chelly and then to Ganado, and going right taking me back toward Interstate 40 and home to Holbrook. Where I wanted to be at the moment.

I stuck the pedal to the floor, and inched up toward eighty with the Plymouth shuddering at times when the tires hit rough road.

Admitting to myself that the storms marching toward me had unnerved me a bit, I tried to relax. Hard to do. While lightning doesn't typically strike cars, I knew that heavy rain could cause all manner of havoc while driving, something I wasn't looking forward to with any zeal.

As I turned in Ganado, I noticed that the giant clouds had surrounded me, with the only sign of blue directly above. South, the direction I was now heading, looked as black as night with the rain below pounding the desert sand.

I could literally see the edge of the storm approaching. Frightening to say the least. So I slowed as I hit the wall of water and immediately felt it jerk the car sideways.

Now driving less than twenty, I could feel the tires fishtail back and forth waiting for me to apply gas to hydroplane. I didn't.

The hail, not rain, bounced off the roof and hood and turned the landscape around me into a temporary winter of white. It was so loud in the car and the visibility so weak, I pulled my foot off the gas and let the Plymouth drift to a stop, yanked on the emergency brake, and waited for some sign that the pummeling would stop, or at least slow down.

It didn't.

For the first time since I'd arrived here, the storm gave me all it had. Thank God I wasn't outside. This I couldn't take for long.

And so, I sat there looking out at the fury of Nature's power assaulting me with its magnificent sadism.

Rivers formed from the melting ice, moving as the earth let them, sometimes breaching the road and pushing me sideways.

The lightning-thunder separations closed in on simultaneous. One hell of a ride. My fear overridden by my awe at least for the moment, I watched as a steer rode by on a sudden wave in the torrent crossing the road.

It was then that I realized the true danger I faced. This was no passing grievance, it was full-out warfare. No prisoners. I knew there was nothing I could do, though my mind raced through the possibilities nonetheless.

And, when the water moved the Plymouth sideways into a culvert next to the road already pushing it with a torrent of fast-moving water, the severity of my situation hit me.

Hard.

While I'd never heard of a desert drowning, I knew I could find myself stuck in a car full of mud several miles from civilization with no sense of the land or what I might do. And that's exactly what happened.

Down into the flushing water, and, like a tinker toy, down the temporary river I went.

Thank God it paralleled the road. At least for the moment. I had the feeling it might suddenly decide to create its own passage. And onward I floated, water now seeping in the doors and filling my shoes. How deep was this damn thing?

A cactus rushed by, going faster because of its size. Then an old inner tube that had been tossed aside. And then, to my true dismay, a jackrabbit who looked forlorn at me for not helping it escape the wall of water that had captured it. Nothing I could do. I mentally attempted to apologize to the long-eared vegetarian as it disappeared as quickly as it had appeared.

And nothing changed. If anything, the storm gained momentum, apparently angered from not having sunk my lonely ship in its sea of water.

Now raining in the form of drops the size of golf balls, the river I found myself sinking in grew deeper. And going downhill where, I imagined, it would join yet a deeper and more merciless one.

So dazed by the suddenness and menace of the storm, I still couldn't yet feel the fear that should have gripped me. I was as a passenger on a rollercoaster, imprisoned in a metal car, hanging on for dear life, knowing I wasn't in control any longer. That life would take whatever turn it decided toward what it had in store for me. That any movement on my part wouldn't make a damn bit of difference either way.

And then, when everything around me had come completely unglued, the rain abruptly stopped, and the Plymouth ground to a halt. The water, however, kept roaring by.

I looked around and discovered I'd somehow landed under a bridge, and that the stream bed, now cement, had somehow caused my car to stop moving.

But the storm ravaged on beyond the road now above me. It's drainage poured down, water striking water so hard that it splashed itself a foot or more into the air. And the leak below me inside the car had increased in force, with the water on the floor now coming up nearly to my knees. This definitely wasn't good.

I looked outside as the cleansing desert sent tumbleweeds, sage, and a pinion tree complete with attached roots downstream. And I wondered if the water I'd taken on would help or hinder me from joining them. I begged for the latter.

It was a strange feeling to think all these thoughts as the world around me disintegrated. Like earlier that day in Walpi, I felt detached, as if I'd split into two people, one of whom was watching all this from afar. Calm and observant, though it knew the other part of me was attempting to suck at my mother's breast or crawl back into the womb.

As if worn out from its relentless attacks, the storm uncharacteristically let up slowly. And, for a second at least, the sun peeked into my rear window lighting the inside of the car like the overhead bulb might.

And I could feel the water around my feet recede nearly as fast as it had accumulated there.

And then it was over.

The desert stopped drifting by, the rain beyond the bridge's shadow lessened, and the water pouring over the bridge above stopped, as if a dam had closed its vent.

And I waited there, wondering what in hell I'd do to get myself out of this mess.

Before I could figure that out, however, some natural instinct overrode my brain and relief flooded my entire body. A heaving, uncontrollable sob soon followed, and I cried.

It was over. I'd survived it. God's fury had pummeled me and once again I'd managed to escape. No knight-errant, I'd not come here in search of such excitement, only to find it nonetheless.

What a trip. An experience I could tell someone about someday. Though I doubted in the telling it would capture the true feeling of what it was like. Of the physical knowledge that whatever I wanted to achieve didn't matter at all. My destiny was not mine to have. It belonged to someone or something else.

A God? Gods? Randomness? Nothing?

And then, as I looked out the window, the sun appeared for real and the tunnel in which I'd parked had drained fully, puddles here and there, but no more running water.

The clouds I could see, the ones in front of me bordered by the bridge on top, had shrunk from the elephantine to the miniscule.

And there I sat, mostly wet, crying, and shaken from my brief bout with death, waiting for what I didn't know. Maybe for something like another storm to come along and fix things, including me. Somehow I knew it wouldn't. For as compellingly relentless as the storm had been, Nature had returned to its taciturn self and demanded that I now take charge. Otherwise I'd suffer again, but this time from my own lack of motivation.

I got out of my Plymouth and walked around and up to the road where I waited for someone with a cell phone to save me.

And, as I stood there, the wind that I hadn't noticed before picked up abruptly and pummeled me with gusts that nearly blew me over.

Never happy this place.

Within a few minutes, though, a car pulled to the side of the road and the driver called out of his window and asked if I was all right.

I told him yes, but that I needed a tow truck to pull my car from under the bridge.

He smiled at that, pulled over to the side of the road now almost dry, got out of his car, and gently looked over the side of the bridge at my Plymouth, jailed there for the moment. And, of course, smiled again. With a sort of awe in it.

He asked me if I'd actually been in the car when this had happened. I told him I had. And his awe increased. Turned out he was a Navajo on his way home when the storm hit and had turned into a carport of a friend of his in Ganado and waited for the rain to flail itself out.

Very nice fellow he, and he called a local repair shop owner with a power winch, a friend of his, and that friend arrived within minutes and hauled my sorry-ass car from beneath the road and back onto the highway.

I tried the ignition and sure enough, aside from the added smell, my Plymouth was good as new. Or as good as used.

So I thanked my savior, asked what I owed either one or both of them, and they both turned me down. Flat. No chance of changing their minds.

I left them standing alongside the road with me once again heading south toward Holbrook and them talking to one another about the events of the day. I suppose this was my introduction to the Navajo world. If it were, then I was well pleased with it.

Seemed the Indians around this part of the world, at least the ones I'd so far met, were both an interesting and empathetic people. I was glad to have made their acquaintance.

16

When I finally arrived back in my room in Holbrook, I thanked God that he or she had thought to help us invent bathtubs. I stripped, drew a bath, lay down in it, and soaked for at least an hour, reheating the tub each time it cooled down with more hot water. I figured that for the moment at least, Holbrook had enough to satisfy at least one such extravagance.

I tried not to fall asleep for I remembered that by doing so I could easily drown. Given my day, the irony from which I would never forgive myself. And I enjoyed every minute of my respite.

By the time I'd completed the ritual, the sun had nearly disappeared and time was fast approaching for me to return to *The Diner*, to try yet new culinary manifestations and see if the mysterious man who sat across the room from me was ready to reveal something about himself.

I dressed in different clothes than I'd worn that day and headed out of the motel toward a different rendezvous with destiny. Or I hoped so.

After three different dinners at my diner of choice, the possibility of my meeting this strange man was almost as ominous a feeling as the storm had been that day. Of course, he'd probably be as shy as a church mouse with nothing interesting to tell me that I hadn't heard many times before.

As I walked, I noticed that either Holbrook had avoided the rain that afternoon, or, as usual, the desert had swallowed up the water and now looked as dry as it had the day I arrived. The green grass I'd seen the day before, poking its heads up through the garden stones, had either withered away or, finding no more to see up here, crawled back down into the earth to wait for another downpour should one occur.

The sign in *The Diner* read 'open' as usual, and I took the three steps to the door in only one of my own, and peeked into the dark-as-always interior.

Whatever I'd expected to see, I didn't.

First, the waitress-cook, normally behind the open area to the kitchen, was not there. Nor was the blonde owner-manager, whatever she was. They were both busy or for some reason absent.

Second, when I looked toward the far booths, the man I expected, the one who hadn't missed a dinner of green algae since I'd been coming here, wasn't in place either.

What the hell was going on?

Then, when I fully entered the room and turned to my far left, toward my own booth, I was shocked to see a fedora slowly bobbing up and down eating with his face turned away from me, and sitting in the seat opposite the one where I normally sat. All this, combined with the day I'd had, gave me a strange feeling in both my mind and stomach.

But how bad could it be? Maybe things were turning around for me.

The man in the fedora had obviously granted me permission to find out who he was. Maybe.

And the rest of them, the two women, apparently wanted no part of it. Or possibly their absence was circumstantial.

So I let the door close on its own behind me, made my way to the spot I ordinarily took, and sat down.

Simple as that. Though the butterflies in my stomach told me different, I was ready for come what may.

I looked at him. Close up for the first time. And what I saw amazed me. First, he didn't actually take note of my presence, just continued his usual pattern of enjoying his green algae.

Second, however, the face I'd assumed was symmetrical and had projected it in my mind from what I'd only seen half of, was not quite that. His nose was bent, as if it had been broken once or twice and not repaired correctly. His eyes, of which I could only see the bottom halves, were of slightly different colors. The wrinkles around his mouth didn't exactly match those at the corners of his eyes.

Third, and this really bothered me, he used his left hand to spoon his soup while his right remained below the table top as if he was either hiding something, or his hand was dysfunctional or deformed in some way.

None of this, of course, was all that disturbing, though a surprise nonetheless. And he blithely continued his eating ritual without recognition that I had joined him at the table.

I decided to wait him out. Of course, what choice did I have? There was no one else in the place. No one to take my order. If I had one, that is.

Given the situation, it wouldn't have surprised me if someone had assumed I'd arrive and ordered for me. And she'd now be delivering it to the table.

But no one did.

So there I was, sitting across from someone who refused to recognize my presence, in a restaurant full of otherwise empty seats, waiting for no one at all to serve me.

What choice did I have except to wait? So wait I did.

And time moved slowly. Very slowly.

Occasionally, the old man sitting across from me struck his spoon against the bowl making a soft dinging sound. Sometimes he'd breathe, which was certainly a good sign. Otherwise I might have taken him for a machine. Some kind of mannequin with robotic parts for spooning algae into its mouth.

Up, in, and down. Slowly. Over and over again.

Surprisingly, I wasn't bored as one might imagine. I was tense, certainly, for I had no idea what was actually going on here. But not bored. And the fact that nothing was going on except his repetitious eating caused me to anger slightly.

Was this some kind of test? And, if so, of what? My patience?

After a late and insignificant lunch of a turkey sandwich in Keems

Canyon and a long ago morning breakfast of eggs, I was starved. But then how could he know about that?

When he finally finished, had cleaned the bowl in front of him clean to the very last sign of algae I could see, he sat back, burped softly, and looked directly into my eyes. As if trying to find something there that would tell him what he wanted to know.

All this without saying a word.

The mystery man, as I'd begun to think of him, had somehow become yet more mysterious. His proximity to me apparently had an inversely proportional affect on me. The closer he came, the less secure I felt.

Then he surprised me again, for I had seriously considered that he would not open his mouth. That such a thing would take a second or third seating across from me to happen.

He asked me, in one of the gentlest voices I could ever remember hearing, if I had any questions. Not that he'd heard I had them, only did I have any.

I was stunned. By the quality of his voice—low, calm, even, slow— and by the slight twitch of his lips as he said the words. As if they didn't come easily for him.

I smiled, hoping he'd return it to me. He didn't. So I cleared my throat to give myself time to think.

What questions *did* I have? What was his name? What did he do for a living? Why he ate the same thing every night? None of these seemed relevant at the moment. So I didn't ask him a question, I made a statement. I told him 'hello,' my own name, and raised my hand from below the table as if to shake his.

An introduction. As pleasant as I could make it.

He, on the other hand, apparently not used to such formalities, abruptly flattened his back against the cushion behind him and widened his eyes as if my hand held a gun pointed directly at him. The look was of shock and even possibly terror.

I was afraid he might abruptly run back across the room or out the door. I didn't know what to do.

Keep my hand there until he recognized my somewhat universal sign of two men greeting one another? Or pull it back to suggest no harm intended?

Fearful that the latter might scare him more, I simply froze and waited him out.

One minute. Then two.

I didn't move for fear it would strike him dead.

Finally, he relaxed somewhat, moved toward me again slightly, and then slowly, very slowly, met my hand with his. His left hand. The same one with which he'd held his spoon. And we shook. Slowly and carefully. With his hand, the one that had looked so strong given his build and the manner in which he'd used it to eat, feeling like a large and very limp lizard in mine.

Again, unexpected.

And we kept this up for several seconds, him no doubt using the same technique he'd used to eat his food.

Me shaking someone's hand as a gesture of friendly acquaintance.

I pulled away first. Gently, but firmly.

And we both returned to our original positions. Looking one another over slowly. Me wanting to hear his voice again. Him, apparently, expecting me to say something more. Ask him a question that he'd previously inferred that I ask. Or something like that.

Not wanting to go through another bout of silence and physical intimidation that was not intended, I initiated the next step. I asked him his name.

He considered my question for a half-minute or so, and then told me it was Tollison Dehia, or at least that's what I heard. He said it under his breath. As if he were ashamed of it in some way.

It was an unusual name, so I asked him what it meant. Why, I didn't know, since I wouldn't have any idea what I would answer if someone had asked me the same about my own name.

He took it in stride and told me his first name had been his father's surname, one of religious roots in England, and that his own surname was Navajo for 'one who goes upward.'

He then spelled it for me so I would understand, I suppose, its unusual nature. In fact he spelled it two ways for me. The first was as I'd understood him to say, and second with 'aaya' at the end rather than an 'ia.' He told me the 'aaya' version was more accurate as it was the Navajo International Language equivalent. But, he said, he didn't really care one way or the other.

This was all very interesting.

However, afraid this would end our conversation or he'd ask me if I had any other questions, I took the initiative and asked him why he had that last name. Did it mean anything special?

And that's the precise moment when things became intensely interesting. Not that they hadn't before this, except now they were interesting from a cultural perspective not just from a simple get-to-know-you perspective.

He actually smiled as he told me that his parents had been Mormon and sent here from Salt Lake City before he was born to, as he put it, educate the 'heathen beasts of the desert' to a more religious and respectful way of life.

And when he'd been born, the only other children he saw were Navajos, and they'd decided his new name, Dehia, based on his parents' profession—teaching people how to go up into the sky and be with God.

It made perfect sense to me. Except, of course, why he'd placed his parents' name before his apparently given name rather than vice versa. And with that, the mystery once again deepened.

He told me that more information would come later, after we learned more about one another. This took me aback.

'Learned more about one another?'

How could he possibly know that would happen? For all I knew, this was a one-shot deal. Find out why this man was in here every night eating green soup and go on my way. Yes, there was something about him that struck me as more than interesting. On the other hand, though, I'd expected to be on my way west soon, and not holed up in an Arizona town on the border of the Navajo and Hopi nations.

But there it was, and I was not about to argue with him. Tollison, as I now thought of him despite his more colorful last name, then asked me to tell him more about myself. And I did.

Slowly, since he seemed to prefer it that way.

I told him about my two fathers, my place of birth about which he knew surprisingly little, and of my bouts with fortune that had ultimately led me to travel the world.

Telling him this may have taken half an hour, though I couldn't actually tell that given I didn't want to look at my watch for fear of making him think I was anxious to leave. And he remained silent throughout, listening with obvious interest and curiosity at points, and never interrupting.

And when I finished, we sat again in silence. He looked into his soup bowl for a long time. Maybe thinking about my story, maybe falling asleep, I couldn't tell because I couldn't see his eyes.

I looked for the cook, manager, owner, anyone else that might be around.

No go.

Maybe Tollison knew where they'd gone. But I wasn't about to break his silence to find out. Nor look at my watch to see what time it was or of the hunger of which my stomach once again reminded me.

When he looked at me again, I saw that he hadn't been asleep. For his eyes were as bright and awake as they'd been when we were talking. It was his way, I suppose. I was used to filling in vacancies with words. He spoke when he was ready to and not before.

Was that it? I didn't know, of course, but what did it matter? I waited in case.

And that's when the manager-owner-whatever came into the room. She'd apparently been back in her office the entire time. Waiting for some hidden clue? Some unspoken cue that it was time for me to eat?

She walked over to the table where Tollison and I sat and looked at me. And then she too took on some strange silence, as if the room itself were purposely hiding the sounds it should contain.

I looked at her. Tollison didn't. And then she walked away again. This time, though, into the kitchen where she began to cook something. My dinner, I hoped. For by now I'd become ravenous with hunger. Ready to eat anything. And given it was *The Diner*, it would most likely be that. Anything.

And we waited.

As if it were the simplest thing in the world to do. Sit and wait without saying anything. Listen to the sounds from the kitchen, the crickets I could hear faintly in the background from outside, and the occasional sound of wood creaking under foot, or the chair, or the table. Simply getting older with time.

Eventually my food arrived, and again, as she laid it out for me, I hadn't seen anything like it before.

I looked at her, waiting for the details. None were forthcoming. I could see that in her eyes.

And to put a stamp on it, she walked back into the kitchen and disappeared. And then, looking at Tollison, from his eyes as well. I was going to have to eat without labels and expectations.

So be it. I was hungry and it couldn't be weirder than anything I'd had before in this place.

Of course, it was. My drink *de jour* was something yellow this time, and certainly not lemonade. I only hoped it wasn't piss from some animal she'd found dead on the highway. For it certainly looked as if it might.

The main course gave me the impression that it had just walked into her kitchen and given itself up. Surrendered. While it didn't crawl around on my plate, the meat wasn't fully cooked.

My dessert was purple and orange, a combination I was more used to seeing on carnival rides or balloons than in bowls on a table. But here they were anyway. So I ate them. Slowly. For there was no way with the built-in heat that accompanied the taste, I could do anything else.

And Tollison watched me. Never saying a word. As if seeing someone eat were somehow gratifying to him. That he might be getting vicarious thrills from it. Or maybe second hand gratification.

It was clear that I'd never met anyone like him—or her for that matter—ever before, and not likely to meet anyone again with such strange habits.

When I finished eating, I looked up into the pleasured face of Tollison and of my blonde cook who'd quietly returned from the kitchen, and must have looked satisfied. For both their faces broke into grins.

And then my cook blessed me with the details of that which I had eaten.

My drink had been made of several uncooked pheasant eggs combined with a rich amount of goat's milk. Not bad.

My salad had consisted of slices of saguaro cactus buds, desert grasses, and several types of pine nuts gathered from the Navajo Mountain area and brought here especially for *The Diner*.

And my main course, the one that had looked alive, was actually a root from a Cholla, one of those cacti that have hooked barbs that when caught in your skin can take several painful cuts to remove. But the root of these plants was tasty and, apparently, medicinal she told me. And would, over time, reduce the possibility of kidney stones to zero. I was delighted to hear this.

Of course, all this was spiced to the hilt with Hatch green chili peppers from New Mexico. Delicious.

My dessert consisted of berries from a vine that had somehow become spliced together to form a new species that no one had yet named. It topped everything off to a tee.

After she'd taken the dishes away and Tollison and I had brushed the table of crumbs, he looked at me and said that we had plenty to talk about and was there someplace nearby I knew where we could do that without being thrown out on our respective butts.

I suggested that we stay put, but he said that his wife would be closing the place soon. His wife? Who was that? The pretty blond lady who'd served me, he said. I told him that she'd told me she was a lesbian.

He smiled as if this were a joke the two of them liked to play on unsuspecting costumers, but didn't say so to my face.

Finally I mentioned a place in my motel that remained open twenty-four hours a day near the front desk that had a table and chairs for guests to relax and talk and would that be okay.

He agreed, and with no further discussion, not even a goodbye to his wife or whatever, we strolled out the door and walked slowly and quietly toward my motel to continue our discussion. Such as it was.

As we walked in the dark, three things occurred to me in rapid succession.

First, I looked up and noticed once again the brilliant ribbon of light known as the Milky Way and considered all the stars I could see. Such a hostile place we occupied. Life so precarious and the tiny capsule on which we rode teeming with such strange forms of it. Something that staggered me with the thought.

Second, that I was now walking along under that canopy with a stranger I knew nothing about and whose quiet demeanor suggested little chance I'd learn much more than I already knew.

And third, that I'd forgotten to pay for my dinner that night.

So I stopped and turned slightly back toward where we'd come. My companion stopped as well. Not surprisingly, he didn't ask me why I'd stopped, or what had suddenly crossed my mind. Instead, and with remarkable insight, he told me that he had taken care of my dinner's bill and, if I didn't believe him, *The Diner* had closed for the night anyway.

How he knew these things was certainly unclear to me. On one hand, he could have reasoned them for himself. On the other, he could have somehow read my mind, and *that* I didn't want to consider.

He was indeed strange. But that gave him no right to my privacy, nor did I even believe it was possible in the first place.

Thus, I decided to believe him and continue on my way without a word of my own. Maybe it was his turn to eat my silence for a change. Not that I was trying to get even, mind you, only note that two could play this game as well as one, and I'd about had it with these spells of silence that were more disturbing than anything he could have said. Why I felt this way—frustrated almost to anger—confused me. But there it was, and I could no more change it than change him.

And then I relaxed. Again for no reason. As a marionette on strings, I felt manipulated in some strange way. And all this during a few minutes walk in the late evening from *The Diner* to my motel lobby.

Curious.

When we arrived, I walked to the front desk and politely asked the young man there, a Navajo with a bright and cheery face, if my guest and I could sit in the lobby and talk for a time. I already knew this was acceptable, though I felt the need to ask for permission for some reason. And, of course, he beamed his approval, and nodded.

And thus began our long journey into a wondrous and fantastical past that I could in no way have imagined no less prepared myself for.

17

We sat around a table on which someone had placed a vase of artificial flowers of such gruesome and obvious fakery that even the dust had apparently spared them its time in landing there. The flowers sparkled in the light from above. They literally danced with reflected beams of color. It was staggeringly disgusting. Someone had even placed them in fake water. I liked it.

And we talked. Or rather Tollison did. Nonstop. Not fast, mind you, but continuously.

First he told me about his parents meeting in Salt Lake City, marrying there, and reveling in their common religion. He knew of this without yet being born because they'd told him so, many, many times over. Clearly, from his vantage point at least, they were a happy couple, joining in a lifetime of love.

Then he told me of their being informed that they would become missionaries and come south to Arizona to live on the Navajo Indian Reservation.

Their mission was to educate the Indians in the ways of Mormonism including the English language, the precepts of the church, and the Word of Wisdom, which meant they should not eat, drink, or smoke anything like tobacco, alcohol, coffee, or tea. In the case of the Indians, this also included peyote and other drugs obtained from the area's plant life.

During their first years on the reservation, Tollison was conceived and born. By this time, his father had established an open-air temple consisting of a hundred or so chairs, a pulpit of sorts, and a kind of earthen rise where a small choir sang each Sunday morning. Tollison remembered none of this, of course, and related it by way of the stories his parents had told him.

Tollison's actual birth was especially eventful since babies came to the local peoples through a kind of midwife. There being no other whites or Mormons in the region around Many Farms where they had eventually settled, Tollison had come into existence with lots of hot water and little else.

He clearly made it, though, and to great sorrow had later become the family's only child, the birth somehow causing his mother to become infertile. This, of course, was not immediately known, but later when it did, his father and mother would cry mercilessly for God's help in changing that state of affairs. Mormons were decreed to be prolific child bearers, and God in his infinite wisdom had somehow seen fit to deprive them of that pleasure.

Tollison then apologized for getting ahead of himself, and returned to his being baptized at the age of eight years, and brought up according to the faith in which his parents had been raised.

And, his father's congregation grew, slowly at first, but then, when other of the Navajos observed the changes in their friends, the followers increased in number.

The Indians learned to speak English as well as their native tongue. And, according to the story his father had passed down to him, Tollison was a happy camper. Loved by his parents, and constantly living the Mormon way.

Until he was roughly five, that is. That's when the sheer numbers of local children and their various mixed beliefs began to occupy their son's mind. To his parents' dismay, of course, but what could they do? Their religion required them to proselytize and otherwise spread the faith. This took immense amounts of time, and with the only babysitters in town being Navajo, their one and only child succumbed to the wild and primitive ways of the natives. Or at least so in their minds.

Tollison then turned to his own memories, and told me of his first one, a day at the lake. Many Farms Lake lies across the highway more or less from the town and an easy walk for those in the mood. To a kid his size, this lake was like an ocean, full of strange fish that an occasional fisherman caught.

The Navajo kids who took him there dangled their legs in the water from a large rock, waded into the lake up to their waists, splashed themselves silly, and generally had a great time of it. Nothing that Tollison could see wrong in that, until he returned home later that afternoon and caught all hell from his parents for running away from home.

He tried to calm them, though it was no use. For them, not being found was the same as running away, and they provided the punishment that went with such a crime. In this case, a good beating to his rear-end.

Tollison then described his family's house for some reason. It wasn't a big house, he said. Maybe only as wide as it was tall and two stories high. The stairwell faced the front door with the living room on the right as you entered, and the dining room to the left with the kitchen off that. The stairs led to two large bedrooms upstairs directly over the main rooms downstairs with, disgustingly, the upstairs toilet aligned with the kitchen sink on the ground floor.

But he'd lived in that house for most of his youth and it represented a special place for him. At the time, the only clapboard residence on the reservation.

To hear him tell it, the town where Tollison lived growing up had only one interesting place besides his Mormon home, and that was the football field. There he could watch the local high school team play, and when they weren't playing use the runner's track that made a large oval around it.

The splintery stands on either side of the field held maybe fifty people each, and less than that during cold temperatures since there were no locker rooms or other protection from the winds blowing up your backsides and into your shirt and down your pants. Or up your skirt if you were a girl.

He told me he was an incredible runner doing well in track and field sports no matter the weather. Many called him the albino Indian, since his Navajo language skills and abilities at running had become so outstanding, something the tribe considered their specialty. Thus, it made him a kind of local celebrity.

As the days, weeks, months, and eventually years passed, Tollison grew into a confused young man. Where his father and mother taught him the ways of the Mormons, the boys and girls with whom he played taught him the ways of the Navajo, the latter not by intention so much, but because that's what they had been raised doing. It was as if what his parents intended to occur was, for Tollison, occurring in exactly opposite ways.

Language came first, of course, for without it the images he saw made no sense.

He also liked the colors, the ceremonies, the calm in the face of destiny with which his friends faced the world. As if they were a part of it. Unlike his parents who were separate and wanted to change all they could about it.

So, with a little help from a primitive sign language and a youthful sense of imitation that all young people have, he began to speak to his friends in their language, not his. This, of course, made his parents extremely unhappy. To see their impressionable son turn into a savage before their eyes as they attempted to change the savages into cultivated westerners.

Try as they might, however, their duties kept them from controlling his falling into the hands of the enemy. Tollison, on the other hand, found ways to confuse his mother and father by only speaking English in their presence and denigrating the heathen culture whenever he could so they'd think he'd withstood the onslaught of primitivism in favor of their much more civilized worldview.

This worked for a time.

However, when he entered the white man's school, administered and taught by his mother and father, he was shocked and angered by the manner in which his parents treated his friends. As if they were animals rather than people. Forcing them away from their own families towards his.

But he had no way to stop it. And thus, his friends, one by one, grew distant. Not only was Tollison best in class—not by natural intelligence but by virtue of his family's culture and thus values—he was also favored by his parents. To his friends this was intolerable.

All this, of course, was natural and easy for me to understand. Every kid went though some of this. Tollison, though, was destined to feel it more because of circumstances over which he had no control.

Everyone was doing exactly what the situation called for. No one in control. Destiny controlled it for them.

Thus, Tollison became an outsider to his friends, a young man perceived as more civilized than them in every way.

Privileged. And nothing would be the same way again. Nothing. What had once been naïve and childlike friendships became hostile, destined to remain that way forever.

The parents of his friends, however, still loved Tollison. He could understand their language and many of their ways. And without their knowing it, he became a kind of bridge between the Mormon way of life and the Navajo one. Explaining away potential hostilities and differences between the two to the adults in ways that most kids of a single culture could not. His parents eventually grew proud of Tollison's bi-lingual capabilities and his understanding of two cultures.

And things quieted down between the ones that followed the Jesus Road, as the Navajo called it—the traditionalists—and the Mormon trio of which Tollison himself was a part. Quieted, that is, until the young white man met an Indian princess that turned him forever away from his parents and their beliefs.

He had been twelve at the time, he told me, and from the minute he saw her he knew his life had changed. She was not only the most beautiful human being he'd ever seen, but her smile and grace was beyond his understanding.

And her name was Haseya, which in Navajo meant 'to rise up.'

Tollison's description of Haseya went something like this.

She was perfect. In every detail. Nothing about her was not perfect. Her smile had a special something in it that defied describing. Maybe it was the dimples in her cheeks, or the whiteness of her teeth, or the way her lips made her seem so honest when she smiled. Her hair was perfect as well. Black as a moonless night and straight as hair can be, it stretched to her hips without apologies. And she used it for expression, sometimes twirling it with her fingers and at other times, especially in combination with laughing, she'd send it flying around her head like a horse might its mane. Her eyes were as dark as bottomless wells, inviting anyone near to enter them for a long, long view of her innocent soul.

And she wore nothing except traditional dresses. As modest as modest could be. As colorful as the desert after rains. And as inviting as a cold pond on a hot summer's day. Even her shoes expressed her being, moccasins of soft deer hide sewn in the most perfect of perfect ways. 'Haseya,' he would say, as he thought these thoughts and expressed them to me.

Like the star-crossed lovers Romeo and Juliet of the Montagues and Capulets, though, their romance was not to be. A white son of a Mormon family and the Navajo daughter of traditionalists could never again see one another. Both families decreed this after discovering the budding romance. No matter the son spoke Navajo, no matter the daughter spoke English, the gulf between them and their families was far too wide a river to cross.

To ensure their separation, Tollison's parents sent him away to a boarding school in Farmington, New Mexico, where he lived nine months of the year and visited only occasionally by his parents. Not vice versa. And, during the summers, Haseya's parents sent her to live with relatives in Teec Nos Pos, a Navajo village in the distant northeast corner of the state, far too distant for them to see one another.

It was the one thing the two sets of parents could agree upon. That their respective children would never see one another again. They could speak of this subject to each other without the least bit of acrimony. And, since they avoided discussing anything else, they got along fine.

Interestingly, and unbeknownst to his parents, Tollison found lots of friends in Farmington, and all of them Navajo.

And so, as his parents imagined him quickly separating from his knowledge of the heathen people, he was indeed becoming *more* associated with them. The whites in the school derided him mercilessly, and his Navajo friends, finding such derision impossible to understand, made him one of theirs. He roomed with them, socialized with them, and sought them out for advice whenever he could. And vice versa. The trust between the young white man and the Indians became an iron chain.

As strong as this chain was, however, it came close to breaking on several occasions. The most severe of these came when the coach of the school's football team recognized in Tollison an immense talent for throwing a football not only for distance but accuracy as well. The coach's dream of a winning season after several losing ones was marred, however, by the names his white teammates called Tollison during the first scrimmage. And Tollison, being by this time a strong minded and strong-bodied young man, took it personally. He made the huddle a perfect opportunity to denigrate as many of his own team's players as possible leading to the distinct impression in his coach's mind that his star player was going to have severe problems adapting to the team spirit.

By this time in his life, interestingly, Tollison considered himself a Navajo. White skinned or not, he would have none of this racism.

And so, try as he might, the coach could not figure out a way to make his potential star player fit in with the rest of the team. That is, until he decided to let the rest of the team go and replaced them with Navajos.

While this didn't make him popular with the families of those he'd 'fired,' he didn't give a damn. One good quarterback was worth ten times the other players. And, as a bonus, not one of his opponent's teams had a Navajo player on them, and thus the plays called in Navajo by Tollison at the line were completely unintelligible.

Thus, when the team won every game they played, the parents of the dismissed team members grew quiet and stayed that way. And, by the end of his first year of school, Tollison was a hero, forgiven for his erring ways by all, and friends to everyone. They won their league's championship game by a huge margin.

When he returned after his year in Farmington for a summer with his parents in Many Farms, Tollison was a happy camper. While he knew by then he would not see Haseya, he'd at least get a chance to be home. Near the lake he'd grown to love in spite of its wicked mosquitoes, and the town to which he'd become attached to as his true home.

That summer, the one between his freshman and sophomore years of high school in Farmington, Tollison tried to reunite with his previous friends in Many Farms. To his great sorrow, however, it was not to be. No matter that he'd made so many new Navajo friends in Farmington, his old buddies could not forgive him for his intolerable behavior when they'd last seen him. Even though that had not been his fault, but the fault of his parents, mainly his father.

He then told me of two major events that took place that summer in Many Farms that would change the shape of his life forever.

The first of these began innocently enough when a friend of a former friend named Atsidi—which meant 'hammer'—came to visit him and asked if he'd like to see the great Canyon de Chelly to the south. He had, apparently, a broken down jalopy that could get them to Chinle and from there they could walk to the entrance of the great canyon.

Tollison didn't know what to make of this and asked Atsidi why he'd consider such a thing given that he—Tollison—was still such an outcast. It turned out, though, that Atsidi was an outcast as well, having broken several Navajo taboos during his young life. He had no friends either, and thought the two of them could get into even more trouble by visiting the canyons of the Anasazi, the ancient ones, whose spirits the Navajo thought still inhabited the canyon.

Tollison agreed, and off they went, despite neither of them getting permission from their parents or anyone else for that matter to do so. By that time, the canyon was already a National Monument, though still part of the Navajo reservation. Entering the canyon required they pay admission and either take a regular tour on a truck, or employ a Navajo guide, neither of which they could afford.

So, after driving to Chinle, Atsidi parked his jalopy off road west of the Monument headquarters and they hiked the long way around to enter the canyon illegally. This latter part, entering illegally, made things all that much more fun for them. But they had to stay out of sight.

They crossed the road that led east to Lukachukai and then into the maw of the great canyon. Once there, instead of heading for the route south into de Chelly proper, they decided to take the northern route into Canyon del Muerto, the canyon of the dead. An appropriate name, he told me, for it was there that the best ruins lay. Unfortunately, del Muerto didn't begin until nearly a mile into the larger chasm, and for that distance they were at the mercy of whatever tourist truck or guide happened by. Luckily, none did.

For the sake of time, they had to skip Newspaper Rock, often called 'The Wall' since it's great precipice suggested that, and it was also covered with petroglyphs and pictographs. The first being figures sculpted into the surface, and the second painted or drawn images. They also skipped Cottonwood Canyon that Atsidi had heard contained an ancient planetarium.

When they finally separated from the main canyon and moved into del Muerto, they'd used more than an hour of the afternoon. A lot of that time they'd spent watching for rangers and native ranchers who might turn them in for trespassing.

Both Atsidi and Tollison knew about Tsaile Creek, the one that ran through del Muerto. Unlike Chinle Wash in the southern branch, Tsaile contained slow sand not quicksand, and was the real terror of the two. But, they no longer had to hide from possible discovery for, with Atsidi along, they could claim him as a guide since anyone they met along this route wouldn't know the difference.

The thousand-foot high sheer cliffs along this branch contained some of the most spectacular ruins and glyphs of the entire canyon complex. Everywhere he looked, Tollison told me, he saw ruins of ancient cities dug out of the walls several hundred feet up from the creek.

Though they had to be careful, a single step in the wrong place could put one of them in deep trouble. While slow sand did what its name implied, once caught deep enough you were really stuck. Witness the truck's license plate Atsidi found on the creek bottom which they discovered was still attached to the back of the pickup pointing downward into God only knew what the deeps beneath them contained. That sobering thought kept their eyes more on the sand on which they walked than toward the walls surrounding them as they hiked the canyon floor.

Their destination according to Atsidi was the famed Ute Raid Panel, about two miles up del Muerto. There, a more contemporary pictograph in charcoal and paint gave witness of the great battle from the mid-nineteenth century, the subject of which had become the source of many Navajo legends of bravery and heroism.

Tollison told me that he'd marveled at these tales for many years in his youth, and seeing the panel told him more of the artistry and history of his people than any other he could imagine. And yes, he did say 'his people,' and as he did I noticed that he'd noticed my surprise. And with that he stopped in mid-sentence. He then waited several minutes in silence as I tried to assemble all he'd told me into a coherent whole.

What, exactly, was he telling me? That he was a Navajo? That culture and tradition were more important than blood?

He smiled then, shifted his weight slightly, keeping, I now noticed, his right hand in his pocket as he did. And readied himself to continue.

Before he did, however, I chanced a remark about what he'd

finished saying. I told him that my view of the phrase 'my people' was a dangerous one. It suggested that a people could belong to one person, as in slavery. Or that 'his' people all held exactly the same beliefs and opinions, something I was sure they did not.

He smiled at me again in that benevolent way he had, of patience and tolerance, and then told me he'd meant nothing of the sort. That he only wanted to stress by that phrase that he had by then in his life discovered that he belonged more to the Navajos than to the Mormons. That his color and blood had little to do with anything except he might get this or that disease more or less than he would otherwise. And what did I think of that.

I mirrored his quiet and thought about it. Culture to me had always been a collection of bad habits. That it did more harm than good to people, and that if we all considered ourselves belonging to the same world culture we'd be a lot better off for it.

But I hesitated.

Culture and language were obviously extremely important to him, and I was in no position to declaim his rightful heir to them. So I kept my peace and waited for him to continue.

And when he did, he told me that that was it. His first story that had so changed him it would remain with him for the rest of his life. That he wished I could visit both Many Farms and Canyon de Chelly one day, and maybe if I stayed around longer, he would be happy to take me there and show me their incredible sights. And sites. And we laughed, for even though we had not spelled the words out, we both knew the little pun he'd told. The homophone. And I told him that I'd like that very much, and what was the next story.

He paused a long time before continuing.

I snuck a look at my watch and noticed that it was half past two in the morning already. The middle of the night.

And noticed the man at the desk was fast asleep from a lack of apparent interest in Tollison's story and the lack of new costumers to the motel. His head lay flat on the counter in front of him, and he was quietly snoring the night away.

18

As I waited for him to continue, I considered my own background of culture and blood. I knew nothing whatsoever about my parents' heritages. Mongrel, I presumed. Each a mix of several ethnicities or at least cultures.

Of course I was an American. And had been raised Catholic. Did either of these count? After all, Americans were by nature confused, and the very word 'catholic' had Greek origins meaning 'in general.'

My schooling had riddled me with God only knew what, and my reaction to the church as I stopped attending Mass had given me scars in places I no doubt couldn't find no matter how hard I looked. Yet, my all-pervasive guilt followed me around like a cat on a leash, struggling to escape while finding it impossible.

Did any of this count? Could I actually relate this to what Tollison had experienced?

His second story took a long time coming, and even when it did, he prefaced it with so much detail I found myself swimming in words, most of which made no sense to me.

Certainly I was tired, but at the same time his voice had a lilt to it that kept my attention.

Not this time. Maybe he'd planned it that way. I couldn't be certain with him.

Whatever the case, it was well past three before he initiated his narrative again. This time with a pained look on his face.

Apparently, that particular summer, his first after a year attending high school in Farmington, had been a major turning point in his life. For now his voice took on an edge that verged on cracking. Like he hoped he could make it through the telling before he broke down. This worried me. After all, I didn't really want to sit here as a man much older than I cried. But I had no choice.

He began his story with a reminder of how young he'd been at the time. Probably fifteen, he said. And, like most young people that age, he was desperately attempting to make the separation between him and his parents clear. To them, to himself, and to the world.

And so, he'd run away from home. This, he said, took place some-time in mid-August, since he was scheduled to return to Farmington in the following couple of weeks. He didn't want to go back there.

So he took off into the high desert with nothing except the clothes on his back and a sandwich in his pocket. Not even something to drink.

He hadn't argued with his parents or in any way indicated his intentions to them. He just did it. Somehow he'd manage to live off the land or be taken in by a friendly family in the area someplace.

As he disappeared into the landscape, of course, he worried more about the problem he was creating for himself. After all, he was fifteen, not a man of the world, and nights got cold out there, even in mid-August. And, of course, there were nighttime critters out in the desert, some of them dangerous. In fact, to some degree, all of them dangerous. From scorpions and snakes to coyotes and pumas. Even bumping into a cactus in the dark could pose problems. Was he really prepared for all that? And on, and on.

After a time, he no longer recognized the land around him. In fact, he wasn't sure that if he decided to turn around and go back home he'd be able to find his way there. The sun was quickly heading for its own bed, and damned if he knew what he'd do then. He could see a sliver of moon trailing closely behind the sun and knew that within an hour all would be dark.

What to do?

He was in Navajo country and knew that these people, his friends whether they knew it or not, liked to live in isolation, even from their neighbors. So finding a Hogan, a mud house with its door facing east, though certainly not impossible at this point, would be chancy after dark.

But as he walked, he found no Hogans, houses, or roads to follow. And, when he stopped and listened for signs of life, he heard only the faint sounds of owls in the distance. Knowing they were not his friends, he worried all the more.

It was then he decided to return home. Explain to his parents it had all been a mistake. He'd gone out for a walk and had somehow gotten lost. Then he was found, and all was well. That is, of course, if he could find his way home in the first place. That was the trick.

He did the best he could by turning one hundred and eighty degrees around and walking in a straight line back towards where he had come from. Hoping all the while that his route here had been straight in the first place.

Night then slowly enclosed him, and the lack of light from any direction made walking in a straight line a problem. Especially since the silhouettes of cacti and various shrubs against the dim starry background made him often take circuitous routes. But, after an hour or so, he saw dim lights ahead, lights he hoped represented the town of Many Farms. His birthplace.

That's when he heard it. The unmistakable sound of an animal moving in the brush somewhere near him. A big animal. One that didn't mind being heard as it approached him. Meaning that it felt confident that if a battle ensued it would have the advantage.

I must admit at this point that Tollison's story-telling skills had me virtually on pins and needles. The manner in which he described his potential assailant, not given its due here in my recounting of it, was truly frightening. I could easily see a large wildcat in the bush beside him ready to pounce. A terrifying image.

In any event, he crouched down into the smallest ball he could make himself and waited for the inevitable. Except nothing happened. No wildcat jumped him, no owl fell from the sky to attack him, no snake bit him, no nothing at all. He waited as quietly as he could, but nothing continued to happen.

Then he heard something whisper. A voice. A human voice. And it said one simple word, 'Bahia.' That was it. A name he guessed. But one he didn't recognize.

What to do? Answer back and discover it was one of the Navajos that had disowned him? Or maybe someone else that disliked him for some reason.

He'd found his home a place of dislocation, not a place familiar.

He answered nonetheless. And the voice came back to him. And he knew that Atsidi, of all people and of wonderful luck, had found him. And they embraced briefly in the cold night.

He was indeed near home. And Atsidi led him there.

They arrived back at Tollison's house around nine that evening, late enough that there would be no doubt that he had either run away or done something else worth punishment.

So concerned about his parents, he almost regretted not staying put in the desert. He knew his mother would give him that hurt look, the one that punished more than anger would. And his father would look away, as if he didn't want Tollison to see him happy he'd returned and was safe.

As they approached the house, Tollison remembered seeing someone out front in the dark. His mother? Certainly not his father. Not big enough. Who else could it be?

As he moved closer, he realized that it was Haseya, the love of his life. What was she doing here? Had she come home early, just to see him? Her parents would be as unhappy with her as his were going to be of him.

He whispered her name, though received nothing in return. He whispered it again. And to this he heard her crying. He couldn't help trying to comfort her.

Had she been alerted that he was missing and had waited for him to return home?

It didn't matter now. He put his arms around her shoulders and did his best to calm her from her tears. She was shaking so hard he couldn't imagine these tears were for him alone.

Was something else wrong? Was her mother or father sick? Had she come out to look for him to help? As he held her, he noticed she was wet. Her tears no doubt, though how could they get on both her arms, and on her back? That didn't make sense. Something was terribly wrong.

So he gently stood back and looked at her face closely in the dim light. It was smeared with something. Wet, with more than tears.

He could smell it now. A smell he remembered from somewhere though could not tell when or where.

So he said her name again. This time, she collapsed. He caught her, and held her for a second in his arms.

What was that smell? What was going on? He pulled her up slowly and saw her eyes were closed and she'd apparently fainted. From what?

He'd come back. They were together again after nearly a year apart. What was the problem?

He reached down behind her legs and picked her up. My God she was small. And light. He hadn't remembered that about her.

Had she lost weight? Why? Did she miss him that much? He knew he had missed her as well, but not so much as to have not eaten.

As he carried her up the steps of his home and placed her gently on the front porch swing there, he noticed the lights in his house were off.

No one home? Had his parents been too busy with their Mormon duties to miss him? Maybe that was good luck. They'd return home and find him exactly where they expected him to be. Asleep in bed. Hungry, yes, though none the worse for wear. A long day, yes, but how could they know about his running away?

As he watched Haseya's shallow breathing, he once again fell in love with her. Even so slight now, she was still a princess. The most beautiful young woman in the world. A gracious swan among swallows.

Then he felt Atsidi behind him, and asked him what he thought was wrong with her. But Atsidi remained silent as silent could be.

He didn't know. How could he? And the mystery shrouded the three of them like a blanket in the quiet night.

Had his parents not missed him at all? Were they asleep upstairs, soundly snoring away?

He bent down and whispered 'Haseya' into her ear. No response. She still breathed, still looked skinny but alive, and she still looked wet. All over. Her face, her dress, her arms. No wonder she was skinny, she'd poured out all the liquid her body held in tears for him.

Maybe his parents didn't care. But Haseya did. And for him at that moment, that was all that mattered.

Tollison then told me he'd asked Atsidi what he should do, but Atsidi was dumbfounded. Now there were two confused rather than one.

So he stepped aside, grabbed the front door knob to his house, and turned it. And found it unlocked.

That was not so unusual given his parents often left it unlocked. Navajos were not thieves. His parents knew that, at least. Ridiculously naïve about them otherwise, but not about that.

So he stepped inside. He shouldn't have.

The smell on Haseya was many times stronger here, he thought. What was that smell? He couldn't place it.

And the darkness in the house made the darkness outside seem like it had been lit by a full moon. He couldn't see anything, not even the couch that he knew was directly in front of him. Placed there for guests when they arrived if they needed to sit in the parlor. And he listened. Intently. For what, he wasn't sure.

He could feel Atsidi's breath on the back of his neck. Very fast now. As if scared out of his mind.

Of what?

So he reached over and flipped on the light switch he knew was right next to the door.

Tollison doubled over then. I could see him holding the arm he kept hidden in his pocket.

Clearly something was wrong. Something about the memory. I didn't know what. I could guess, of course, and had, several times.

What had he seen? What was that smell? What was wrong with Haseya? What should I do to help Tollison now? Whatever had happened had happened a long time ago. But for him, now, it was as real as if it were happening this minute. This instant. I could somehow see that. And feel it myself. This was a strange and terrible moment. One I couldn't bear for long.

I looked over at the deskman. Still sleeping on the counter in front of him. I looked at my watch. Almost five in the morning.

Was this the same day I'd driven through an amazing storm in the desert and found myself under a bridge south of Ganado? Was this the same day I'd earlier visited an ancient village in the sky on the first mesa of the Hopi?

Now I wanted to help Tollison. But somehow I couldn't. There was no help for him, apparently. At least until he told me what had gone wrong that day so long ago in Many Farms.

And then everything stopped. By everything, I mean for me and Tollison. Not that we stopped breathing for we didn't. Nor did we stop living, for we continued on. But for one terrible moment, we stopped being *separate*. It was as if he was sharing a moment in time with me.

It wasn't him in that house so long ago, but me.

And when I saw what I saw, what he'd seen, I could feel, as surely as if they were my own, his parents lying in pools of blood.

That was the smell. Blood. On the floor with pieces of his parents' bodies scattered about. They'd been hatcheted to death by someone who'd gone insane.

The word 'violence' couldn't describe what I saw. It was beyond horrific. And I felt it. Like a knife had pierced my heart.

And then, before I could really get a handle on what I was seeing, a screaming voice entered the room wielding a huge butcher knife.

Without my saying anything, feeling anything, doing anything, that huge knife came down on my right hand and I felt pain. Real pain. Shooting up through my arm up into those centers of my brain that react when something violent occurs to your body.

And I passed out.

19

When I woke, I swore I saw that scene again before I adjusted my eyes to look at Tollison, in his typical farmer's outfit and wearing his fedora. He was apologizing to me over and over again. And next to him was the sleeping man from the desk asking me if I was all right.

I was fine and didn't actually know why Tollison was apologizing. And as all this was happening, I noticed that the sun had risen and the clock on the wall said six, which I assumed and hoped meant six in the morning. The rest of the room looked empty at the moment.

I asked Tollison why he was apologizing and he told me that he had no idea that his telling of the story would affect me so. That he hadn't meant it that way. That I shouldn't take it personally.

I told him nonsense, if anything it had been my fault and he should feel happy that he was such a great storyteller. By this time, the man had gone back to the desk or counter or whatever, since a couple had appeared and wanted a room for two days.

Then I made the mistake of attempting to sit up. Too soon, apparently, and I fell right back down again, banging my head against the arm of the couch.

After a second shaking my head, I asked Tollison how long I'd been out. And he told me no more than a half hour, probably less. And was I sure that I felt all right.

I told him again that I did, and he moved back to his chair giving me some room to breathe. And I remained silent for a time, trying to recollect what had put me in this state.

I remembered the dead bodies. *That* I managed to recollect. The fact that someone, presumably Haseya, had entered the room in Tollison's house and had cut off my, or his, right hand, however, had put me out. Too much. That, and the feeling that somehow I'd replaced Tollison and had shared his pain with him.

As I tried to sit up again, I felt a little dizzy. But I made it this time. I tried to clear my head, but wished I hadn't. For there in front of me was Tollison, holding up his right arm in front of me with a stump where his right hand should be. As if he'd read my mind and answered my question by using that simple gesture.

It had been real. Not a dream. And I felt like vomiting.

He reached for me then with his good hand and apologized profusely again. I wondered why he did such things if he knew I would react this way.

Shouldn't he know this? Maybe he truly didn't. I couldn't tell.

The feeling slowly went away, and I closed my eyes for fear he might tell or show me something else that had happened so long ago that would drive me over the cliff again.

Too much going on for me to handle. This simple man with such a kind voice had lived such an amazing life. I couldn't have carried that as a memory no less an actual occurrence for so long. What held him together?

As I thought these things over, I knew by looking at him that the story was far from finished.

And, damn him, he was determined to tell me the rest.

After all, there he was minus a hand, standing in front of his father and mother minus their heads and other parts, with a friend behind him and, presumably Haseya, his lovely princess having committed these insane crimes.

And no one to arrest her. Or take her to a hospital. Or him for that matter.

And we'd left it there, like a soap opera going to commercial. It was nowhere near over. And though I knew the chances were good I'd most likely fall into the pit again, I also knew I had to hear the rest of this story.

Then he surprised me by saying that he and I both had to get some rest and that he'd meet me again that same evening for dinner. That I should get some sleep now and, if I felt I had the strength, go see Window Rock, the political center of the Navajo Nation and see the window and the bronze statue of a Navajo code-talker there. And then up through Fort Defiance and along the south side of Canyon de Chelly. Maybe take the White House Ruin Trail into the canyon. It was wonderful. I could sleep, do all that, and still be back in time for a meal to die for at *The Diner*. And what did I think.

I was too tired to argue. As much as I wanted to hear what else he had to say, I couldn't. Not then. Not after what I'd been through.

So I watched him walk out the front door and into the morning sun and, after waiting until he'd disappeared around the corner, took myself back to my room and proceeded to lie down on the bed there and fall soundly asleep.

And, surprisingly, not dream. At least that I could remember.

When I woke, it was noon and my stomach was growling in protest that I'd missed breakfast and too many other meals lately to make it stop.

So I cleaned up, wandered out to what was now a crowd of people hungry for lunch, and eventually found a seat near the back for a meal of something nearly as unrecognizable as the food in *The Diner*. The name attached to it was Buffalo Wings. Though it looked nothing like parts of any buffalo I'd ever seen.

I remembered then that some varieties of worms will eat themselves if they can't find food. I figured the wings were better than me, so ate them.

All of them.

After that, I headed out on the Interstate east toward Window Rock just as Tollison had told me to do. All the while looking for errant clouds that might trap me under a bridge somewhere.

I found none. A perfectly clear day.

I wound my driver's side window down as the temperature rose into the high nineties. Dry heat, as they say, but still damn hot.

Just before the New Mexico border, I took a left off the Interstate going north and quickly found the turnoff to Window Rock, the 'window,' and the statue of the code talker, an image of one of the gallant Navajos that, using their own incredibly difficult-to-learn language, had completely defied Japanese attempts to decode. And helped win the war. Ironic that, given their own history of defeats at the hands of the U.S. government less than a hundred years previous.

I stopped to get gas for my guzzling Plymouth and headed north again. As I did, the wind picked up. Mysteriously since the sky had not changed. Still no clouds, and no hint of rain.

With my window open, the force of air against my arm and face was enough to imagine a wind. But I could tell it was the real thing, since the car would rock occasionally and I could see newly stacked sand on the road's shoulder scatter across the asphalt. Nothing to worry about, though, except that winds can predict oncoming storms, something that after yesterday I didn't want to encounter again.

As I passed through Defiance, turned west, and the wind really started to blow, I thought more about what Tollison had told me in the wee hours and what it might mean.

Haseya had obviously gone nuts, murdered Tollison's parents, and then for some reason retaliated against him by cutting off his hand.

Given what he'd told me about her, the Navajo culture, and his parents, it was improbable if not impossible to believe. But I believed him. Not only because of the manner in which it had affected him and me both, but the manner in which he'd told me. And the arrows that pointed directly to her as the one who'd done it. And because I could not pin it on anyone else.

Why hadn't she killed her own parents instead? And why she'd gone so out of her mind that she'd decided to slice up Tollison after he'd seen what she'd done?

It made no sense. Neither did murder in the first place, though sane people can do insane things.

And the wind picked up more violently. I could now see curtains of sand in the distance, walls of the stuff apparently coming in my direction. I'd heard about Arizona dust storms, even from my distant Brooklyn, though never imagined I'd see one. Like those planet-wide winds of dust on Mars that last for days, weeks, or months that drove astronomers, particularly amateur ones, nuts for lack of clear images of the surface. Certainly what I was witnessing wouldn't be that bad. Couldn't be that bad.

When I reached the south rim of the de Chelly branch of the canyon, I was immediately impressed. Not as wide or as deep as the Grand Canyon to the west I guessed, but still inspiring.

I took the first turn to a lookout I could, and saw Spider Rock spire, a seven hundred and fifty foot high freestanding rock pinnacle that I'd seen several times on television commercials. They hadn't done it justice.

At the Wild Cherry Canyon turnoff I saw the incredible thousand foot high vertical walls and the dribble of August water that wandered about in the sand below.

And each time I looked up, I saw the wall of dust in the wind coming closer. Like the clouds and rain the previous day, there was a menacing warning quality to it that made me want to get the hell out of there as quickly as possible.

I didn't give in to it.

My Plymouth offered perfect protection, it being so close to the ground and having such a low center of gravity.

When I reached the lookout toward White House Ruin and the sign inviting visitors to take a guide-free walk down the canyon wall on a trail, I couldn't resist. While the dust still threatened, looking all the more ready to add a foot to the height of the canyon walls, the temptation to see one of these glorious ruins up close was too much to resist.

The walk down, though somewhat windy, proved trivial. Though I knew I might suffer from my calves not having had much recent experience walking downward, every step took me into the past. Where I wanted to be at the moment.

As I approached the ruins from the south, I could see the two steps of dwellings. The first one only slightly up above the wash on the canyon floor, and the second maybe forty feet up the canyon wall. And, as I had when I'd entered Walpi village on the third mesa the day before, I got that strange feeling of entering a different dimension. At least a different time zone.

Then a strange feeling washed over me without my control. Not only of great age. After all, I'd seen many examples of that on my tour of the world. Something here so out of my perspective, that I couldn't handle it. Of disasters and conquerings of which I could only guess.

And then I saw it. A shadow passing across one of the glassless windows on the upper level. Not possible given that I couldn't imagine anyone, even a small animal, scaling the cliffs to that height. It moved so quickly, I couldn't actually verify I'd seen it. But I knew it was there. It had happened. Someone was in the ruins. Watching me as I watched.

I stood there for at least ten minutes, and nothing else moved. I could have stayed longer, except something had slowly dimmed the sun behind me to the west. I looked up, and the pinkish sky told me my time here was up. That whatever had followed me this day, might actually do me some harm. So I turned and ran back up to my car. No small feat given its nearly thousand-foot altitude above.

Once there, though, I listened to my inner voice and, not wanting to be trapped here in a dust storm the apparent size of the one approaching, I quickly drove west through Chinle and then south, back toward the way I'd come on my first day here, and into the parking lot at my motel almost simultaneously with the sand hitting the window beside its front door.

By then, the sky had disappeared into a brown cloud and the glass rattled with the ferocity of sizzling bacon in a hot frying pan.

I smiled at beating the weather to the punch for a change.

Then I turned to the desk and there behind it was the young Navajo girl, looking as she had the first time I saw her, wearing a bright and colorful native dress of some sort. More innocent and beautiful than anyone had a right to be.

Ashamed at my age of admiring someone so young, I returned her smile, but only as I turned away and headed back toward my room.

Everything I saw had hidden meanings, it seemed. Storms chasing me around the desert. Young native maidens standing behind desks. A one-handed man telling me stories of murderous scenes from his childhood. A blond woman of mysterious background. A strange and wonderful diner I'd become attached to serving the most flavorful aberrant meals. And villages, canyons, and holes in rocks that had decided to convert me from a rational man to a shaman of some kind.

What the hell was going on?

20

I sat on the bed in my room for a time watching the wind blow the dust and sand toward the south with a fury I couldn't have imagined possible.

Several times I swore I saw tornadic-like spirals form and dissipate, bending this way and that like a real tornado might.

And I thanked whatever God there may be that I had made it safely back from de Chelly. And a prayer that my car would survive the wind's damage.

That I would again be able to see out of its pockmarked windows. I had money, yes, but not enough for a new car. At least not here in Holbrook, even if they had a dealer, which I doubted. And the light slowly diminished and the sun set though I could not see it do so.

I took a long bath, washed thoroughly, and dressed in my last clean set of clothes, reminding myself as I did to visit a neighborhood pay laundry to wash my others at my next opportune time.

Then, of course, with some dire level of curiosity firing my energy, I left my room and headed once again for *The Diner*, wondering what lay in store for me there. This time. Something unexpected I knew. Both culinary and narrative.

By the time I got outside again, the dust storm had moved on toward the south and I could see the stars blinking above me like the sparkling eyes of an audience waiting to see what I did next.

And when I stood again on the threshold at the top of the restaurant's three steps, I swallowed, and turned the door handle, hoping for good news on all counts.

And, of course, what I saw surprised me yet again. No way I could ever had imagined such a thing. Not in this place or any other.

Every plastic seat in a booth and every chair at a table were filled with all manner of people. Young and old. People of different races, colors, hairdos, clothes, and everything else you could imagine. And they were talking, laughing, and eating and drinking with such ferocity and abandon that I could hardly imagine this was the same place I'd eaten in for the past few nights.

What the hell was going on?

Had word simply gotten around that *The Diner* was the place to get barbecued frog tongues, or eyelashes of hummingbird, or frozen eagle eggs?

I looked for the blonde woman that owned or at least managed the place, and found her in one of the booths, clinking glasses with someone I didn't recognize.

Were Wednesday nights free dinners for all? Had the entire town gathered here? For what? Was she giving away cars tonight? Come one, come all? Alice still lives here and she's giving away the store?

Maybe that was it. Was she selling the place?

And then I felt a tug on my shirt from behind me. I looked there and saw Tollison in a booth. Smiling up at me. And I closed the door, faced the bacchanal, and asked him what the hell was going on.

He got up and encouraged me to leave with him, walked me a distance from the diner, and told me that it was its final night.

The final night of what? What did he mean, final night?

And he told me. It was *the* final night. She was closing *The Diner* for good. Forever. He hadn't known about it or he would have told me. She hadn't told him. She'd told the whole town but not him. How he hadn't heard about it was beyond me, except he hadn't. After all, he'd told me she was his wife. And now, after he'd had his meal of algae, he'd discovered he'd had his *last* meal of algae. Not one more serving of it left for him. And then he looked like he was ready to cry. And, for once, I could see his point. I was about to cry myself.

I asked him why she'd made this decision. And he told me.

Had I not noticed the few customers she'd had my previous nights here? She couldn't make enough money to pay the rent. Though he readily then admitted that couldn't have been much in the first place given the state of the building.

We both stood there, listening to the muffled voices cheering on the inside, and together wondered what the world had come to. We were a pathetic sight. How long had he been coming here, I asked him, and he told me that it was too long to remember. And we watched some more.

Then, apparently disgusted with himself for making such a big deal out of this, he asked if we could return to the motel and continue our discussion there.

I agreed that would be best given the circumstances, and we made our way in the dark silently toward the motel.

As I looked up at the sky, I noticed that the storm of sand had now left residue behind, an overcast not of moisture, I guessed, but of planet earth. At least planet earth as Holbrook understood it. And, apparently, most of northeastern Arizona.

When we arrived in the lobby of the motel, the young Navajo girl had been replaced by the same man who'd been so gracious to us the night before. We briefly discussed having dinner in the motel, though neither of us was very hungry given the circumstances.

Our plans for dinner as demolished as they were, we sat in the same places we had the previous night when things had gotten so out of hand.

As much then as I wanted him to continue his story, I needed to hear more about *The Diner*.

And Tollison agreed.

First and most important, I insisted on knowing who the blonde woman was. Really his wife? A lesbian? His sister? Enough of this game. I, at least, needed to know the truth of the matter, and he owed me that much. At least that's what I told him.

And, of course, in his inimitable style of discourse, he sat there, staring at the table between us, silently thinking it over.

This was a game I imagined on his part, but it was damn frustrating from my point of view. What could I do about it though? You can lead a horse to water, except you can't make him talk.

So, I gave up, sat back on the couch, and thought about other things. My trip here. Through Oklahoma, Texas, and New Mexico. He must have heard me mentally change subjects then, for he looked up suddenly and told me the blonde woman who owned or ran *The Diner* was his mother.

I knew that couldn't be, and told him so.

He then said she was his niece, his niece in law, his grandmother, and so on, each time followed by a refusal to believe it from me.

It was getting downright ridiculous by this point. So, he stopped and told me she was all of these things. That, of course, made less sense than anything he'd said previously. So I shook my head back and forth. Slowly.

But he announced resolutely that he'd told me the truth. I continued to shake my head. And he repeated himself. Over and over and over again, no matter my insistence to the contrary.

Finally he stopped, I stopped, and the conversation, of no surprise to anyone who might have been listening at that point, stopped.

And then he said it again. She was all of those things to him. Though instead of ending there, he continued by telling me that over the years he'd known her, she'd been like a wife, a sister, a mother, an aunt, and so on. At different times. Same place—*The Diner*—but at vastly different times over the years. Because that's what he needed her to be. Even though he'd not told her his story, she discovered it somehow or maybe guessed it, or parts of it, and wanted to help him. He'd been, after all, in a sorry state when they'd met and she, for some reason known only to her, had decided that she was the one, the only one, who could help him. And she had.

I asked him how could she be a lesbian then. To that he had no answer. He told me flat out that when she'd played his wife, she'd been as much of a wife as any wife could be. And he smiled and opened his eyes wide to make the point further. In other words, they'd made it happen and he'd not dreamt it. For sure.

Then he added that for all he knew, her abilities at mental shifting of gears could easily have led her in that direction after she'd met him. He was, after all he'd been through, a sorry example of a man.

I did not want to explore this any further and told him so. Except to know her name. Then he surprised me further. After all she'd done for him, she'd never told him her name. She only told him to come to dinner at her diner every night and someone would be along to help him. I asked him if he'd done that, and about the result. And he told me he had. And that I was looking and listening to the results.

To this I had nothing whatsoever to say. I was no savior. I was a spoiled rich kid from the east coast having little hope for myself no less anyone else.

What could she have seen in me?

He told me he had no idea, except that I had shown an interest, listened, and was an empath.

I asked him how she could have known these things about me.

And he responded by telling me that he had no more idea about that than he had ideas about how she knew how to help him by giving him whatever he needed in life.

It was then that I begged him to stop talking about her. None of this dialog was doing anything for either of us. And that we should let it be. He agreed with a flourish of his hand-less arm.

And with that out of the way, we got down to business. I reminded him of where we'd left off only this morning, where his hand had been cut off, no doubt by Haseya after she'd brutally murdered his parents.

He remembered, and to show it, he once again put his head in his hands and appeared to return to the actual state of mind of seeing parts of them there, scattered about in pools of blood.

Thank God he decided to leave me out of it this time, so I could continue to listen without passing out.

When he looked up at me, his eyes were moist and I could tell he'd been crying. Softly, to avoid my having to participate in his grief.

Then he began talking in that way he had of continuously speaking as if reading from a prepared text. He'd apparently been taken to the nearest hospital in Chinle, a few miles south of Many Farms. There they stopped his bleeding and wrapped his wrist tightly, gave him heavy doses of antibiotics and painkillers and kept him for two days.

During that time, the local area Navajo Tribal Police Captain—the Navajo Nation had not yet been established—interviewed him, and as was the custom took his word as gospel and left him alone.

He had no idea what had happened to Haseya. Being drugged for pain most of his stay, he couldn't remember much of what occurred while he stayed in the hospital, but did remember that Atsidi and his parents picked him up and took him home with them for further recuperation. It was from that time on that Atsidi called him Bahia and so did everyone else. And Tollison took Tollison as his first name, and placed Bahia as his last, for it belonged there.

As he healed, Tollison told me that he developed a love-hate relationship with the Navajos. After all, he was only fifteen years old and had seen the results of the murderous actions of a Navajo girl who he thought he loved, and then watched her cut off his right hand with a large butcher knife.

While he knew she was crazy, he couldn't forgive her for this, and part of him blamed her parents as well. They were a traditional Navajo family, and thus the entire tribal population was partially at fault.

It was not just she who did it, it was the beliefs of all who'd taught her what she knew. Thus, he rebelled against Atsidi's family, not Atsidi himself, for that would have been impossible given what Atsidi had done for him.

And once again he ran away. This time not into the desert, but to the scene of the crime. His own house, which had by then been cleaned of the bodies of his parents. And he stayed there for some time, living off the money his parents kept in a cookie jar in the kitchen and otherwise staring out the window at the land beyond. The only place he'd ever known, having been conceived and born there. Being white and Mormon, learning the language of the heathen, as he now thought of the Many Farms people.

As Tollison described it, these were the darkest hours of his life. Reading couldn't keep his mind off things. He could barely think. And when he did, he broke into tears and screamed at the God who he thought had somehow punished him for a crime he'd not committed.

He forgot about his football team in Farmington and about returning there for school. School was the furthest thing from his mind. All be wanted was to sit, eat occasionally, and stare out the window at the desert he remembered so fondly.

One day, as he was looking out the window though not really seeing anything, he heard a sound coming from the upstairs of the house. A soft sound as if it were not meant to be heard. Possibly a mouse that had somehow gotten inside? Or a snake maybe?

After a while, though, he heard no other sounds and eventually returned to his empty stare.

Then he heard it again. This time louder. A shuffling. Something bigger than a mouse or snake. Much bigger.

At first he thought, hopefully, that his mother or father might have returned to him. Not dead after all.

Then he looked at the stump at the end of his arm and realized the absurdity of that. That he was not safe after all. That most likely someone or some*thing* had entered his house while he was sitting in front of the window feeling sorry for himself and gone upstairs to steal what it could find there.

So he stood, and carefully, very carefully, walked across the kitchen and through the doorway, once again listening intently for the sound to repeat itself.

And it did. This time louder still. He looked up the stairs toward where the sound had come from, and continued to wait. For something to show itself, or another sound that might indicate what it was that had interrupted his day.

And the seconds ticked by. Like a mouse tiptoeing its way to hide in a closet. Clearly this was no mouse, though, for he heard the sound yet again. A brazen one this time, with the clear intent of being heard. No doubt about it. No hesitancy, no fear, no curiosity involved.

Someone or something had invaded his house and was not shy about admitting it. Tollison had no idea what to do. He couldn't run from a sound, no matter how big the creature that made it might be. After all, in his current state, he himself might be the cause of it sounding louder. Imagining things that weren't there.

And where would he go anyway? He hated everybody.

His once princess Haseya may have committed the actual crimes, but one way or another she'd been taught by the culture into which she'd been born and raised. *These people* had murdered his parents.

So he stood his ground and waited. Wanting to go up the stairs except not willing to take the chance. He wanted to force whatever it was to make the first move. Show itself, so he'd know what he was up against. After all, who in their right mind would attack something completely unknown?

It was then that the creature did make itself known. Not by sound this time, although it was that as well, but by stepping out from his bedroom door at the top of the stairs and presenting itself.

In all its menacing glory.

It was tall, many feet taller than Tollison. It was big around, like it had eaten something twice its size. It was furry like no wild animal Tollison had seen before except in pictures and photographs. It had a snout of great proportions with its teeth barred in a sinister and malevolent way. These teeth dripped with saliva or something from whatever it had last eaten. Its coat of black fur was stained with all manner of gruesome remnants of its previous conquests. And it growled with a ferocity he'd never heard before or imagined hearing now.

It was a bear. Though not a bear. Standing up like a bear might, but on the legs of a man, not a bear.

Tollison's own legs wouldn't move. Couldn't move. For he knew this creature. He'd heard of it as a young boy. It was yee naaldlooshii. A *skinwalker*. A shaman of such evil, that it murdered just for the fun of it. And often ate its victims. Everyone he knew knew about skinwalkers, though few if any had ever seen one.

Now Tollison had. And standing at the top of his stairs growling deep in its throat. The devil had somehow gotten into his house and with its mouth drooling in anticipation of a good meal now stood above him with nothing except twenty-two steps between the two of them. Between the beast and death.

His description of the skinwalker had so terrified me, that a sudden pain in my stomach felt like the beak of the dreaded tarantula was eating me from the inside out.

Tollison willed his feet to move, though they would not. He'd never believed in the skinwalker. Thought it was a fable made up from some Navajo's nightmare long ago.

But this one was for real. And it took its first tentative step down to the landing just below the second floor, grabbing and hanging onto the bannister as he knew it would. After all, skinwalkers were actually evil men or spirits of men, not really bears or whatever they turned into when it came time for them to hunt their victims.

They wore the skins of animal. After all, they were yee naaldlooshii. Skinwalkers.

He tried to run. To escape this mad creature who'd kill him if it could. But he still couldn't move.

And so he watched as the skinwalker made its way step by step down the stairs to its waiting victim. A victim somehow hypnotized by its presence, like a fly caught in a spider's web waiting innocently for the slaughter to begin. For the skinwalker to tear him to pieces, shoving its snout into Tollison's belly to drink his blood and eat his flesh, all the while snorting in both victory and pleasure at its conquest.

It was then that Tollison noticed something incredible that made him laugh. On top of the huge bear's head sat a hat. A human hat. Several times smaller than would fit on the bear's head. A fedora the Italian's called it he remembered for some reason.

Three things then happened in rapid succession.

First, the skinwalker tripped slightly so unnerved was it by Tollison's sudden laughter. And this trip caused the animal to lose its balance, pull its hand off the banister, and fall. This, in turn, loosened whatever grip the fedora had on its head and it literally flew through the air and hit Tollison in the chest. This, in turn, caused him to instinctively grab it with his good left hand.

The second thing that happened was that the skinwalker slid toward Tollison with twice the rapidity with which it had walked before, making the bear much more angry than it had been.

And third, all this sudden action caused Tollison to lose whatever it had been that held him frozen in place and sent him charging out the front door of the house as fast as his legs would carry him.

As he ran, he could hear the skinwalker regain its standing position and follow him. He didn't dare look behind to see if this were true, but knew it by the sounds the animal made.

Coming ever closer due to the long length of its legs and the larger steps it could take. And across the desert the chase continued.

As he ran, Tollison—now wearing the fedora the skinwalker had accidently passed to him—had no idea where he was going.

Would he find someone to help him, or wander into the desert as he had that time he ran away from home only to find his parents murdered on his return?

Then, however, he noticed that he'd intuitively run toward Atsidi's Hogan. And as he did, even as the skinwalker was almost upon him, he saw Atsidi working the cornfield.

He screamed Atsidi's name for help. But Atsidi didn't hear him.

Didn't look up. And the race continued. With the skinwalker's rancid breath causing the hair on his back to rise, he stumbled into Atsidi's Hogan and, immediately exhausted, fell to the floor.

Once there, he waited for the inevitable. The skinwalker to have his feast. For it didn't matter if anyone saw the beast do it, the monster had to have his fill of the evil that Tollison had become.

Nothing happened. No more sound except his own breathing. Fast now from his running.

And then the sound of Atsidi's mother rushing into the room and kneeling by Tollison's head saying, toh-bah-ha-zsid askii ta-gaid amá, or 'afraid boy without his mother.' And she sat back on the heels of her feet and laid Tollison's head in her lap as he slowly cried himself to sleep, all the time saying over and over, yee naaldlooshii, yee naaldlooshii, yee naaldlooshii, yee naaldlooshii. Skinwalker, skinwalker, skinwalker, skinwalker.

When he woke he was in a bed in a room of the Hogan with Atsidi sitting by his side. They remained in silence for a while, as is the custom in the world of the Navajo. Some whites called it the *Navajo quiet*. No need to fill silences by saying things that didn't matter. And they sat that way for some time.

Then Atsidi told Tollison that he was welcome to stay in their house for as long as he wished. That as far as he and his parents were concerned, Tollison was an atsilí, a brother to Atsidi. A member of the hak'éi, or member of the family.

That night he ate dinner with his new family, speaking only Navajo and trying to laugh with them as they told stories about relatives he'd never met and friends from out of the area belonging to different clans and different chapter houses.

He learned that he had joined the Bit'ahnii or the Folded Arms Clan and belonged in the Many Farms Chapter House. He knew he didn't *really* hold these honors, but didn't care. The Hogan was warm and friendly. And he'd taken the place of Manaba, Atsidi's sister, who had died from pneumonia when she was a year old.

For the first time in many years, and certainly for the first time since the murders of his parents, Tollison felt comfortable. Nothing about the family he'd been invited to join had anything but the ring of authenticity. It was real. He was loved. And he gave the love back in kind.

Then, on the fifth day of his stay at Atsidi's Hogan, he learned he was to have an Enemy Way Ceremony held in his honor. To cure him of the evils in his mind.

He'd heard of the Enemy Way, and that it was often held for Navajo soldiers, men returning from war to shed the ghosts of enemies they'd killed. He hadn't killed any enemies, at least as far as he could remember, but the manner in which his new family told him these things, he could not turn them down.

The Enemy Way he discovered was as important as the Blessing Way, the other side of the coin so to speak, the latter being to honor the blessings of young girls for their entrance into womanhood.

What shook him to the core, though, was that he was to share this Enemy Way with another person, Haseya, the one who'd murdered his parents and cut off his hand. This he had trouble understanding, though he knew the way of the Diné—the Navajo people. Curing people of their sickness that had caused them to commit crimes, rather than placing them in prison like whites did. And that the way to cure people of their most egregious crimes was by giving them an Enemy Way Ceremony. In a way, it was only reasonable that the two of them should share this ceremony given that they both had, in a way, suffered from the same crime. Unfortunately for Tollison, it meant he would relive the murders throughout his cure.

Atsidi told him that Enemy way ceremonies always lasted an odd number of days, typically three, five, seven, or nine, few shorter than three and fewer longer than nine. Due to the severity of the crimes involved in this particular case, the planners of the ceremony chose seven days as the duration. Seven continuous days and nights of talking, dancing, staging mock battles, singing, chanting, sand painting, praying, and thinking. All this to cure the two of them of their chindi, or ghosts of the dead. The tribal council also set aside another week for the preparation of the site where they'd decide the ritual would take place.

Truth be known though, Atsidi said these ceremonies were simply excuses for the tribal elders to smoke peyote and visit with relatives they rarely otherwise got a chance to see. That from what he'd heard, the only curing that really got done was of the loneliness of those same elders.

But, as the day for his Enemy Way to begin approached, Tollison almost ran away again, so frightened was he of having to spend, as he put it, three hundred and thirty six consecutive hours alongside the person he loved and hated so much all at the same time.

On the night before the festivities began, while the tribal elders held a meeting to plan the healing, Tollison stared out his stepparent's Hogan window wondering why this was happening to him. After all, here he sat, a one-handed young man ready to begin the prime of his life, and having no idea who he was.

A Navajo or a Mormon? In love or in hate? Lost or found? And the world outside the window provided no answers. No rumble of thunder, cry of an owl, or a simple whoop of a coyote.

Just before falling asleep, it came to him that it wasn't the lack of things that bothered him so much, but the reverse. There were too many possibilities.

21

A t this point in telling his story to me, Tollison, who'd buried his head in his hand as he'd spoken, now raised it, looked at me, and begged my forgiveness for taking so long and talking about so many things.

I told him I hadn't noticed. Then we both looked at the clock, now reading well after midnight.

It was then I realized I'd already been brought under the spell of his soft slow-sounding voice twice during his descriptions—that being his encounter with the skinwalker and the reaction of Atsidi's mother when he'd arrived. Those moments had captured my imagination such that the time had passed unnoticed.

He then asked me how much detail I wanted to hear about the Enemy Way Ceremony. And that he didn't want to bore me with too many cultural minutia.

I told him I'd leave it up to him, but in no way had I been bored by his narration thus far. I couldn't imagine being bored by whatever he wished to describe about the Enemy Way.

But I did take a restroom break, passing the once again sleeping front desk guy. The white guy in his early twenties who apparently didn't spend his days sleeping, but partying his ass off.

When I returned, Tollison was sitting where I'd left him, looking out into the dark night as if recollecting the skinwalker that still hounded him after all these years.

When I sat down again, I looked at him. Steady, calm, though still clearly within his story. Ready to continue.

But I wanted something else. At least for the moment. So I asked him if he had known any of the people that had filled *The Diner* that evening when I'd come for dinner and found it overflowing. A party in full swing.

He told me he had no idea who those people were. No one he saw looked familiar.

I asked him if he had any guesses.

His only guess, he told me, was that she'd been to each one of them as she'd been to him. That it was her way. That maybe they'd come from all over, not just from Holbrook, to pay their respects.

I asked him again if she'd warned him of the event, but then remembered he'd already answered that question. The only thing about it was that it had been unpredictable. That obviously was the way of the blond owner or manager. Whatever she was.

And then I asked Tollison to continue with his story. At whatever pace he wished. And not worry in the least about boring me. Nothing he could say would or could do that.

And he smiled, and continued.

The Enemy Way Ceremony, he said, had prescribed events for the most part, though in no particular order. Anyone could attend and contribute and thus change the manner in which the events played out over the seven days—in this case—that it took to complete.

The ceremony began at dawn, he said, the day after the planning meeting took place. And that's when he saw Haseya for the first time since she'd killed his parents and cut off his hand. He described her as emaciated and withdrawn and yet, somehow, still radiant. She kept her head bowed and wouldn't look at him. Ashamed of what she'd done? To say that Tollison was conflicted would be an understatement. I could read it in his body language as he described the meeting. But, try as I might, I couldn't visualize the star-crossed lovers in my mind's eye.

The two of them were then driven to a stranger's home—at least to them—to make an offering of a foot-and-a-half-long juniper branch decorated with eagle feathers and colorful yarn called a staff. Tollison later learned that this stranger had agreed to receive the staff in advance, thus becoming the medicine man for the ceremony. While this process could take up to three days, Tollison told me it took only one in his and Haseya's case. Maybe because she was a rarity, as Enemy Way Ceremonies typically involved males not females.

That night, the medicine man began the Enemy Way songs and the dancing began in the location where the ceremony was to take place.

A young native woman who initiated the dances wore traditional attire. He remembered her, he said, as he could see out the door of the Hogan where he and Haseya were and she looked, as Tollison described her, much like the young lady in the motel I'd seen twice.

Was I imagining this?

During this time, the patients spent most of their time alone or with friends inside the Hogan. Now Tollison grew unusually quiet. He clearly didn't want to discuss the situation with Haseya.

I could tell, though, he knew he had to.

So he did.

At first, he said, he wouldn't speak to her or her to him. Visitors, mostly family of one or both of them would come and go—in his case members of his step family—and wish him or both of them good luck. Or talk about things going on in the village they belonged to. Many Farms in this case.

When no one was around, neither spoke. About anything. It was strained, he said, and he didn't get much sleep.

On the fourth day, however, Haseya asked Tollison a few questions. In Navajo, of course. Most of these were simple.

How did he feel? Did he notice any changes? Was he hot? Nothing of any importance as far as he was concerned.

At first, he didn't answer her. Eventually, however, he decided that was stupid and he said a word or two to show he'd heard her.

These conversations, if you could call them that, often lasted most of the night. While he didn't mind that, since sleeping was not going to come easily anyway, he still found talking to her unsettling.

On the fifth day, both he and Haseya had grown so tired that they forgot their differences and began acting as they had before the murders took place. This was obviously difficult for Tollison to talk about, though his voice continued on nonetheless.

Mostly they spoke of things they'd done when they'd been purposely separated by their parents. Tollison told her about his football team and school in Farmington, and Haseya about her summer visits to Teec Nos Pos to stay with her relatives.

Almost immediately, he fell in love with her all over again. He could barely see in the dark Hogan, but that wasn't the point. It was hearing her voice and listening to her tell of the beauties of the land and the Navajo Way that so captured him.

Then, as gravity to a fallen rock, they virtually fell into the night of the crime.

And Haseya came unglued.

She cried so much and for so long that Tollison had no idea what to do. He couldn't comfort her. Not after what she'd done. Even though he wanted to. Badly.

Instead, he cried as well. Not so much for his dead parents, surprisingly, but for her. That was the thing, he told me, over and over again.

In the end, it was as if by killing his mother and father she'd killed herself. She'd committed suicide. It was insane to feel that way. He knew that. But that was how it was. She was dead, no matter what he felt for her in the Hogan at that moment.

After that, they stopped talking. It was a terrible time. He wanted to forgive her. He couldn't. Enemy Way Ceremony or not. Staff or not. His childhood love or not. It couldn't be. Why? Because he was a Mormon?

No. That wasn't it. As a Navajo he couldn't forgive her. Was that true?

After all, Navajos did not hold grudges. They didn't need to forgive people. They cured them. Healed them because people who committed such crimes were sick and needed to be healed. Not imprisoned.

So was this, then, because at the heart of it, he was a white man, and no matter that he'd been born on Navajo land, been raised in the Navajo tradition as least to a degree, and now had a Navajo family, he was forever—by blood and parentage—a gringo? Someone who could never understand the Diné. And this, of course, made him even sadder.

And the Ceremony progressed, day after day, with neither speaking to one another again. And with all the songs, all the incantations, all the dancing, all the meals and discussion around those meals, and all the chanting and prayers, and the visitations, nothing changed. Nothing at all happened. To either of them. *They* did not change.

The ceremony had not worked. And they both knew it. They looked at one another on that final day as they were being led to the center between the visitor's campground and the Hogan where they'd been housed for so long, and demonstrated that fact to one another. Unspoken words that they could not be, never could be, and they both knew it.

For a reason even they could not understand, she'd been partially turned to the white way and he to the Indian way and that was it. Simple and complex as that.

And so the Enemy Way Ceremony concluded. And she returned to her family and he to his, such as it was.

And time proceeded as it always did. Forever forward. Never backward, as he'd once hoped it could.

Their love had perished that night with his parents. Never to be rekindled.

Tollison had, I noted, put his face in his hand again and looked like he was sobbing.

I'd expected, since surprise was his way and everyone around me these days, that he would look up then and smile, and then tell me they'd gotten back together again. Finally somehow resolved their problems. True love.

And, surprisingly, that's exactly what he did. He looked at me, smiled, and told me that they had gotten back together again.

I couldn't believe it. A true love story. It wasn't possible. This was a joke. I knew it, and he knew I knew it.

But no, he said. Not long after the ceremony was over, maybe two or three weeks later, they met accidentally in town. Her parents saw no reason any longer to send her to Teec Nos Pos, and he certainly was not going back to Farmington. So they met.

They exchanged greetings and—and this was really a surprise to me—he asked her if she would like to visit Canyon de Chelly with him. That he'd been there, especially to Canyon del Muerto, and was already familiar with the land and the ruins. Not that this was a date or a chance to relive their young love for one another, or anything of the sort. Simply two people having been born in the same village, wanting to spend time away to see new sights.

I was dumbfounded on hearing this and told him so. He made their arrangement sound so innocent after the discussions they'd had in the Hogan during the ceremony.

He told me that that discussion had somehow released the venom, freed them from the evil spirits, and, while there was no way they could ever truly love one another again, he, at least, saw this as a way to ease the tension between them. And he made this case so convincingly, that I bought it. After all, it did make a certain kind of sense.

I should have known then that his previous description of their parting from the Enemy Way did not agree with his current one, but by then I'd stored that earlier one away for the time being.

And so, he told me they borrowed Atsidi's father's car with some trepidation and concern on Tollison's part given the possibility that for some reason he might not be able to return it. Why he felt this way I couldn't figure, but left him alone to tell his story.

So he drove the two of them to Chinle and to the mouth of de Chelly, remembering as he did the time that Atsidi and he had had visited there earlier that year.

As he drove, he told me, they said nothing. That it was not a tense drive, but one of being Navajo.

Nothing to say. Nothing said. Of course, they had plenty to say *really*, but nothing that would, in the end, have meant anything. To either of them.

As they walked into the entrance of the main canyon, Tollison kept a lookout for rangers and tours, but saw none.

Unusual. Then they passed where Newspaper Rock and Sleeping Duck Ruins lay waiting. And he noticed the sky was the most beautiful he had ever seen it. And cloudless.

The sandstone rocks gleamed their rusted orange-pink color, and the lazy Chinle Wash was its wandering self, never quite knowing which way to go in the ever-changing shape of the broad belly of the canyon.

When he looked at Haseya, she smiled, and he knew as well that she could see it and feel it.

But he knew it wasn't really true. That Haseya was still a murderer and always would be. And that forgiving her or not, nothing could ever change that. That nothing would ever be the same again between them. But a single day in a canyon didn't mean much, and there was no reason not to enjoy it. After all, everything didn't have to be for the sake of something else. Things could be independent.

Couldn't they?

So they walked up the canyon and took the northern branch into the canyon of the dead, something he hadn't wanted to think about and therefore had put out of his mind.

Haseya followed his lead, probably unaware that the canyon was called del Muerto. Labels meant nothing anyway.

As they walked, he pointed out particular things to her. The patina stains on the high walls made by falling rain spilling down from above over hot rocks. And the various caves and ruins where they spent time looking over the glyphs.

The late summer's heat was not so bad, and the sun had already begun its yearly move southward for the winter. So they made it to the fabulous Antelope House on the north side of the canyon by mid-afternoon. Here, the masonry was incredibly structured, standing three stories high in places. He explained the Anasazi—the ancient ones in Navajo—at least as much as he knew, and it was good to see her white teeth smiling broadly at the age of the ruins. But looking a little worried at the same time. For the chindi, or ghosts of the dead, could still be around somewhere.

They finally sat in a green meadow under a nearby cottonwood tree and enjoyed the shade and cool wind that now blew down the canyon.

And he thought he could feel her wish that this was a fresh moment for them. That nothing had existed before this time. That it was only them, with no memory of anything that had gone before.

It was then that he noticed the clouds forming to the east. Large cumulus clouds with dark flat bottoms full of water.

So he told her they had to leave. That late summer storms could unleash their rains and cause flooding in the canyon.

He had no idea why he told her this at that moment. Surely she knew this, having—like him—been raised within six or so miles of this very place. Maybe it was to warn her they were in a canyon that had narrowed somewhat from the one they'd entered. Or that del Muerto Creek, the sands on which they now sat, could become a roaring torrent of water, turning a lovely afternoon into a deadly nightmare.

Whatever the reason, they gathered what few things they'd brought along, and headed west again as fast as they could without running.

Before long, however, the sun had disappeared behind clouds and lightning brightened the sky with thunder exploding in their ears.

The storm definitely arrived faster than they could escape it. No way could they make it back to the car before the rains came.

So Tollison told her they had to begin climbing. He'd never been in the canyon during a storm before, but logic demanded that high ground was a safer place than near the creek.

They found a spot strewn with boulders and wound their way up them as fast as they could. Eventually, of course, the boulders got fewer and fewer, and the sheer wall of rock above actually bent outward slightly preventing them from climbing any further. During this time, the storm shuddered and shook with its mighty winds and blasts of thunder, and the canyon depths became yet darker under the canopy of clouds.

Then the temperature dropped. Significantly. Enough to make Tollison aware of having worn summer clothes not expecting such a change.

And then the rain fell. Not hard at first, but it didn't have to. The water below them was already rising from heavy rains up stream, and what had been a lazy creek had now become a shallow but raging river.

The waters were driving hard to the west, and all of the culverts and canyons that fed the Tsaile churned those waters into furious torrents, adding to the creek thousands of times over before it reached the two of them.

He and Haseya, cold and wet by now, huddled together among the rocks watching helplessly as the suddenly accumulated waters below them rose up the sides of del Muerto.

He could feel her heart beating through her body as they watched the angry river grow.

He could sense her fear as if it were his own.

And then, as they watched what they could not control, he felt strangely as if they were one. That maybe, somehow, God had finally smiled on their presence in the universe and brought them together again.

But, of course, that was foolish. For the water below them filled the lower canyon so quickly and with such ferocity, that his moment of belief disappeared in the sudden collapse of many of the boulders beneath them. Luckily, the one on which they perched stood firm. So far.

Before he knew what had happened, though, he could feel Haseya slipping away from him.

Then, before he could do anything to stop her, she fell into the raging river.

He tried to reach her, but stretched his missing right hand out for her and, of course, it did no good.

She'd spun off the now lone rock they'd found and into the waves of water splashing by.

He screamed at the top of his lungs for God to intervene. To help them.

She yelled that she couldn't swim. He could. But he knew that by attempting to save her he'd only drown as well. After all, a one-handed swimmer trying to catch a non-swimmer in this mess? Not a chance. Or so he told himself.

As he watched her helplessly splashing, he willed himself to take the plunge. Unfortunately, just as he'd not initially budged under the threat of the skinwalker in his house, he couldn't move this time either.

And before he could blink, she was gone. Under the water. What could he do to save her? Was it too late? Was it that she had to die this way, unsavable by the man with the missing hand that she herself had cut off?

He thought these thoughts even as he knew that at that very moment she was probably already gone.

Or nearly so. Or dead. Alone. Without him.

And, as he realized that once again life had delivered him unto yet more impossible tragedies that he couldn't endure, a shaft of lightning hit the water slightly downstream and earsplitting thunder deafened him.

The wind surged violently and pushed him back against the cliff in case he himself had the urge to fall into the water and drown.

For God, or the gods, would not have it. His was a life meant to suffer. No mercy. Not for him. And he sat down and cried as the storm began to subside and the river shrank nearly as fast as it had risen. The canyon had belched out its poisonous waters into Chinle, and along with it his beloved and hated Haseya.

Tollison at this point cried again, and I could both hear and see the sobs wrack his body with the sound of the thunder and the disappearing waters in his mind.

I'd not become him this time, but I'd felt his pain. Maybe as strong as he had. At that moment, the sheer heaviness of his grief weighed on me, him, the motel, and Holbrook.

It was nearly impossible to bear.

But I waited. For what, I didn't know. I guess for him to stop crying. For the man at the desk to stop sleeping. Or for the sun to peek up over the horizon since the clock read just past six in the morning.

I had once again survived a story told by a man who'd lost everything he'd ever had and somehow survived.

But as what had he survived?

22

When Tollison once again raised his head toward me with tear-streaked cheeks, I hesitated to say anything. But I had to. He'd left his story with so many questions.

So I asked him what he'd done then.

And his answer was so simple, so jarring, it caught me completely off guard.

He'd waited until the water approached normal level, walked out of the canyon, driven off in Atsidi's father's car, eventually found his way to Holbrook down south, parked the car, wandered around looking for a telephone, found one in a small diner near the motel where we now sat, called the Many Farms Chapter House and left directions on how to find the vehicle, ate a very strange dinner given him by a very strange blonde lady, told her his story which she listened to with great interest as a mother might, and, over time, grew a beard, found another place to live, and met me.

And that was all there was to it, he said. End of story.

I was once again taken so off balance by his naïve and simple explanation that I doubted I'd heard him right.

Hadn't the Many Farms authorities looked for him? Had someone found Haseya's body? Had he never once returned to the place of his birth? Had he ever again seen a skinwalker? And on, and on.

The answers came back clean and easy. No, to all of them. And, he added for my clarity, he hadn't exaggerated any of it. And he'd told the truth about the blonde woman in *The Diner*.

Then I asked him the most dangerous question of the night. Why had he chosen me to tell his story to?

And to that, he had no immediate response.

Then he said that he'd not actually made the choice. She had. The unnamed woman in *The Diner* had decided I was the one.

I asked him how she could know this.

And he told me what I thought he would. That he had no idea except he trusted her and no one else. That she'd know.

Of course, that made no sense to me at all. Not much I could do about it, though. Making Tollison talk was like trying to pull teeth from an eagle's mouth. If nothing was there, nothing would come out.

I couldn't believe it. We were done. I'd heard his story. Tragic and wonderful at the same time.

Instead of declaring we were completely finished, however, he asked me if I was up for breakfast before we went to sleep for the day, or at least the rest of the morning.

Why not, I said, and started to lead him into the dining room that was now opening for the day.

Instead he suggested we return to *The Diner*.

Since this made no sense given the all-night party that must have continued after we'd left, I asked him to reconsider.

He told me that our hostess would indeed be there and quite prepared to serve us the house finest.

I reminded him that probably meant filet of bat's wings, sirloin of catfish fins, and scrambled watermelon seeds. He didn't think that was very funny and proceeded to lead me there anyway, walking and not talking.

When we arrived, I was surprised to find *The Diner* sign still in place and the open sign right where it had always been.

And up the steps we went and into the dark interior, which, at this time of the day was completely empty except for the blonde manager-owner-whatever, busy in the kitchen as if she knew we'd arrive at that precise time.

I asked Tollison how he'd known this.

He said they'd been friends for a very long time, and had gotten to know one another's work patterns.

So we took our seats as she entered the dining room with both her arms covered in steaming full dishes and her hands glued around three glasses, not two.

I immediately assumed she'd be joining us. And she did. And at my table, not his across the room. We all had basically the same three plates full of God knew what.

One looked like the aforementioned filet of bat wings. The second was cutlets of some kind of meat I wasn't sure I wanted to know what. And the last was eggs of something still in their half shells waiting for us, I presumed, to decide how to eat them.

I looked at her for instructions, but she gave no hint of either telling me what I wanted to know, or once again using her forefinger to punish me for asking.

And so we ate together. Without a word said. Just our sloppy personal habits of using our silverware how we'd each been taught in our youth.

It was, of course, delicious. How she did it I had no idea. I was once again sure that were she to open another diner in the middle of nowhere and served nothing except road kill, it would be famous within a week.

When we finished, I felt elated, probably from having some food after missing dinner the previous night. Almost giddy, as a matter of fact.

So I asked my usual question about what we'd eaten. Tollison waved her off and told me it had been several dozen butterfly wings, fried caterpillars, and the special for the day, brazed catfish balls. I didn't ask about the last one for fear he'd tell me. And to drink, we'd had nectar of carnations dipped in beer batter.

I watched as the amazed blonde nodded her approval of Tollison's guesses. I was too tired to give a damn, though not too tired to ask a few more questions of our hostess, for from indications given the previous night, this might very well be the final time I saw her.

I began by expressing my sorrow that The Diner was closing and how many years had it been. She immediately looked at Tollison and warned him with her forefinger as she had done me several times in the past.

It turns out, as she told it, that the closing had been only for the name of the place, not for the place itself. Tomorrow *The Diner* would become *The Vestige*. She'd remain the manager and owner—so I had been right all along—with the treats to be equally as bizarre as they'd ever been.

Many people, she told me, had been led to believe that her restaurant was the actual diner of the two in town, and the one by the Interstate had eventually taken umbrage at her duplicate name and threatened a lawsuit.

She didn't believe the restaurant had a chance, but couldn't see her way to fighting a battle with a large chain. This had, she added, happened several times in the past due to the extraordinary nature of her foods.

While she told me this, I watched Tollison who stared at the ceiling in self-defense.

I wasn't near through asking her questions, so continued on the same line with how she could stay in business when she had so few customers. Two was as many as I'd counted except for the previous night.

She told me that business picked up around nine in the evenings, and then went until maybe three in the morning when the place was full. So, while Tollison was telling his story to me, in two installments yet, *The Diner* had been the hottest place in town.

I then popped my first serious question. What was her name? And to that she had no answer. She shut up like Tollison had the habit of doing.

Of course, I knew she spoke Navajo as well as him. Maybe she was one of the white ones that had been born on the reservation before it had become a nation, and for some reason had turned away and moved to Holbrook.

Pick your own name for me, she said. Any name would do, as long as I kept it consistent. She'd hear it and recognize it was me. And that would do.

I asked her if that's what she did with all her customers and she nodded yes. All except Tollison, however, for he was special.

And what was his name for her, I asked, but she waggled that finger of hers at me and told me that it wouldn't be special if she gave it away.

I looked at him. After all, he'd told me about how he actually didn't know her name. Then, I nodded. I knew he'd told me the truth. He didn't know her name, only the name he'd given her. And I had no right to know that.

So, without giving it much thought, I looked at her and said, 'Mary.'

At first she was uncertain whether that was a guess on my part as to her real name, or the name I'd chosen to give her.

So I repeated it. She got it then, and said the name over several times under her breath. She nodded, and told me it was a perfect name. That no one had ever given her that name before, and why had I chosen it. Since I had no idea, I told her it was the name of Jesus's mother, the one who'd given a virgin birth.

That made her laugh out loud. Apparently, none of that equated with any version of herself she held.

Then she once again rolled the name over by repeating it softly, and telling me it was perfect. She would accept.

I abruptly asked her if she'd been a hippie in the sixties. I fully expected her to stare at me again and shake her head, but she didn't. Instead, she grinned and said Berkeley. I had expected her to say Woodstock since that was closer to where I lived, though Berkeley was just as good.

Then she told me of the LSD. And I, stupidly, corrected her. It was LDS. Church of the Latter Day Saints. The Mormons. But too many hours spent with Tollison. She'd meant lysergic acid diethylamide, or acid, or lysergide, or INN, or LSD, Timothy Leary's drug of choice.

She then reminded me that the average human brain has about hundred billion nerve cells, and that the average human head weighs about eight pounds.

And that, of course, led me to my final question before hitting the sack.

Why had she chosen me, of all people, as the recipient of Tollison's story? To hear the tragedy of his life?

And that caught her short.

She'd had to have known he'd tell me of her approval and that I would have to ask, yet she looked shocked that I would do such a thing.

She then stared down into her lap and waited. I didn't help her by filling the air with empty words. No way was I going to let this opportunity pass without an answer. I had to know what she'd seen that made her choose me, of all the people she'd met since she'd first encountered Tollison, for him to tell his extraordinary story to.

When she raised her head up, she had a far-away look in her eyes. Not a sad or happy look, one that told me she'd had to search the recesses of her mind to find an answer. Maybe I was beginning to learn something about the Navajo Way. From two white people no less.

Then she told me that I'd passed her first test. That I'd eaten her 'out there' food as she called it without any questions. And before she'd told me what it was.

Trust, she called it. A simple sense of trust.

Her second reason was that once told, I didn't immediately leave and attempt to vomit. Therefore, she could not only trust me, but knew that I had t'áadoo yináidzid, or no fear. I was fearless.

Finally, she said I was neh-hecho-da-ne, friendly. A trustworthy, fearless friend that could be counted on. That, she said, she'd seen in my eyes.

I'd never looked at myself in that way before. And, like the name Mary had been for her, I bowed my head and stared down toward my lap, thinking it over. While I was not someone to be easily fooled, it seemed that she was telling the truth as she saw it. And, if I was right, all good reason to believe that I deserved to hear Tollison's story.

When I looked up at her and again him, they were both smiling.

I decided to change that quickly, and asked her what difference did it make that I was all those things? I would be leaving shortly to continue my way west. To the Grand Canyon and on toward the great Sierras of California. I was a vagabond and, while hearing Tollison's story had been a once in a lifetime event for me, I would soon forget it and life would go on as it had for millennia with no more notice of Tollison's life than there'd been before these past two days.

In other words, so what.

That's when her face lit up with a brilliant smile, and I knew she was about to spring something on me.

I was a surprisingly willing victim.

A trustworthy and fearless man of my word and once informed of her intentions and maybe his, I could not refuse whatever it was she or they both wanted me to do.

Without hesitation, she said it. The purpose of my visit to Holbrook, Arizona, and *The Diner* according to Mary.

Tollison wanted me to write his story for all to read. He'd lived with his pain for so long he could no longer bear it. The time had come for others, not just me, to learn of it. To have it printed in a book and therefore become truth for the world to witness.

I was, of course, completely dumbstruck by what he said. Nothing could have been further from my mind at the moment.

So I reminded them both that I was not a writer. Maybe I'd penned a few articles in graduate school, but those had been scientific journal pieces, simply academic jargon-filled repositories for how certain experiments had proven successful. Not stories like they expected. There were far better historian-authors that could do a better job of writing Tollison's story than I.

They didn't deny that. It would be my first attempt, and in being so would be an honest, brave, and reliable accounting. And that's all they wanted. I was perfect for the job.

I countered with my naiveté, my inexperience, my simple writing style, all those things that would make readers disbelieve what they read.

They, of course, countered with those factors being the very reasons they'd chosen me. I knew I'd been cleverly trapped. The two of them against the one of me.

And then they hit me with the *coups de gras*.

Tollison couldn't write it. After all, he'd been right-handed before it had been chopped off, so with only his left remaining, he could no longer write it out with a pen or type it on a computer keyboard.

And Mary couldn't do it, for she had a restaurant to run. She had to gather what the desert provided and turn it into the wondrous meals that kept her in business. And, she added, keep Tollison alive, for he couldn't work.

All this served on a poor unsuspecting traveler on his way from Long Island to San Francisco was too much to take. I was had and they and I knew it.

Then Mary asked me whether or not I believed Tollison's story. I told her that I did. With the possible exception of his rendition of the skinwalker. I believed that he believed he'd seen it, and that he also believed it had chased him from his home and back to the waiting arms of Atsidi's mother. It had sounded real enough. But I didn't buy it because I was a rational man raised in a world of science, not of superstition.

I think she liked my answer because it was honest and she understood my reluctance to believe in such things.

She told me then, as if I'd already agreed to write the book, that I could handle that in whatever way I felt best. In fact, none of my readers would likely believe in the skinwalker either, so my own disbelief might actually help them through that part without raising suspicions that the rest of the story might be false.

And with that, the door closed and was locked behind me.

I was trapped and shackled. In a short time I'd gone from world traveler to author without ever having to get a degree or work my way up the ladder from reporter to columnist, to short-story writer, to biographer. I'd made the trip in less than ten minutes.

With that unsaid promise made, Mary announced that we should drink to it, and she returned to the kitchen, grabbed three full glasses of something red and pre-made giving me the distinct impression of her knowing I'd accept their offer, and brought them out to us for a toast.

And we clinked our glasses and drank the liquid to the bottom.

It was, of course, delicious.

I shook my head at her then. I didn't really want to know what I'd consumed. The milk of rose petals, the nectar of wild flies, or the drippings from poisonous oleander bushes. It was none of my damn business. I'd survive or not survive. I'd been christened an author of a great story, and it was time to celebrate and not worry about my impending death, should it come to pass.

I then suggested, at around eight in the morning, that I needed to sleep. We could speak more of this later in the day when I'd had some rest.

And we agreed to meet once again at *The Diner*, or whatever it was now called, around one for lunch and discuss what we'd meant by our agreement.

Before I got to my feet though, she asked me if I knew that "I" was the most spoken word in the English language.

I told her I did, and that "You" was the second most spoken word in the English language. An interesting duality, and a revelation on the human condition, I thought.

We split up then, I back to my motel room, and the two of them remaining in *The Diner* to clean up, I presumed. And, guessing that was where Tollison slept, I imagined they might take some time off from their duties as well for both of them to sleep.

23

As I walked past my back window toward the front of the motel, I could have sworn I saw a shadow pass in front of my bed. Between it and the glass. I stopped and watched, but once again saw nothing. Possibly a maid a work, tidying up my room, thinking that I'd already slept and was now out eating my breakfast. My reverse days and nights had no meaning for those with real jobs. And, when I opened the door to my room, it was empty.

Where was that shadow? Like the ones I'd seen in the ancient dwellings and ruins. Moving past windows in the dark interiors, ephemeral as well.

Neither here nor there. Neither now nor ever. Always getting lost in the darkness which it apparently sought as natural as day the night.

Then I saw an owl in the early morning's light out through that same window. But from inside out. A great horned owl, aiming its hooked beak at something nesting in a creosote bush nearby.

After a pause, I heard a sudden deadly rustle of branches followed by a flutter of wings, and the owl took off again, a mouse now wrestling helplessly in its claws. Nature's way of trimming overpopulation through pain and death, its beauty so deeply flawed I could never forgive it. Not that it gave a damn whether I did or not.

I lay down on the bed and slept soundly. No dreams. Of skin-walkers, great Noah-type floods, or anything else that would remind me of Tollison's strange life. I was too tired for that. Too exhausted from surprises.

When I woke, the clock told me I'd slept longer than I'd planned. It was nearly two in the afternoon. Since I hadn't undressed and knew breakfast, lunch, or dinner awaited me at *The Diner*, I immediately headed there to see what culinary concoctions Mary had created for us today.

I felt great as the sun lit me, and the blue sky seemed to lift me up in all its glory. Not a cloud in the sky, or a slight breeze in the air.

A glorious day. As I walked, I remembered back to that innocent day when I'd decided to stay in Holbrook, most of which I now reminded myself, I'd still not seen.

So much had happened in so short a time. I'd met at least two strange characters, experienced storms of horrific dimension, heard a story that I'd never forget no matter what I'd told Mary and Tollison, and changed my career from wanderer to author. All in a few days.

When I arrived, the sign was there and the perpetually 'Open' card rested below it. I looked the building over carefully. The dark wood had gone mostly to splinters with, I imagined, a small termite hole here and there. What I might have one day called a dump was a special place among special places. And, as I stepped up the steps, I wondered what I would find inside.

An empty room? Mary and Tollison waiting for me? A crowd of infinite dimensions? All the chairs, tables, and booths gone with no sign that anyone had ever occupied the place at all? So many possibilities. And with things going as they had, none of them were all that remote.

So, of course, I was surprised again. For what I found was Mary in the kitchen busy cooking, and a man in a fedora sitting across from where I usually sat, eating a bowl of green algae with a tablespoon, mechanically bringing that spoon to his mouth, sipping, and then returning it slowly for more. He had finally gotten his algae again. And it pleasured me to see him eating it so eagerly.

I took the seat opposite him, kept my peace, and watched him eat while Mary cooked without saying a word.

The Navajo quiet had caught on. Saying nothing sometimes says the most. It meant that not only was there nothing to say, but that not saying it was the most important thing one could do. And with that bit of idiocy, I closed my eyes and took a brief nap.

When I woke a second time that day, Tollison had finished his meal and Mary had brought us a fine lunch as his next course and my first.

I thought I recognized what some of the plates and bowls contained, though didn't want to bother Mary with my guesses. So I began eating. Not a word said. No hellos, no how's things going, no nothing. No need to say these things. Not among friends.

And I ate, having not realized how hungry I'd gotten. The food, of course, provided flavors and joy I couldn't have imagined possible. I was sure at one point that some of it must contain a natural narcotic for I zoned out. I didn't actually fall asleep, but felt like I was looking at myself from the outside in. From above the table at the three of us eating there. Still enjoying my meal though somehow aloof from it as well.

When I finished eating and my two selves had rejoined, I sat back and relaxed. I was full, not stuffed.

And I wondered how I would ever get along in life with the knowledge that I'd never have a meal like this again. And, with that, I vowed that no matter what happened from here on out, I'd find the time to return to Holbrook every so often to once again sample the food of whatever this place would then be called.

When I looked up, I found Mary and Tollison staring at me in a quizzical way.

Had I said something in my slightly drugged state to confuse them?

If I had, I decided to make it right. I looked at Mary and told her that it took more calories to eat a piece of celery than the celery has in it to begin with.

She blinked. Didn't smile. I must have said something before that that hadn't made her happy.

Tollison then interrupted my soliloquy with the comment that we had one more task to accomplish before I could leave town and begin my work on his or my or our book.

As I'd learned to do during my visit, I looked at him, waiting for him to ask his question or make his statement, and let the silence between us become the words I would have a few days before said.

Tollison then looked at Mary and she him.

Apparently they had a secret language of looks that I didn't and probably couldn't understand.

At that point, Tollison told me that we—him and me and not Mary—had to visit Many Farms and Chinle that afternoon, for there were still many questions that needed answering before I could begin writing.

For example, where had the body of Haseya gone?

Had they found her? If so, where had they put her? In a cave? A grave? What?

He had to know these things and so did the readers of the book I would write.

I asked him how long had it been since that day when she'd drowned, and he took his time actually counting on his fingers.

He then told me it had been sixty years since he'd last seen her.

I reminded him of the poor record keeping that many desert communities maintained. That we were most unlikely to find anything about her in the records. Computers had been only recently invented. And on, and on.

He maintained that he had to know. Maybe she hadn't drowned. Maybe she'd somehow managed to make it to Chinle and found her way back to her mother and father. This had never occurred to me and, though I couldn't imagine such a thing, it was possible after all. Anything was possible given the story he'd told me.

There were other things that needed to be done as well. Loose ends, he called them, but wouldn't elaborate further.

And, almost as if ordering me to do so, he told me that we would take my car, that I knew the way since I'd told him of my trip there my very first day in town, and that it wouldn't take long.

I watched Mary as she listened to Tollison speak. She was somehow at peace with his decision. After all, finding Haseya alive might drive Tollison nuts and she might never see him again. They'd been friends for so long it hardly seemed fair that on such short notice he would drive away with a stranger never to return. And, as I watched her watch him, it was clear that no such thoughts had entered her mind. That all she wanted for him was to chase away the ghosts that still haunted his memory. Come what may.

And so, without further words spoken, Tollison and I stood and walked out the door and into the bright sunny afternoon toward my car in the parking lot of the motel.

As we walked, I yelled back in Mary's direction saying something to the effect that Winston Churchill was born in a ladies room during a dance.

I hoped she hadn't heard me.

Not a cloud in the sky. Not even a slight breeze in the air. A perfect day for traveling. Though the heat was uncomfortable, it wouldn't bother us. We were on the final leg of a grand journey.

Or at least he was. I was along for the ride.

We joined the Interstate traffic and headed east, and I asked him what he really expected to find.

He told me that he had no idea. Sixty years is a long time. People are born and often die in that time. If she were alive, she'd be in her mid-seventies as was he. At best, it would mean that he hadn't let her die after all. And that would make him happy.

He then surprised me by saying that if she were alive he would not want to see her. No way could he withstand that shock. Not only because of her age, but of the emotions that it would arouse in him. Of the love. And the hate. He couldn't take that.

And then we drove in silence to the turnoff north toward Ganado, the turn toward the three mesas, and the turn north that would bring us to Canyon de Chelly and not far beyond that to the Chapter House in Many Farms where the records of the village were kept.

I stopped for gas in Ganado. Noted that the wonderful sky had not changed and most likely wouldn't this time of day—by then three in the afternoon—and bought a local area map to ensure we wouldn't get lost looking for the Chapter House and any other building or location we might wish to visit.

Once back in the car, my meandering thoughts got me to ask Tollison to elaborate on any other spots he might want to visit.

He told me that depended on what I discovered at the Chapter House. I realized, therefore, that I'd be the one doing the searching, not him. That even with his gray beard and the time that had passed since he'd been there, he couldn't risk being seen.

I could certainly understand that, so didn't put up the fight I might have had I not heard what I now called 'The Story,' so much larger than life the tale had become to me by then.

And I could feel for him, and feel his reluctance to meet a lost friend or a relative of Haseya that might still be around. While these things didn't appear likely to me, who was I to question his motives?

On the outskirts of Ganado, I noticed something interesting. A Church of Jesus Christ of the Latter Day Saints, a Mormon temple, standing off the road to my left. Apparently the Mormon's drive to educate the heathen had not stopped up north with the people in Many Farms. Would I find other such places scattered across the region?

With the windows in the Plymouth down to keep the wind blowing and us at least a little cooler than the outside heat, it was too noisy to do much of anything except yell, and neither of us wanted to do that. So we fell into silence again. And through Chinle we drove and on the final few miles into Many Farms.

Once there, I consulted the map I'd purchased that had separate sub-maps for the various towns in the area, and found the Many Farms Chapter House.

With no idea whether chapter houses were open most of the time or closed except for special occasions, we drove there straight off.

As we did so, I noticed Tollison slowly sliding below the window, peeking out occasionally, but otherwise keeping low. He'd removed his hat to stop the wind from blowing it off, and I found it remarkable, now that I thought about it, how it had maintained over the years. It still looked fairly new. The only things giving it away were the slight streaks here and there, similar to the ones on Tollison's face, and the fading leather from the sun. I also noticed Tollison's thinning hair, growing toward baldness. None of this, of course, had anything much to do with our journey, but it kept me awake while I drove the highway I'd already driven twice during my stay. Once each direction.

I found the Many Farms Chapter House without much trouble and it was open. No return visits or extensive waiting in Many Farms necessary.

So I asked Tollison what he wanted me to ask.

He told me he only needed the records of Haseya from the years during which he'd known her. And maybe for any other mention of her in their records. He also told me he couldn't remember her second name if, in fact, he'd ever known it in the first place.

So I took what little information I had with me into the building and waited my turn behind a large man with folds of fat around his middle, and an elderly woman who I thought might disappear in front of my eyes she was so slight. Both Navajo, and both quite shy of the well-built man at the desk. A young good-looking Indian with a long black ponytail down his backsides.

Their requests were brief, and I soon found myself facing the ponytailed man who'd so far spoken only in Navajo.

I had no choice but to speak in English and wasted no time in telling him what or rather whom I was interested in. And, from his immediate reaction, all I'd needed was a first name.

He told me, without looking anything up, that Haseya had become a legend around these parts. That she'd been involved in some kind of multiple murder many tens of years ago, and then had disappeared and never heard from again.

Maybe she'd run away.

Maybe she'd been killed in the brutal rainstorm that had occurred around the last time she'd been seen.

Maybe something else entirely.

Though as far as he knew, that was it. He asked me if I wanted to have him check to see if anything had come up recently he hadn't heard about.

I told him I thought it might be a good idea.

Apparently, the file was small because he returned in less than a minute with nothing to add to his story.

I asked whether there was any other place I might find further information on her in town.

He told me that her parents had long since passed, as had the rest of the clan alive at that time. He guessed the relatives he knew knew nothing more than he did.

So I thanked him and returned to the car.

Tollison was, of course, eager to discover what I'd learned, and disconsolate to find I'd learned so little. Of course, the notion that Haseya's body had not been found fed his notion that somehow she'd survived.

Now he had to know, and Chinle was the place for that.

Before we drove there, however, he wanted to have a look at the house where he'd grown up.

I couldn't imagine how seeing that again could possibly help matters. Even I was reluctant to see the place where he'd run away from home, returned to find his parent's slaughtered, and then had his right hand cut off and later seen the skinwalker. But we were here, and that was that.

He explained where the house was and I drove there following the map I'd purchased in Ganado. Like the chapter house, it too resided on the main highway south of where we'd parked.

As I drove by, I discovered that the map we'd used was out of date. All we found was a platform of cement, vacant of house and any other sign that one had once been there.

Tollison sat up and looked out his open window. I thought I heard a sniff from his direction, but couldn't be sure given his head was turned away from me.

So I asked him if this was the place. He nodded his head and told me to continue on to Chinle. That the answer had to be there.

I continued south and toward what the map told me was the Chinle Comprehensive Health Care Facility off 191 to the west a little less than a mile.

And we promptly got lost. Chinle was a modern American town. A Burger King, Best Western and Holiday Inn motels, Catholic and Baptist churches, and a Farmer's Insurance building.

I'd missed these on my first visit to get gas here.

All the comforts of home.

And that Americans on average eat eighteen acres of pizza each and every day.

We also found the Rough Rock Chapter House next to the Veterinary Clinic and the Nation's Fleet Management offices, which I assumed meant tending to the open-air vehicles that rode the floor of Canyon de Chelly for visitors to see the great ruins.

When by four in the afternoon we discovered the hospital, or what passed for one, I got out and repeated roughly what I'd asked in Many Farms. Any word on Haseya over the many decades that had passed since her disappearance.

They checked their records and told me that what I'd described sounded like the great flood some sixty years ago, that they had searched long and hard at that time for missing persons and survivors, but had found no one.

The person who told me this was a young white woman of maybe twenty years age whose great grandmother, now living in Pennsylvania somewhere most likely, might have had a better chance of giving me the information I wanted than her.

When I returned to the Plymouth, Tollison was now sitting up, apparently unconcerned that anyone here might recognize him.

I told him what they'd told me, and off we went to the local chapter house to make sure we'd left no stone unturned.

And the same story there. No records of any bodies recovered during that time, and no one ever registered with them by the name of Haseya.

When I told him this, he looked more than apprehensive. He looked downright disturbed. As if the thought of Haseya still being alive somewhere was too much to handle.

While on one level I could understand his sentiments. However, I also felt that time could heal at least most wounds. Certainly if she had somehow survived the disaster, she'd be a different person now than she'd been then. Of course, I didn't believe she was alive at all. She'd been carried out with the wild current and deposited, dead from drowning, somewhere far from the site and no doubt deep in the sand where she still lay. Though I didn't tell Tollison that.

And it was then that he sprang his true reason for our trip. He wanted to show me the canyon. At least the del Muerto branch. Just as he'd shown it to her.

I told him how many horses in the team it would take for me to accept that invitation. While the sky was empty of clouds and the sun still high enough to make such a trip possible, there was no way, particularly after what he'd told me last night—my God was it only last night?—that I would go into the 'canyon of death.'

Not now. Not tomorrow. Not ever. He smiled at me then. In that calm and patient way he had.

And there we sat, a standoff in the parking lot of the Rough Rock Chapter House in Chinle, Arizona. Like two cowboys readying for a gun-fight. For someone to draw first.

And then he pointed toward the east. At first, I didn't get what he meant. Then I saw it. The National Monument Visitor Center.

We were less than a mile from the entrance to Canyon de Chelly.

Still at least four hours from dusk and an easy walk of twenty or so minutes from Newspaper Rock, Sleeping Duck Ruin, and all the other amazing sights of the north canyon I'd not yet seen.

And I remembered my previous visit to the canyon, only a day or two previous, to the south branch down to White House Ruin, and that with the raging dust storm following me I'd made it safely back to Holbrook.

So I heaved a big sigh, nodded my head, and within a minute found myself locking the Plymouth doors and readying myself for a simple hike on the sand. A hike that he'd already taught me a lot about as he described his visit here some six decades ago with Haseya.

The slow sand and the high walls of the canyon scarred with patina from the scorched rainfall on them.

The Anasazi Ruins positioned up those walls in places where no one could scale without climbing gear today. And we walked. Across the Chinle Wash into which Tsaile Creek joined, and down the throat of the canyon entrance, both without paying our fees which Tollison guaranteed no punishment would come if we were caught.

I reminded him that this was a National Monument not a Navajo bastion, but it didn't matter. He knew his Navajo skills would bail us out. And besides, no one came into the 'del Muerto Canyon' except fools.

I needn't have reminded him of what that made us, because he wouldn't have cared.

We took off our shoes and wandered barefoot in the shallow waters of the wash. I tried to worry him about the slow sand, but he paid me and it no attention.

And we made good time.

We passed Newspaper Rock and stopped for a moment to take a look. It was indeed a sight to behold.

Before long we hit the separation between the lower de Chelly branch with the spire and the White House Ruins, and the upper del Muerto branch with the Ute Raid Panel, the Antelope House, and the distant Mummy Cave. Here the water got slightly deeper and Tollison told me we'd need our shoes again, and to stay out of Tsaile Creek.

He sounded like he'd been here a week ago, so familiar the surroundings and authoritative his voice.

And I followed him, thinking as I did that it had only been a short time since we'd left the car and that no matter what kind of storm we encountered, we could make it back safely. The sky above, though now only a corridor of blue rather than a distant horizon, showed no clouds. Dust or otherwise.

We were safe. At least for the moment.

And it was at this time that I damned myself for being suckered into the canyon. Given my previous experience with that storm out to get me, how could I have been so stupid to let Tollison talk me into coming with him? I should have tied him to the car door and took off directly back to Holbrook. But, like a tiny ball and a mallet tethered by a rubber band on one of those solitaire Ping-Pong games, here I was, hiking into hell with a novice devil leading me there.

As we plowed forward, the sun behind us slowly inched toward the west, or at least it seemed that way to me. I must have looked skyward at least once a minute, yet nothing appeared up there. Not a single cloud in any direction. Maybe my concerns were undeserved.

Occasionally something would bother Tollison and he'd go off trail, if you could call it that, and look over a rock or a bush that appeared interesting or strange to him. I imagined him scavenging for her body then, but I had no real inkling of what he was up to. And, by that point, he'd charged so far ahead of me that he couldn't have heard me if I'd yelled.

The trail we followed was slight at best. Faint hoof marks here and there and a subtle sense of footprints blotting them out in spots. Occasionally a bush was bent in unnatural ways indicating something large had passed. Mostly, the path meandered, then disappeared entirely, and then returned. Until, that is, it disappeared completely, no doubt toward some hidden exit up a culvert in the canyon walls. The alluvial fans of sediment at the bottom of these culverts gave the impression of having weathered great floods in the past. Not a comforting sight.

As we passed Antelope Ruin, the last of the spots I remembered him telling me about before he'd met his disastrous fate with the rains, I wanted to tell him to stop. We'd come to a halfway point in our journey and now was the time to turn back.

Before I could form the words, however, he moved out of sight.

Not good.

I needed my guide, no matter his age or his previous experiences in the canyon.

So I hurried after him as fast as I could. Only once did I glance at the ruins as I passed them. And once, and this I could not believe, I saw a shadow pass by one of the open windows up a cliff in one of the rooms of those ruins. Well beyond any way anyone could have climbed up or down from below or above. It simply wasn't possible.

And, for some reason, as with the other sightings I'd made of moving shadows, this one gave me chills. Maybe it was simply shadows crawling swiftly across the canyon from the sinking sun and the increasing sense of danger from my losing sight of Tollison.

So I ran. No way did I want to be in this canyon alone. Not now. Not ever. This wasn't my battle. This may be his. But not mine. I took no sides in this war. I was an innocent bystander.

Somehow, though, I got the feeling I was actually a part of the story itself. That it wasn't finished. That we were here to do that. Once and for all. Finish the damn thing. And I wanted no part of it.

Suddenly a swarm of dragonflies flew off the shallow water of the creek and headed in my direction. Having heard they'd been clocked at over sixty miles an hour, I hit the deck as quickly as I could. My love of trivial facts may frustrate some, but for me I couldn't count the times this kind of knowledge had saved my life. Or, at the least, appeared to have saved my life.

Of course I was then confused as to whether damselflies, less quick than dragonflies, could kill a man as well. Maybe they tortured them into giving up by using their fabulous colors and fluorescent ways.

When they'd finally gone, I got up on my knees and looked for Tollison again.

And, if I hadn't been worried before this, the sight of a small innocent single cloud moving quickly across the sky nearly made be faint.

I'm not a courageous man.

Nor one that liked to face unseen odds and unknown perils. I'd traveled the length and breadth of the world and seen almost every kind of marvel it had to offer. And yet here I was, in my own backyard so to speak, and for the first time feeling that fear of having no control. That evil or good or some combination of both would overtake me and determine my destiny.

That I had little choice in the matter.

I finally saw Tollison up ahead waving for me to catch up. Had he found something? The body of Haseya? Or the place where he'd lost her to the current in the raging water?

I didn't care at that moment. I was simply glad to see him. Actually to see anyone beside the shadow following me, and the possibility that where one cloud had formed, many others could easily grow.

I ran as fast as I could, not at all looking where I was on the floor of the canyon. Forgetting that Tsaile Creek was famous for its slow sand. For it was then, when I'd reached the fastest speed I could go, that I tripped and fell face first into the placid waters of Tsaile and got myself completely soaked.

The pool of water couldn't have been more than a couple of inches deep.

The sand below that water, however, was as much water as it was sand, and I could feel it grab me with a thousand tiny fingers, and with the help of gravity and my weight pull me into its belly.

I struggled to pull myself out of its grasp. The harder I struggled, though, the worse it got.

Every push with my hands and arms against the sand, the deeper they drove into it and the harder it was for me to maneuver them out. At the same time, I couldn't remain there. For even doing nothing, I was sinking. Slowly, yes, but sinking none the less. And bodies lying down are not bodies standing up. Standing, I was six feet tall and it would have taken many hours for me to sink my full height. Lying down as I was now, I was maybe eight inches and half of that already under water. My stupidity had put me in the worse position possible.

I quickly looked around for something to save me. A limb of a tree to grasp. A rock. Anything to find purchase and stop the inevitable.

Unfortunately, the creek had washed the canyon floor clean of such things. It was as flat as one could imagine right up to the walls on either side of me, maybe twenty feet in both directions. And of no help whatsoever.

I tried to splash my feet free of the sand's grasp. Then my arms. Finally my head, now lying sideways to keep as much of my mouth out of the water as possible.

No go.

I gave myself two minutes at most. And then I heard the calm voice of Tollison nearby.

He patiently told me to stop moving. I did.

Then he said to pull my right hand out of the water. I gurgled that I couldn't. Yes, he said, I could. That I was trying everything at once. Just do this, he said. And I did. And surprisingly my right hand came free.

Then he told me to grab something that I could now feel scratching the back of that hand. And I did. As tightly as I could.

And then something magical happened, like those days so long ago when my father had taken me to Coney Island in Brooklyn when I was a kid.

I moved. Endwise. Feet first. It didn't seem possible.

I wanted to ask him how, though couldn't raise enough of my head and thus my mouth out of the water to make a sound no less ask questions. And, before I knew it, I was lying on dry sand. The only water around being that which was then draining off my body.

I looked back and into his smiling face. He'd done it. He'd saved my life. But how? And I asked him that.

He told me it was easy. I was pushing up and down, both things that slow sand knew all about and could react to. He, on the other hand, had slid me across the slick sand and water. Something the sand and water knew nothing about. The action fooled the creek and I was safe.

In that instant, I became aware of something more than strange. The man that stood before me was not only a white man who'd happened to be born in the world of the Navajo, but an actual Navajo. White skin or not, Mormon parents or not, he was an Indian. And no one, not even Navajos could take that away from him. I could see it in his eyes. I could hear it in his voice. I could feel it in my bones. I wasn't an expert to know it. But it didn't take an expert. He'd somehow crossed the line.

And with that realization, and the fact that he'd saved my life, thunder came rolling down the canyon so loud that the wind it caused blew bushes near me over enough for the ends of the branches to touch the sand. And the trees near the walls of the canyon bent sideways.

I looked up into the once blue sky and saw that it had turned so dark that the lightning that then split it down the middle was as a knife slicing through one of Mary's algae soups.

The words frying pan into the fire came to me at that moment.

And apparently to Tollison as well, as we both looked at Tsaile Creek where I'd just been saved, and saw the water literally rising under the rain that was undoubtedly pouring into the canyon many miles to the east.

I climbed to my feet using Tollison's legs as support and we both turned and headed for the nearest wall with fallen rocks at its base to climb.

The immediate resonance with the story of him and Haseya doing the same thing so many decades ago was not lost on me. But God had apparently seen to it that whatever thoughts I might have were not important any longer.

Survival was the name of this particular game.

I followed Tollison as closely as I could as we climbed the rocks toward the base of the mighty wall. After all, he'd survived such a flood in the past, I hadn't. He'd know what to do. And so up we went. And none to soon, as the waters below climbed as fast as us if not faster.

There was, of course, only so far we could go. The rocks had fallen from the rim and at a certain point the canyon itself took over and prevented any further possibility of climbing.

I didn't like the thought of attempting to go higher or of falling into the now churning waters below. There would be a certain point, however, if the storm continued to rage, that we'd have no choice. The canyon would get its way.

My hands gripped the rocks with a frenzy I didn't know I had. And up we went. Further, faster, and with the water licking at our heels. Quick glances at the sky proved fruitless. The rain had begun in earnest and filled my eyes with pain when I did.

The reflections of lightning slashed across the rocks and the thunders, too many to count, followed as if in unison with the light.

A torrential rain. An impossible situation. And all this too much to take.

I suddenly found myself out of body, looking down at our painful attempts to escape, and feeling giddy at the joy of living to the fullest. Of experiencing all that life held. Of not caring if the experience itself would end that life.

And that's when we came to the end of the line. A large rock perilously teetering on a pile of lesser rocks below it. Maybe six by six feet, it allowed a view of the quickly filling canyon that no one living would believe. Thousands of tons of water passing us by in a second. A terrifying sight. And it continued to rise, now only inches below our feet.

Then, between claps of thunder and jets of light, I heard voices calling to one another.

I immediately knew I was dying. Sudden hallucinations before the final instant.

I was wrong. I turned, and there standing before me were two beings, not one.

Tollison, of course. And in front of him, almost lying back against the cliff, was the ugliest creature I could ever imagine existing. It had the snout of some kind of bear, and the coat of some other animal, but the eyes of a human.

I screamed. But no one heard me, the storm too loud. Was this the damned skinwalker? We'd come this far on our quest for safety from the storm only to find a skinwalker?

What the hell was I thinking? A skinwalker? It couldn't be. Of course I didn't believe it. Skinwalkers don't *really* exist. Or if they did, they existed only for Navajos, not for white men like me.

Except there it was. And staring malevolently at Tollison. Readying its teeth to sink them into his neck or his body or his legs or maybe his one good hand.

It was then that I knew I'd joined with Tollison again. I was seeing what he was seeing. That his mind had worked its magic on me.

Of *course* I was hallucinating. Who wouldn't under the circumstances?

But the skinwalker seemed real. And deeply menacing. And immediately dangerous. More dangerous than the waters behind us.

Suddenly the world froze. The rain ceased falling on me. The sounds stopped sounding. The skinwalker didn't move. And Tollison stood there like a statue.

I expected the heavens to open, the sun to shine through a sudden opening, and God to speak to me.

But it didn't happen.

What did happen was an insight into the universe that shrunk my understanding of human culture, of what was happening to me now, the entire universe, into something far less than the size of a pinhead.

A moment of epiphany. For there, staring directly at me, was my father. I looked into his kind eyes and knew it could be no one else.

I almost collapsed from surprise at seeing him. And, of course, I cried.

I knew he was dead. But that smile. His. And now he held out his hand toward me—the same one he'd used when he'd walked me to the carnival on Coney Island that first time.

Too much to take. Overcoming my disbelief. What was going on?

But I reached out my hand to his just as I saw a crack in the façade. Something in the way he squinted slightly. Or maybe the way he held himself. And the spell disappeared.

I blinked. Probably shouldn't have, for when my eyes opened again, it was not my father but my mother I saw. Crying. As she had that afternoon at my father's memorial.

How could this be? Was I making these things happen? But why would I? There was no way I wanted to relive seeing them again. Especially on this terrace of death.

And I blinked again and Chloe, the woman who'd left me for better and richer digs, appeared. She opened her eyes wide and then squeezed them shut abruptly. Irrationally.

What the hell was she doing here? How could she possibly have found me in this canyon? I blinked again. Yet when I opened my eyes, Chloe was gone. In her place? Paulette.

I was clearly hallucinating these things, though I didn't really feel so. She reached out for me with those arms of hers. As if to couple in the way we had in the past. And she stepped toward me.

I looked into her eyes, and it wasn't Paulette. Or at least not the Paulette I'd known. There was malevolence there. A kind of perfect hate. Paulette had not been a lover, she'd been a lustful partner in crime, if what we'd done was a crime. Twice over. But it wasn't. That was the Catholic in me.

So I stepped back. And nearly slipped into the still rising waters behind me.

It's what she'd wanted. I could not only see that in her eyes, I could see it in the way her fingers and hands reached out toward me. More to push than to hold me or pull me toward her.

This was insane. Not a dream. Not a nightmare. Not my imagination. This was *magic*. The most intrinsically evil magic I could ever imagine.

So I looked for wires. All the tiny possible hints of how someone could make this happen.

Then I looked over at Tollison. At his now inseparable skinwalker. She or he having enveloped him in a hug.

I yelled for him to stand back. That this was not real. Though it was clearly still very dangerous. But my voice would not come.

When I looked back toward my skinwalker, Paulette had been replaced.

I should have guessed. My step-grandmother had taken her place. The witch. The shrew. The bitch. A true skinwalker. *Finally*. Holding a bright red satin scarf. Dry as bone. Somehow protecting all of us from the rain by a hidden umbrella.

And no sooner than I saw her, that bright red satin scarf disappeared, and in its place were two open and spread hands with the thumbs overlapped, hiding the longer one in back.

So I glared into her eyes like a mongoose into a cobra's, gritting my teeth and growling. Two could play this game.

Then, in one simple explosion of understanding, everything came clear.

None of this was real. Not me. Not Tollison. Not Mary. Not life. Not death. Not anything.

Looking for truth was meaningless. Looking for meaning was meaningless. There was no truth. No lies. No meaning. No answers to questions. No questions in the first place.

Magic. Incessant, forward moving, magic.

And time had apparently stopped for me to get off the roller coaster should I choose to do so.

Then, as if my bubble had burst, everything rushed toward me again at record speeds, as if filling a cavity of empty space I'd momentarily occupied.

The rain pounded on me with savage energy, the skinwalkers growled at the top of their lungs, and Tollison pleaded with a pain I could feel in my bones. The water raged with renewed vigor. The lightning flashed so near it nearly blinded me. The thunder roared with such fervor I couldn't really hear it anymore. The water rose at twice the rate.

And I was alive again. In time. And happy to see it so.

Tollison turned toward me with an imploring horror on his face. Asking me to help him. And how could I refuse? He'd saved my life in the once small Tsaile Creek.

So I told him to stand back, I would slay the giant killers.

I didn't say those exact words, but the desperation of the situation before me was not lost on him.

He stood back.

And, as the evil things in front of us suddenly stared at me, I laughed in their faces and yelled, 'Go away!'

Why not?

We were dead, the water lapping over our shoes now. We were all dead. What did it matter? What did anything matter?

The skinwalkers made deep guttural sounds, so loud the thunder above us tamed before them. Maybe I'd made a mistake, I thought, as Tollison now huddled behind me for protection from whatever they were.

If I'd really thought the skinwalkers weren't real, I changed my mind. For one of them took a step toward me and I could smell the rancid odor Tollison had mentioned to me the first time he'd told me of the grizzly thing he'd seen. And its mouth dripped with saliva and long teeth showed from under his upper lip. As if he was contemplating biting my head off.

Then I heard Tollison yell from behind me, and in a voice quite different from him than I'd heard before, he said, 'there she is!'

For some reason, that sentence made some kind of sense to the skinwalker, for he looked where I imagined Tollison had looked, into the waters rushing along the rocks beside us.

So I turned to look as well.

And there, below me, as if in a dream, I saw the Navajo girl I'd seen at the front desk of my motel, now in the water, opening her mouth as if calling for help. A beautiful siren drowning in the deadly current.

Even though she was under water, her lovely native dress ballooned out from her legs and her wonderful black hair unwound from its ponytail and flamed out from her head wildly.

She was dying, too.

And it was then that I really knew I'd somehow joined with Tollison. My thoughts were his and vice versa.

'Haseya!' Tollison yelled. 'I have to save her.' His voice was wild with a mixture of passion and terror.

I yelled to him that it was some other girl. Not Haseya.

And as we argued, she slowly passed us going downstream, all the while silently repeating her calls for us to save her. By now, though, she'd gone completely under.

Tollison turned back toward the skinwalker, and yelled at him, 'All right, I *did* kill them. But *she* cut off my hand. She tried to stop me because she didn't think they were dead. I *did* push her into the flood. I had to. She would have told them about me. I couldn't trust her to keep quiet forever. But she's not dead. Tell me she's not dead!'

Then he turned back toward me, wanting I suppose, even in that desperate moment, to make sure I wrote his story the way he wanted it written, and yelled at me that he'd told me the truth, that this was but one lie in a story otherwise full of truths. Only one lie among truths. Certainly the presence of this monster now standing in front of him was proof of that.

He was crying as he screamed this. For himself, for his parents, for Haseya, for everything.

I was dumbstruck.

Was this version now the truth?

Or was it the skinwalker's intimidation?

Was he lying to protect us from one catastrophe only to fuel another?

Was the skinwalker responsible?

I had no idea what was going on. So I turned to see the skinwalker's reaction, and to tell him that I no longer believed in him, and that he should stop appearing in windows of long dead palaces of the Anasazi to frighten me.

But the skinwalker was no longer there.

So I again turned to Tollison. And he was no longer there.

I looked at the rushing waters in time to see him flailing way with his good hand and diving after his Haseya.

All this had occurred so quickly, I hadn't had time to process it. But the gods were not through with me yet. The rain continued to pour down on me. The waters of the Tsaile continued to rise, up to my knees and now to my waist. So hard did they wrack my body, that I couldn't possibly continue to fight them.

And so I didn't.

I let go.

And out into the water I fell. To rush downstream with the rest of the flotsam and jetsam.

As dangerous as the water had seemed to me on the rock against the wall, it was not so much a danger as I swam in it, especially going downstream.

So I relaxed and let the water take me where it wanted to take me. Why fight it? As long as I could float, I was safe.

So I dogpaddled a little and pushed away the detritus that rushed by, generally taking a passive approach to it all. Something I could never have done if I'd not already been so close to death so many times in so short a span of time.

As I bruised myself against underwater bodies I could only guess as to their source, encountered an occasional whirlpool that formed and then dissolved in less than a minute, and swallowed a mouthful of dirty water now and again, I just let the aberrant river take me toward the mouth of the canyon with as little effort as I needed to expend.

And I saw no others along the way. No Tollison. No Haseya. No skinwalkers. No bodies.

As the current pulled me along, I thought of what Tollison's story was *really* about.

Love and hate.

Passion and fear.

Opposites constantly struggling for supremacy in the human zoo of emotions.

How Tollison, enraged with hate for his parents' unwillingness to understand his love of Haseya, had driven him to murder them and then turned his passion for Haseya into fear of her.

Of our lives driving us forever into these conflicting desires. Nothing was one or the other, but both at the same time. With supremacy given to the one that apparently served us best at the moment.

Had my lack of reaction to what Tollison admitted to me—that *he'd* killed his parents and not Haseya—resulted from something I already knew though not admitted to myself?

Had I liked Tollison too much to see the truth?

And was the skinwalker merely a representation of Tollison's hate, fear, and ultimately his pain for not being able to love Haseya enough to stand up to his parents and remain in Many Farms in the first place, even if it meant possibly losing their love for him?

And, while I waxed philosophically about these complex emotions and what they might mean in the true state of the human-imagined universe, I considered that Tollison's skinwalker might have only wanted his fedora back.

And with that, I laughed out loud and, for an instant, what had been so tragic only a moment ago, was actually funny.

A comedy instead of tragedy.

Maybe Dante had been right after all.

"The banners of Hell's Monarch do come forth towards us, therefore look. If thou discern him. As, when breathes a cloud, Heavy and dense..."

And God spared me.

The water slowly receded, and after nodding goodbye to the Antelope House that had been spared by its height above the creek, the waters met at the convergence of Chinle Wash and Tsaile Creek and once together in the broader canyon diminished to the point where I could actually walk upright.

And thus, with the storm stomping off to the west, and the sun making its final appearance of the day below it, I hiked the final miles out of the canyon to safety.

24

I looked for their bodies as long as the fading light held and then
returned to my car, drove through the still muddy streets of Chinle,
and back to the Comprehensive Health Care Facility. Once there, I
told the nurses quickly of our exploits.

They didn't care about our not having proper admission or guides
to take us into del Muerto, only about potentially having two or more
possibly still-alive beings in harm's way.

So I accompanied them in an ambulance, even as trucks, jeeps,
and whatever else took to the canyon's sands.

And with bright headlights, we spent the rest of the night looking
for Tollison, Haseya, the skinwalkers—though I didn't call them that—
and even the young Navajo girl at the motel where I stayed in Holbrook.

But we found no one.

Not a sign that anybody had been stupid enough to hike up the
canyon with the weather forecast for heavy rains in the area.

All the rest had taken shelter, most in their homes.

They eventually told me that one of the searchers had found a
torn necklace of pearls somewhere near the head of the canyon, but he
knew something about pearls and they'd proven to be fakes. No reason
to keep fakes that by any account had no form of identification on them.

And that was the last I could take of the mess I'd gotten myself into.

I asked them if they'd found anything resembling a hat. A fedora to be exact.

No one there, apparently, had ever heard of or seen a fedora, so I had to describe it for them. Then, after nearly ten minutes of questions, they told me that no one had found a hat at all anyway. And there went ten minutes of my life I'd never get back.

Apparently the flood had taken them. Haseya for a second time if I were to believe Tollison after his lie. And maybe the young Navajo girl I'd seen in the hotel wearing the fake pearl necklace.

Or had I really seen her? Did she even exist? Or was she actually Haseya and I had become Tollison for those brief few seconds I saw her standing there in the hotel lobby?

But there was no way to find out the answers to any of these questions.

Life was all out of answers. At least for me.

At dawn, they sent me back to Holbrook in my car and told me they would continue looking for three more days and nights, and if they found anyone, dead or alive, they'd phone me there.

And I left them. Still in my waterlogged clothes and half-baked brain. And drove through the quiet morning sun with no clouds in the sky in any direction.

By the time I arrived back in Holbrook, it was noon and, for an instant, I thought of going to *The Diner* for a quick bite to eat to tell Mary what had occurred. But I was so tired, I couldn't do it. I went instead to my room and hit the bed like a dead man and passed out.

Once again I didn't dream. No need to, I guess, since my daily activities had out-dreamed my subconscious. The two had changed positions.

When I woke, the sun had disappeared, and I was hungry as a bear waking after a long hibernation.

So I showered, dressed in used clothes not so dirty as I'd made those I'd worn to bed, and walked to *The Diner*.

Or thought I had. For when I got there, the building I found was locked up tight as a drum.

No signs in the window. Nothing to indicate I'd eaten there the day before.

Mary had apparently decided to close up early. Taken a day off between her former restaurant and her new one to be.

But I was not to be discouraged. I stepped up to the door and tugged on the clearly locked handle there. And, to my amazement, either I was stronger than I imagined or the lock was weaker than it should be, the door opened as easily as it had when Mary was still in business.

The room was dark as always, but with the lights outside showing me some of the interior I could still see the lack of tables, chairs, and booths, and any other sign that the diner had ever been here at all. It was an empty shell. Just that.

And, as I stood there, I heard the scurrying of mice or rats running around in the dark, perfect prey for Mary's strange stews should she have been around.

I had clearly passed over into another time zone. Maybe this was the best dream my subconscious could come up with.

Not bad, I thought.

Certainly not good enough to scare me.

Not after what I'd already been through.

As I stood there, the door behind me swung further open and the light behind me illuminated the room a bit more.

There, across from me, was the oval window with a tiny ship in it with sails.

I hadn't made that up.

With that, though, I walked back to my motel and asked the clerk at the desk, someone I didn't recognize as having been there before, what had happened to *The Diner*.

The young man told me that nothing had. It was still there and doing a fine business.

I told him that it wasn't still there. That I'd just visited it, and the place was empty of both people and furniture. And its signs even.

He looked at me strangely, and told me he'd eaten in The Diner only last night, and not to tell the manager of the motel that he'd taken the food of its competitor over that of the food in the dining room in the place where he worked.

I told him I wouldn't, and then explained that I wasn't talking about The Diner on the Interstate, rather the one down the way in an alley off Holbrook's main drag.

He'd never heard of the place.

So I tried *The Vestige*, remembering then the new name Mary had devised the morning before.

He'd never heard of that one either.

I was getting desperate, and so asked him about the strange dark-wooded building in that alley that I'd found locked up.

And that one he knew. Told me it had been locked and abandoned for as long as he'd been in town which was well over twenty years now. That he'd been born in Holbrook, and so he should know.

Giving up, I decided to once again try the food of the motel's dining room. And so I did. Meatloaf, plenty of ketchup, a glass of beer, and a salad of yellow lettuce that looked as if it had been picked some-time around when Tollison had been born.

It was dreadful.

When I asked the waitress for coffee, I also asked her if she'd ever heard the name Tollison before. At first she shook her head no. Then she told me that it sounded familiar. Something about a legend she'd heard as a kid. About a man who'd drowned in a flood decades ago and that I should ask someone at the local newspaper office. That they might know.

I thanked her and gave her a special tip.

Knowing that the newspaper office, a weekly I imagined, wouldn't be open this late, no matter what day of the week it was, I headed for my room and found myself still tired. And I slept away the night without dreams.

The next morning, I asked the person at the front desk, yet a different one than I'd encountered there before, if any calls had come for me from Chinle.

He told me none had. No surprise there. And I ate scrambled chicken eggs with large doses of Worcestershire sauce and chili. Wasn't bad, though it still made Mary's cooking seem like heaven.

Then I wandered down to the local press and asked for the editor who, luckily, happened to be in and happened to be nearly as old, I guessed, as Tollison.

He certainly remembered the story. Young white man raised by Indians whose parents were trying to convert the savages to Mormonism up near Many Farms. He'd murdered his parents, had his hand cut off by his girlfriend as punishment for his crime, and run off with her, an Indian if he remembered right, and no one had heard from them since. Word was they'd both drowned in the Tsaile during the belly washer they'd had that year. He made it sound like a quick third-page newspaper story.

I sat with him on one of the chairs on the front porch of the building and told him my version. Not detailed, but the basic structure of it. He was a kind man, I knew, for instead of calling me a nutcase as I returned to my car, he kept on saying the words 'mighty interesting' over and over again.

Mostly to himself.

Sometimes I think I can still hear him saying those words when I recall Tollison, Mary, Haseya, and the rest of them.

It was a magical time of my life.

And I believe that something had happened. So much so that I've kept my promise to Tollison and his tortured soul by recounting the incident in writing his story down.

To finish, though, I spent the next two days in my room before I checked out of the motel and drove the Interstate toward the Grand Canyon thinking about all the loose ends I'd left behind.

Who was Mary? Did she exist or was she somehow an amalgam of all the women I'd ever known? Or Tollison had known?

Was the lock on *The Diner*'s door so easily broken because I'd eaten there before?

And if I had, what had I eaten? Spiders, and mice, and rats?

Was Tollison still alive? Had he actually told me the story I'd heard? Or was he a spirit in the air and I happened to pick up his signal like a lost radio station in the desert?

If I'd imagined him and the rest of it had been a true vision, had I really been in the canyon and survived a flood?

Certainly if that had been a vision, many others had shared it with me. And if it had been a real flood, where did the vision and reality meet?

Which part was which part?

By the day and date on the calendar on the wall of the motel, I'd been there enough days for it to have all occurred. If it had been a vision, where I had been all those days?

In my motel room staring out at the desert? If so, how could I have seen the First Mesa?

Survived the storms in the Crystal Forest and up near Ganado?

Had those been real, and only Tollison and I spending the night hours talking in the motel lobby imagined?

I didn't ask anyone these questions. Not even the owner of the motel if they had a night person on the desk that fit my description of the man who'd slept the nights away. So what if they had one? He'd been asleep. What did it matter?

But so many unanswered questions. It's difficult to write such a detailed report of such an experience and end up with so many loose ends. Untied loose ends. Loose ends without any acceptable answers except that maybe I'm nuts and maybe I'm not.

As luck would have it, though, God was not through tying up *his* loose ends.

For when I stopped for lunch in Winslow, the town next in line going west from Holbrook on the Interstate, I happened to take a look at one of the maps I'd bought a few days before I'd left. And, as I ate, I let my eyes wander over the details of the various places I'd been. All was in line with what I remembered, except for one minor detail.

Where my motel I stayed had been, none was marked.

Of course, this was an old map and my motel was fairly new. It may have not been built yet. But things were so strange that I had to see for myself.

With a very disturbing feeling growing in my brain, I drove back to Holbrook, turned down the main drag, and tried to squelch the incredible fear that it wouldn't be there. That God was indeed cleaning up after the mess he'd made. Fearing that maybe disappearing the motel, I was next.

I needn't have worried, though. The motel *was* there. Right where it should be. Looking the same as it should look. As I remembered it.

To make sure, however, I went inside and asked the man at the desk—a different one than the one that had checked me out—if someone with my name had stayed there for the past few days.

He looked me up in the book, and found no record of anyone named me having been there during that time.

I asked if I could look at the registration book, and he turned it around for me to see.

And there, at least, was proof I hadn't stayed there.

For no one had. The pages were all blank. The motel had been empty. So God *had* been cleaning up after himself after all.

I should have been shocked by the results of my question, but I wasn't. When so many things make no sense at all, one more doesn't matter. Except, of course, for my fear that I was next to go.

As I squeezed into the driver's seat of my Plymouth, something in the passenger seat caught my eye.

A book. It hadn't been there when I'd left the car. Of course, the windows were open. Anyone passing could have dropped it in as they walked by.

But who?

And, as I looked at the book, I noticed it had been squared up perfectly to fit the seat, not randomly tossed inside. Placed just so, with the title lined up so I could easily read it when I sat down. Not an accident or an impulse. A determined gesture to force me to see it there.

It was a black book except for the title printed in large red letters on the cover.

A hardback book without an author's name. Nor a publisher's identification mark. New. Not a crease, or a dog-eared page, or a grease mark on it. Not even a fingerprint I could see in the reflected light from the sun. Impossible not to catch your eye.

The title read simply, 'The Meaning of Dreams.' Straightforward. Impossible to misinterpret. Particularly for me.

And at that moment I knew who'd placed it there. Who'd been responsible for most if not all of what had happened to me.

To some degree, I'd already figured most of it out anyway. But for some reason, that person had felt it necessary to put the candles on the cake. To make sure I knew what was really what. Or who was really who. For it then occurred to me that it wasn't ever *really* about the what, the when, the where, or the why. It was *always* about the *who*.

So I left the book in its place, backed the Plymouth out of the parking lot, and then drove it into the street fronting the building I'd just visited.

As if nothing had happened at all. Of course, nothing *had* happened at all.

Just a man finding a book he hadn't placed in his car in the middle of nowhere on another hot late summer's day in the Arizona desert.

I headed as fast as I could out of town, noticing as I did that the newspaper office was still in place as well.

As I drove toward Winslow a second time that day, I half expected my right hand to begin disappearing, or the tires on the Plymouth.

But nothing happened at all.

Maybe God, in his infinite wisdom, had decided that enough was enough. I was not a threat to reveal his mistakes, and that whatever had leaked through the continuum from the past riding on the back of a man tormented by his secrets, had vanished except for my memories of it.

That no one would take me seriously, no matter what I said or did. That life on this world was again safe from leakage of spirits from one dimension or whatever to another. And, as I continued my journey, much was lost to me due to my preoccupation with Tollison and his nightmares.

These were sacred moments of beauty. Not so much of the things I'd seen, but in the people I'd met. For traveling the world as I had, I'd only now discovered that whatever beauty I witnessed, it was not in the perceived nature of Nature, but in the perceived nature of life. And, of course, in the culture of 'lives' in which I lived. It was no longer a collection of bad habits, but an eternal battle between good and bad habits. Of life. And, of course, of death. The paradox of paradoxes. That whatever set of truths we think we know, there is a lie that damns us to the eternal search.

And the rest of my trip went relatively uneventfully. At least compared to my visit to Holbrook and Navajo country.

And I've survived to write this accounting of the events of those few days in northeastern Arizona.

And I can say that I have put to rest my curiosity of the events described here. I'd learned a lot of magic in my youth. Enough so that many who see me do it are convinced that I have actually made things appear or disappear. I cannot not imagine that there are others who can do much better than I.

Was it magic then? Was it culture? Was it nothing at all? Each of these reasons had occurred to me as a revelation during my experiences with Tollison in the canyon of death, and before and thereafter.

Had I spent those days delusional in my motel room? Or sitting in my car in the Petrified Forest?

Of course, knowing my penchant for minutia, maybe they had occurred. Like numbered Ping-Pong balls in a moving circular bin waiting for me to chance choosing one to select a winner in the state lottery. Didn't really matter which one, except, of course, to the winner of the moment.

My final remembrance of my stay in Holbrook was a view of a coyote as I passed him by. Not as thin as the one I'd seen earlier on my stay.

And I swear he had a toothy grin on his face.

Readers Guide

1. Why did the author choose to have his protagonist tell a story rather than use dialog and other more traditional means used by novelists?

2. What rationale did the author use to have *The Diner* serve such extravagant and hard-to-imagine dishes?

3. The one name in the book never revealed is that of the protagonist. Why avoid using his name?

4. What role(s) do skinwalkers play in the novel?

5. Is Canyon de Chelly simply a convenient place for the two floods to occur, or does its choice here have some special significance?

6. Violent weather seems to follow the main character around no matter where he goes. What might it represent in this novel?

7. What relationship do the mother of the main character and the mother of his stepfather have?

8. Why spend an entire chapter on the protagonist's around-the-world travels? Does it matter? How?

9. The main character's primary girlfriends play small roles in this book. Do they serve a purpose and if so what?

10. What role does the book *The Meaning of Dreams* play, both near the beginning and its actual appearance at the end?

11. Why Big Sur for the car accident? Could the choice of place be changed and have any effect on the novel's plot or outcome?

12. What role does religion play in the novel, particularly given that two have prominent roles beside Navajo traditions?

13. The author develops 'magic' near the beginning of the book. Does its reappearance near the end suggest something important for understanding the plot's meaning?

14. Spiders rarely appear again following the protagonist's fear of them in the first chapter. Do spiders symbolize something important, and, if so, what?

15. Why does the coyote seem to smile at the end of the book? Do coyotes play other roles here and why use them as such symbols?